DARKNESS, SING ME A SONG

ALSO BY DAVID HOUSEWRIGHT

DARKNESS, SING ME A SONG

DAVID HOUSEWRIGHT

 MINOTAUR BOOKS ⚐ NEW YORK

DARKNESS, SING ME A SONG. Copyright © 2017 by David Housewright. All rights reserved. Printed in the United States of America. For information, address St. Martin's Press, 175 Fifth Avenue, New York, N.Y. 10010.

www.minotaurbooks.com

Designed by Devan Norman

Library of Congress Cataloging-in-Publication Data

Names: Housewright, David, 1955– author.
Title: Darkness, sing me a song / David Housewright.
Description: First edition. | New York : Minotaur Books, 2018.
Identifiers: LCCN 2017041312| ISBN 9781250094476 (hardcover) | ISBN 9781250094483 (ebook)
Subjects: LCSH: Private investigators—Fiction. |Murder—Investigation— Fiction. | GSAFD: Mystery fiction.
Classification: LCC PS3558.O8668 D37 2018 | DDC 813/.54—dc23
LC record available at https://lccn.loc.gov/2017041312

Our books may be purchased in bulk for promotional, educational, or business use. Please contact your local bookseller or the Macmillan Corporate and Premium Sales Department at 1-800-221-7945, extension 5442, or by email at MacmillanSpecialMarkets@macmillan.com.

First Edition: January 2018

10 9 8 7 6 5 4 3 2 1

FOR RENÉE

TIMES INFINITY

ACKNOWLEDGMENTS

The author wishes to acknowledge his debt to Pat Donnelly, Tammi Fredrickson; David P. Peterson, Forensic Science Supervisor, Minnesota Bureau of Criminal Apprehension; Janet Waller, and Renée Valois.

DARKNESS, SING ME A SONG

CHAPTER ONE

She was tall, slender, impeccably tanned; strawberry hair fell in waves to her shoulders. I knew she was older than fifty years, yet she could easily have passed for forty and probably did. Possibly she'd had work done, but if so it was very well done indeed. Even while dressed in an orange jumpsuit over a white cotton tee and without makeup, she looked like she could be advertising beauty products in a fashion magazine. I wondered how she managed it. Most people, you put them in jail for forty-eight hours, they look like hell. Probably her money had something to do with it. Eleanor Barrington had plenty.

I met her in an eight-by-eight interview room at the Ramsey County Adult Detention Center in St. Paul. She sat in a metal chair at a metal table, both anchored to the concrete floor, and absentmindedly pulled at her collar. David Helin sat across from her, a legal pad and pen arrayed in front of him, although he didn't do much note taking. I was leaning against the cinder-block wall, my arms folded across my chest, trying hard to quiet the questions that had been bouncing around in my head ever since I heard that Mrs. Barrington had been arrested.

"When do I get the hell out of here?" she asked. Her words were sharply spoken and produced a disconcerting echo as they bounced off the gray walls.

"Soon," Helin said. "Maybe tomorrow."

"Tomorrow? What's the holdup?"

"Bail was set at two million dollars—"

"Write a fucking check."

"It's easy to come up with two hundred thousand dollars in cash, the ten percent that the court demands up front. But we must also provide an audit of your assets to prove that you can cover the remaining amount, and that's taking time—"

"God damn it."

"I'm working with your accountants—"

"I'm going to start firing accountants and lawyers, too, if I don't get out of here and soon. The toilet in my cell doesn't even have a seat on it."

"You need to understand the State's position," Helin said. "You have a couple of houses scattered around the country and another in Martinique."

"They think I might run off somewhere? Why would I do that?"

"A woman was killed."

"I don't care. Why should I care? Some dead whore on the street."

"You knew the woman," I said.

Helin's mouth tightened at the sound of my words. I was there to be seen, not heard, yet he did not interrupt.

"You spoke to her many times," I added. "She had been dating your son for over six months."

"What's your point?" Mrs. Barrington asked.

"You seem somewhat callous about what happened to her."

"Bitter. I'm fucking bitter."

"Why?" Helin asked.

Mrs. Barrington sighed an exasperated sigh and rolled her large, hazel-colored eyes toward heaven.

"I told you. How many times do I have to tell you? The bitch meant nothing to me. She was just a trick my son was banging. I really don't give a fuck that she's dead; don't really give a fuck who killed her except that people are blaming me. It's *very* annoying."

"Witnesses claim they overheard you threatening to kill her," Helin said.

"Just talk," Mrs. Barrington answered. "Haven't you ever done that? Said I'm going to kill that bastard, going to kill that bitch? You get angry, you say things."

"You had reason to be angry."

"Damn right, I had reason. Didn't I, Taylor?"

She stared straight at me as she spoke, expecting me to nod my head in agreement, expecting me to say, "Yes, ma'am." I did neither.

"She was a fucking whore trying to rip off my son, trying to rip me off," Mrs. Barrington said.

This time Helin turned in his seat to look at me, seeking confirmation.

"All we know for sure is that her name wasn't Emily Denys and that she didn't grow up in Albert Lea, Minnesota, or attend the University of Iowa," I said. "In fact, there's nothing to prove that she even existed thirteen months ago."

"See," Mrs. Barrington said.

"That doesn't mean she was bitch or a whore or a thief."

"She was a liar."

Yes, I told myself, she was a liar.

"Our problem right now—do you know a woman named Alexandra Campbell?" Helin asked.

"No," Mrs. Barrington said. "Why should I?"

"The county attorney interviewed her this morning. She lives across the street from Emily Denys. She claims she saw you get out of your car, walk up behind Denys, shoot her in the back of the head as she was unlocking the front door to her duplex, walk back to your car, and drive away."

"That's bullshit. Why would she say such bullshit?"

"We'll ask her." Helin turned in his seat to look at me again. "Right?"

"Yes, sir," I told him.

"Wait," Mrs. Barrington said. "The killing took place two days ago. If she saw me—if she saw someone do it, why didn't she come forward then? Sounds to me like someone got to her."

"Are you suggesting that she was bought off?"

"If I know nothing else, I know what money can buy."

"A possibility we'll explore," Helin said. "In the meantime, there's the matter of the murder weapon. Denys was killed by a bullet fired from a nine-millimeter handgun. Mrs. Barrington, you purchased a nine-millimeter handgun seven years ago at Joe's Sporting Goods. A Ruger LC9 to be precise."

"After my husband died," she said. "I kept it in the house. In my bedroom."

"Where is it now?"

"What I told that smirking asshole of a policeman, I don't know."

"You said it was missing."

"I preferred to think of it as being mislaid."

"You were unable to produce the gun when the police asked for it."

"It wasn't where I thought it would be. I don't remember seeing it for years. I might have moved it and forgot where."

"Did your son and daughter search the house like we asked?" Helin said.

"I don't know."

"I'll call them—"

"You know what this is? This is that bitch of a county attorney trying to make a name for herself by going after the one-percenters. Prove she's a woman of the people. Yeah, and then come knocking on our doors looking for campaign contributions when she runs for higher office."

"Mrs. Barrington?" I asked.

"What?"

"As you say, you're a wealthy woman."

"Not fucking wealthy enough that I can buy myself out of jail, it seems."

"What happens to your estate if you're"—I nearly said convicted; instead I said—"incapacitated."

"The estate is held in a family trust as per the instructions in my husband's will. As it stands now, I have complete control. If something happens to me—wait. What are you saying? That my children did this?" She stood abruptly, a mother bear protecting her cubs. "What the fuck are you telling me?"

Helin was just as quick to his feet. He grabbed my arm and hustled me out the door.

"I'm going to talk to Taylor for a moment," he said over his shoulder. "I'll be right back."

Once we were outside the interview room, the door closed, Helin turned on me.

"What the hell was that, Taylor?" he asked.

"Do you believe she's innocent?"

"Yes, I do, as a matter of fact. She's an incredible piece of work, but yes, I believe she's innocent."

"Then what happened to the gun?"

He thought about it for a few beats.

"The fact that it's missing is either very convenient or very inconvenient, depending on your point of view," I added.

"You're doing your job, thinking like a private investigator," Helin said. "Good for you. I'd ask you to find the damn gun, except—I'm not entirely sure I want to find the damn gun."

Because you think she's innocent, I told myself.

"Are you sure you want me to keep working the case?" I asked.

"Why not?"

"You know the county attorney is going to call me as a witness for the prosecution. I'm going to have to testify that Mrs. Barrington hired me to check on the background of the girl her son was dating and that I reported that Emily Denys—we don't actually know who she was, but we know who she wasn't."

"That's not a problem, don't worry. The CA can only call you as a fact witness. She can only ask about what you just told me. Beyond that—you can testify to what happened before the body was found, but not say a word about what happened after. The work you do for me on behalf of Mrs. Barrington is protected. My privilege is your privilege."

"Attorney-client confidentiality."

"Exactly right."

"Yet the CA is making a big deal in the media about Mrs. Barrington hiring a private investigator to stalk the victim."

"That kind of talk will never reach the inside of a courtroom, trust me."

"Makes me took like a douche, though."

"I'm sorry about that. But Mrs. Barrington might be right. This reeks of a grandstand play on the county attorney's part. The fact the police have been unable to identify the girl—I don't know."

"Maybe the CA knows something we don't."

"It wouldn't be the first time. Find out what that is, will you? I'm not sure how much longer I can keep Mrs. Barrington in jail."

"You're the one delaying her bail?"

"You heard her in there. If the media gets hold of her, the woman will poison her own jury pool. The mouth on her—and she's so damn beautiful, too."

"It's always a pleasure working with you, David."

"Yeah, we're both wonderful people. Eventually, I'll get a chance to depose the State's eyewitness. For now, see what you can learn about her, what she knows. If you can shake her up in the process, I won't mind a bit."

"The best time will be tomorrow right after breakfast," I said.

Helin stared at me as if he had no idea what I was talking about.

"I read it in *Psychology Today*," I said. "People are more likely to be helpful in the morning right after they've had breakfast."

"We'll talk tomorrow. Oh, and if Mrs. Barrington should ask, tell her that I just tore you a new one."

"Taylor."

The sound of my name as I was stepping out of the front door of the Ramsey County Adult Detention Center caused me to pivot. A woman dressed in a matching skirt and jacket was approaching fast, followed closely behind by a tall, thin African American sporting a mustache. I recognized them both—which is why I let the door close between us. I waited for them beneath the steel poles flying the American and Minnesota flags.

They came out of the building in a hurry. Ramsey County Attorney Marianne Haukass walked briskly toward me, her heels making a clicking sound on the concrete, which made me think that was why she wore them. She halted a few feet away and pressed her fists firmly against her hips.

"Didn't you hear me?" she asked.

Her hair trembled in the breeze like the flags above us. It was too dark to call her a blonde and too light for her be a labeled a brunette. I never liked the term "dirty blonde," yet in her case . . .

"Yes, I heard you," I said. "Hi, Martin. Good to see you again."

Martin McGaney stood behind the CA. He gave me a little head nod in recognition.

"What are you doing here?" Haukass asked.

"No license holder shall divulge to anyone other than the employer, or as the employer may direct, except as required by law, any information acquired during—"

Haukass raised her hand like a cop was stopping traffic.

"Enough," she said. "I really don't want to hear it."

"I'll be on my way, then."

"You're making a mistake, Taylor, continuing with this case. If you were smart, you'd drop it."

"Is that a threat?"

"A friendly warning."

"We're friends?"

"You've been helpful to my office," Haukass said. "You're the one who broke that car theft ring, the one that used wreckers to cruise the streets, towing to chop shops vehicles that were parked illegally or that they found broken down on the freeway. I'd hate to see you get into trouble."

"What kind of trouble?"

"I heard that a complaint might be filed with the Department of Public Safety; that you might be forced to explain your involvement in the murder of Emily Denys to the Private Detective Services Board."

"Is that all? For a moment there, I thought it might be serious."

"I heard the complaint alleges that you engaged in fraud, deceit, and misrepresentation while in the business of private detective. You're one for quoting regulations. You know what that means."

"My license could be suspended if not revoked. That's serious, all right. Especially if I'm then asked to testify about that stolen-car ring you mentioned. If my testimony is discredited, won't that hurt your case?"

"You can see why I'm concerned, then."

"Marianne," I said.

I purposely used her first name. It's an old cop trick. It removes a suspect's dignity and makes him feel defensive, inferior, and often dependent, like a child seeking a parent's approval. It lets the suspect know who's in charge around here. I don't know why this is true, yet personal experience tells me that it is, especially among people who expect to be called mister and sir and ma'am.

"Marianne, despite the BS you've been ladling out to the media, Mrs. Barrington hired my firm to do a simple background check on Emily, asking for no greater depth than if she had applied for a position with one of her companies. That's not unusual. I bet we get a hundred calls a year from people asking us to investigate the boys and girls they meet in bars or on online. We charge five hundred to a thousand dollars a pop depending on how extensive the service. In my humble opinion, which I'd be happy to share with a jury, anyone who has something to protect, like, say, Mrs. Barrington, would be foolish not to do a background check on the individuals who ingratiate themselves into their lives. So, you see, I was acting well within the scope of my employment."

"*Holland*," the county attorney said, emphasizing my first name as strongly as I had hers. "Is that going to be your defense?"

"It has the virtue of being true."

"We're all adults here. We all know that truth often has little to do with it."

"I know this to be true—a murder case would normally be handled by the assistant county attorney who heads the criminal division of your office. Instead, the Ramsey County attorney, a woman without prior criminal trial experience, has chosen to prosecute the case herself. Probably because it's high profile with the promise of substantial media attention."

"If you say so."

"I do say so. Something else—you're new to the job, so when you behave like a heartless bitch playing politics with people's lives, you think a lowly private investigator like me should be surprised; he should be frightened. No one is surprised. No one is frightened. Ask your man here. McGaney's been around. He'll tell you you're just another in a long line of heartless bitches—both male and female—intent on using their position solely to build a tough-on-crime rep that'll carry them to political glory. Now, if you should genuinely care about people, that would surprise me. That would shock me to my core."

Haukass tried hard to hide her anger and almost succeeded. She started to speak, stopped, started again, her words dipped in honey.

"Don't say I didn't warn you," she said.

She turned and walked briskly back toward the detention center. McGaney followed, yet not before giving me a grin.

"You just can't help yourself, can you?" he said.

CHAPTER TWO

I opened the door, the one next to the sign that read FREDERICKS & TAYLOR PRIVATE INVESTIGATIONS, and stepped inside. Freddie was happily working the PC mounted on his desk. I remembered a time when he hated computers. Somewhere along the line he caught the virus, though, and now he was the best at running background checks and skip traces, hunting identity thieves, vetting jurors, uncovering hidden assets, and even conducting cyber investigations—all from the comfort of his stuffed swivel chair. He looked up when I entered the office.

"Taylor," he said.

"Freddie."

"How'd it go?"

"We're still on the clock."

"You make that sound like it's a bad thing."

"I don't know, Freddie. More and more I'm thinking this is one we should walk away from."

"We could, but that would be establishing a whaddya call, dangerous precedent, quitting a lawyer midcase. Besides, I like Helin."

"Me, too."

"He's been very good to us."

"Yes, he has."

"Way I look at it, we're workin' for him, not the client. The way I always look at it."

"I suppose."

"So, we're on the same page?"

"Sure."

"You best take a look at this, then."

Freddie called up an article that appeared on the website of the St. Paul *Pioneer Press*. The headline read:

MURDER VICTIM WAS HIDING
UNDER ASSUMED NAME

"Did they get that from the cops?" I asked.

"Doesn't say, but whenever a pretty white girl gets killed, reporters like to run a picture, interview the family and friends, get folks to say they never expected nothin' like this t' happen in their neighborhood. Maybe they figured it out for themselves."

"The CA might have told them off the record. I've come to admire her sneakiness."

"Don't know 'bout that. Paper does say how a PI gave up the alleged victim to the alleged killer."

"Did it print our names?"

"Just yours."

"Swell. Does it mention anything about a license review?"

"Is there gonna be a license review?"

"The CA says so."

Freddie smiled a big toothy smile. "Never a dull moment, huh?" he said.

I went to the coffee machine we shared, one of those expensive suckers that brews one cup at a time, and fixed myself a mug of Chocolate Caramel Brownie, a flavor provided by Cameron's Coffee. Cameron's used to be located in New Richmond, Wisconsin, but had since moved to Shakopee in Minnesota, just southeast of the Twin Cities. I, on the other hand, was in the exact same place I was six years ago. I sat behind the same desk and swiveled the same chair to look out the same window.

The view of downtown Minneapolis had changed. Me, I hadn't changed at all. Or maybe I had. What did I know?

"How long have we been partners now?" Freddie asked. "Five years?"

"Why? You thinking of throwing an anniversary party?"

"I'm thinkin' we've been involved in some serious shit since we joined up."

"Some serious shit before that, too."

"What we learned, people usually kill out of anger. Even if it's over drugs or what you call gang related, it's usually cuz someone is pissed off."

"Okay."

"This Barrington, Eleanor Barrington, she was supposed to have popped the Denys girl outta anger cuz she thought the bitch was rippin' off the son—what the papers said."

"Freddie—"

"How come the bullets weren't in front, then? You pissed off at someone; usually you shoot 'em straight on. You're facin' your anger, so to speak. But little Emily—one bullet in the back of the head, no sign she even knew it was comin'."

"Meaning what?"

"Maybe she wasn't murdered. Maybe she was assassinated."

"A professional hit?"

"Not necessarily. What I'm saying, the way she was killed, it wasn't personal. That's the thing."

That's what I missed when I was working alone, the reason Freddie and I agreed to become partners despite what you might call a stormy relationship—was it really five years ago? It gave me someone to talk to besides myself, a second opinion to balance the voice in my head.

I wagged my finger at him.

"You just might make a decent investigator someday," I said.

"Comin' from a seasoned professional like you, that's mighty fine praise. Makes a brother all warm inside. Gotta ask, though—if a poor black child without no proper education can figure it out, how come the white man's police department be laggin' behind?"

"Kind of makes you think the county attorney might be up to something, doesn't it?"

"All I know, a prosecutor callin' out a private eye in the media for no good reason—I've never seen that before, have you?"

"No, I haven't."

Freddie made a production out of resting his index finger against his cheek.

"Makes a man go hmmm," he said.

Freddie was still hemming and hawing when the door opened and a woman with Asian features walked in as if she owned the place, which, if you go strictly by Minnesota's property laws, wasn't entirely untrue. She was carrying a one-year-old infant.

"Hey, hey, hey," Freddie chanted. He rose out of his chair and reached for the child. "There's my little man."

He took the child from the woman's arms. The woman raised her cheek to be kissed. Freddie had to bend down nearly a foot to reach her. He buzzed her cheek, then returned to the chair as he waved the child through the air. The child was laughing. I wasn't surprised. Freddie had been known to crack me up, too.

I couldn't pronounce the woman's given name, much less spell it, so I called her what everyone else did.

"Echo," I said.

"Hello, Taylor."

She moved across the office to my desk. I stood up to give her a hug. She was nearly a foot shorter than I was, too, a Chinese girl who moved to the United States with her mother two dozen years ago.

"What brings you downtown?" I asked.

"We're going to Lake Calhoun for a picnic and to listen to some music."

"Yes, we are," Freddie said. He was speaking to his son as he continued to wave him around. "Yes, we are. We're going to the park. Taylor, look how big he's getting."

"Think he'll play football, like you?"

"Not a chance, uh-uh, he's not." Freddie pulled the child to his chest. "End up like me, all-everything until he trashes a knee and becomes an AP in the air force because he's too dumb to make it through college without an athletic scholarship? No sir. He's going to be smart. He's going to play basketball."

"Is he going to become an actor, too?"

"Heck no."

Heck. I had never heard Freddie curse in front of his wife.

"What does his grandmother say?" I asked.

"Never mind his grandmother."

"What do you mean?" Echo said.

"Haven't they told you? Freddie's mother wanted her little boy to become a famous Hollywood actor. That's why she named him *Sidney Poitier* Fredericks."

Echo chuckled at the suggestion. "I did not know that," she said.

"Never mind," Freddie said.

I took the child away from Freddie—he seemed reluctant to let him go—and I waved him around a little bit myself.

"When you get older, the stories I'm going to tell you," I said.

"I'd like to hear them myself," Echo said.

"No, you wouldn't," Freddie said.

He pulled the child from my arms and cradled him.

"Did the bad man frighten you?" he asked.

"Is it true that you once put a gun to Freddie's head?" Echo asked.

"Actually, I put a gun to his big toe while he was lying in bed, but in my defense, it was only after he whacked me on *my head* with his gun and left me unconscious in an alley."

"That happened?"

"God's truth."

"No big thing," Freddie said. "Water under the bridge."

"How did two ever get to be friends?" Echo asked.

"What makes you think we're friends?"

"You've worked together for how long now?"

"I saved his sorry"—a quick glance at Echo, and Freddie said—"butt."

"You did?"

I held up two fingers. "Twice," I said.

Echo's eyes flew from me to Freddie and back again, and I wondered, doesn't the man speak to his wife?

"We're going to the park," Freddie said. "Yes, we are. We're going to the park."

"Taylor, come with us," Echo said.

"I don't think so."

"It'll be fun."

"You'll have more fun without me."

"That's for sure," Freddie said.

Echo called his name and gave him the look some wives reserve for husbands that embarrass them.

"It's true," Freddie said. "Taylor's been a stick-in-the-mud ever since he broke up with Cynthia—for the second time, I might add."

"Stick-in-the-mud?" I asked. "Is that street?"

"Fuuuuudge," Freddie said, although I don't think that's what he meant to say.

"C'mon, Taylor," Echo said. "Come with us."

I shook my head.

"Freddie's right. You've been moping around for months. She's just a girl."

"Have fun, you three."

CHAPTER THREE

I still had a landline in my apartment, and not out of any sense of nostalgia. It was because I wanted a number that family, friends, and charities could call, leaving my cell phone strictly for business. The last thing a guy wants is to interrupt a due diligence investigation because some nonprofit is desperate to record his opinion on global warming. I can take it or leave it, by the way.

The phone was ringing when I unlocked the front door. I would have let my voicemail pick it up, except the monitor told me who it was, and I knew she'd only call back later.

"Hi, Mom," I said.

"How did you know it was me?"

"I have caller ID."

"You should wait for the person to identify herself. It's only polite."

"What can I do for you, Mom?"

"Does it have to be something? Can't I call just to see how my son is doing since my son never calls me?"

"I've been busy."

"You're always busy. You should visit your family more."

"It's kind of tough since you live in Fort Myers, Florida, and I live in St. Paul, Minnesota."

"Not us. Your other family."

"What other family?"

"Your brother."

"Oh, yeah. How's he doing?"

"Why don't you ask him?"

"I've been busy."

"*Holland Taylor.*"

Whenever my mother uses your full name, you knew you're in trouble.

"You haven't spoken to your brother and sister-in-law—and your nephews—in weeks," she said. "And don't tell me you're too busy. You're just being antisocial."

"Me? Every time I go over there they tell me how irresponsible I am, how I need to grow up and behave like an adult, how I need to be more like them, with a sensible job, living in a sensible home in a sensible suburb, living a sensible life. How social is that? Besides, I don't need them to tell me those things. That's your job."

"You never listen to me."

"You never listen to me, so we're even."

A third voice said, "Don't sass your mother."

"Dad," I said. "You should clear your throat or something so I know when you're on the other line."

"Are you still seeing that woman?" my mother asked.

"That woman?"

"You know who I mean."

"Cynthia Grey?"

"Yes, that one. Cindy."

"Cynthia. No one ever calls her Cindy, Mom."

"Why not? What's wrong with Cindy? A girl like that, can't be called Cindy, who's a partner in some hoity-toity law firm that takes up three whole floors of a building in downtown Minneapolis where you can't even park unless you pay a man twenty dollars? We never liked her."

"Dad liked her, didn't you, Dad? Many times you told me she was a looker. Wasn't it you who always said I should find a rich girl who could take care of me in my old age?"

"Don't drag me into this," Dad said.

"Did you say those things?" my mother asked. "Well, I never. You, Holland Taylor, you can do better, don't think you can't."

"Just to settle your nerves, I haven't seen or spoken to Cynthia in months."

"That's good."

"If you say so."

"Who are you seeing now? Tell me."

"No one."

"Lee says she has a friend. A very nice girl."

"Who's Lee?"

"Letitia Taylor? Your sister-in-law?"

"Oh yeah, yeah, yeah . . ."

"Well?"

"Well, what?"

"Are you going to call her?"

"Who?"

"Lee—to ask about the girl."

"Probably not."

"I'm not going to force you."

"I appreciate that."

"It's just—I've been worried about you. We've all been worried about you. Ever since Laura was killed, and Jenny, too. Since the drunk driver . . . It's getting to be an awfully long time ago."

"Nine years, seven months, sixteen days."

You'd think that after all these years I would have lost track. Only it was how I calculated the passage of time—before Laura, Laura, after Laura.

There was a long pause on the line before my mother spoke again.

"It's time for you to find someone new and settle down," she said.

"I'm going to say good-bye now so you don't accuse me of hanging up on you."

My mom was clearly speaking to my father when she said, "He never listens to me."

"Leave the boy alone," Dad said. "He'll figure it out."

"Good night, guys," I said.

"You can at least call. You never know, she might be a wonderful girl."

"Good night."

People talk about Jewish mothers. They've got nothing on God-fearing Catholic mothers, I promise you.

The knock on my front door came so quickly after I hung up the phone I thought my visitor might have been waiting for me to finish the conversation. I opened the door to find my neighbor's eleven-year-old daughter holding a plastic sandwich bag containing a carrot and a few leaves of lettuce. She was smiling brightly.

"Hey, Mandy," I said.

"Hi, Taylor. Can I feed Ogilvy?"

"He'd starve without you. Call him."

Only she didn't need to. As if on cue my gray-and-white French lop-eared rabbit hopped into the room. Amanda squealed when she saw him—as she always did—and knelt on my hardwood floor. She held the carrot above the rabbit's head.

"Beg," she said.

Ogilvy stood on his hind legs, holding his front paws forward like a dog might.

Next the girl waved the carrot in a circle.

"Roll over."

The rabbit rolled over.

She rested the carrot on the floor.

"Play dead."

The rabbit rested on his side, sprawled out in front of her.

"Good bunny," Amanda said.

She sat cross-legged on the floor, the skirt of her private-school uniform forming a nest that Ogilvy happily crawled into. She fed him the carrot out of her hand.

"He's so smart," Amanda said. "I never knew rabbits were so smart until I met him."

"If you can only get him to stop chewing on my computer cords, I'd appreciate it."

I propped my front door open so anyone climbing the staircase outside could see into my apartment. The door to Amanda's apartment was directly across the landing. I was 2A. The Wedemeyers were 2B.

"Is your mother working late again?" I asked.

"I guess so."

"Are you hungry?"

"I had an apple before I came over. Do you think Ogilvy would eat an apple?"

"I have no idea."

"What do you feed him when I'm not around?"

"I throw some alfalfa into his cage. Sometimes I'll feed him popcorn."

"How come you don't feed him carrots and garden stuff?"

"I have you for that."

Amanda stroked the rabbit while he ate, starting at his nose and moving her hand all the way to his tail. I withdrew to my kitchen and started thinking about what I was going to eat myself. The kitchen wall had been cut down at one time so I could see over it into the living room.

"How'd you do on your test?" I asked.

"I got an A."

"See. I told you not to worry."

"My mom says I do well because I worry."

"There might be something to that."

"Taylor, do you like my mother?"

"Yes, I do."

"Do you think she's pretty?"

"I think she's very pretty. Not as pretty as you, though."

"She says you're nice."

"That's good to hear."

"She says you're nice because you let me come over and play with Ogilvy when she's not home and because you carry heavy stuff for her and helped when the car wouldn't start in the snow that one time."

"I was just being neighborly."

"You should go out on a date together."

"Where would we go?"

Amanda gave it serious thought. Finally, she answered.

"My mom really likes music. Do you like music?"

"Yes, but I don't listen as much as I used to."

The sound of someone on the landing caused the girl to turn.

"Mandy," a voice said.

"Hi, Mom."

I walked into the living room just as Claire Wedemeyer did. She was dressed for business in a linen suit; a heavy bag hung from her shoulder. She gave me a high-wattage smile. It was the only thing that mother and daughter seemed to share. Otherwise, they didn't appear related at all. Amanda was all sunshine and wheat fields. Claire was a dark and brooding forest—except when she smiled.

"I'm so sorry," she said.

"For what?"

Claire rested her hand on my wrist. She was one of those people who felt the need to touch the person she was speaking to. I found it annoying when we first met. Now it didn't bother me at all.

"For Amanda always coming over, imposing on you like this."

"It's no imposition at all. I enjoy her company. So does Ogilvy. Don't you, Ogilvy?"

The rabbit didn't answer. He had finished the carrot and was now chomping on the lettuce leaf that Amanda held in her hand.

"You're very kind," Claire said.

"Mandy is always welcome here. So are you, for that matter."

"I told Taylor you two should date," Amanda said.

Claire released my wrist and took a step backward. "Mandy."

Claire closed her eyes and muttered something that I didn't hear. I smiled at her. That's what she saw when she opened her eyes again.

"Kids," I said.

She touched my wrist.

"Amanda, honey, time to go home."

The girl hugged the rabbit to her chest and set him on the floor.

"Bye, Ogilvy," she said.

Amanda stood up.

"Can I feed him again tomorrow?" she asked.

"Anytime you like," I said.

"See, Mom. It's okay. Taylor likes me. He likes you, too. He said so."

Claire closed her eyes again.

I smiled some more.

She opened her eyes.

"Good night, Taylor. Thank you for looking after Mandy."

"It was my pleasure."

She turned to leave my apartment, but the exit was blocked by a woman dressed in a black sports jacket, white shirt, and jeans. A gold badge in the shape of a warrior's shield was anchored to her belt.

"Excuse me," Claire said.

"No, excuse me," said the woman.

They sized each other up in an instant, and from the expressions, I doubted they would ever become friends.

"Claire Wedemeyer," I said. "This is my friend Anne Scalasi. Anne, my neighbor Claire."

They shook hands without pleasure.

"You're a policewoman," Claire said.

"Assistant chief, St. Paul Police Department," Anne said. "Why? Does it matter?"

"Not to me."

"This pretty young lady," I said, "is Amanda."

Anne stooped to shake the girl's hand, but Amanda didn't respond.

"Are you the one who arrested my daddy?" she asked.

Claire's hand found Amanda's shoulder.

"I don't think so," Anne said.

Claire steered her daughter toward her apartment.

"Good night, Taylor," she said.

A moment later, mother and daughter were safely inside their apartment, the door locked behind them.

I ushered Anne inside and closed my own door.

"What the hell was that?" Anne asked.

"A very awkward moment, I'd say."

"Her old man was arrested? For what?"

"This is the first I've heard of it."

Anne pulled a pen and notebook from the pocket of her jacket. I knew what she was planning.

"Don't do that," I said.

"You're not interested in finding out what happened?"

"Not even a little bit."

"It'll take one phone call."

"Let it go."

Anne returned the writing material to her pocket.

"Are you sleeping with her?" she asked.

"Oh, Annie, c'mon."

"I bet she wishes you were."

"What makes you think that?"

"I felt a vibe when you called me your friend."

"Is that the trained investigator speaking?"

"Do you know the last time I actually ran an investigation? Lately, Taylor, I feel like a machine, crunching numbers, studying statistics, budgeting man-hours, how many, where, when; defending policy. Do you know what I have under my command? Family and Sexual Violence, Property Crimes, Homicide and Robbery, Youth Services, Special Investigations, Gangs, Narcotics and Vice, and the Safe Streets Task Force. Yet the closest I get to an ongoing investigation these days is a morning eBrief."

"You should never have accepted promotion."

"It was a means to an end. Speaking of which, I hear you're in trouble again."

"Who told you that?"

"People who know that we were partners back in the day. People who are watching to see if I reach out to you."

"What people?"

"The ones who want me to become the first female police chief in the history of the St. Paul and the ones who don't."

"Just out of curiosity, are you going to help me?"

"No."

"I didn't think so."

"We have an understanding."

"Yes, we do."

I found the Maker's Mark and poured a couple of inches into two glasses. Anne slouched on my sofa and fluffed her auburn hair. Ogilvy rammed her ankle with his head, which was his way of demanding attention. Anne leaned down and scratched him between the ears.

"Hey, you," she said.

The rabbit started grinding his teeth. Most people find that disconcerting, but Anne had been around the lop-ear enough to know that it meant he was content.

I gave Anne a glass as I settled in next to her. She took a healthy pull of the bourbon.

"Remember that time we were in homicide?" she said. "We put on our blues and snuck into the St. Paul Saints baseball game, pretending that we were working security?"

"I remember."

"Do you still follow the Saints? The Twins?"

"Not like I used to. I don't have anyone to share it with."

Anne leaned in and kissed me. I draped an arm around her shoulder and kissed her back—a careless kiss.

"I saw Martin McGaney today," I said. "He's working as an investigator for the county attorney's office."

"I know. He always was a suck-up."

"I remember when he worked for you."

"I remember when you worked for me."

"A long time ago."

"It seems like a long time."

We kissed again, putting more meaning into it.

"Where's Ash?" I asked.

I didn't mean to break the mood. I was just curious.

"His Lordship Ashley Leighton Redman?" Anne said.

"He's not really a lord."

"He acts like it. Last I heard he was in Singapore. Or some place. I don't know. He travels, you know that. Designs buildings all over the world. I see him one week out of three. Before he left this time, he asked me to think about resigning."

"So you could travel with him?"

"So I can stay home twenty-four/seven and manage his household."

"That's ridiculous. He knew what you did before you were married; knew that you were trained at Quantico and once worked for the Minnesota Bureau of Criminal Apprehension and all of that."

"He didn't know I was going to become important. He actually said that—'I didn't know you would become important.' Here I thought I was always important."

"Divorce him."

"Just like that?"

"Why not?"

"How did that work out with you and Cynthia?"

"It's not the same thing."

"You weren't married, but you were living together. You sold your house in Roseville to move in with her."

"The house was too big for me, and it was filled with—"

"Memories of Laura and Jenny."

"Yes."

"You moved in with Cynthia for two years, broke up, moved out, and bought a condominium. A year later you two reconciled, you sold your condo at a loss, moved back in with her, and broke up again. Now you're living in an apartment less than a mile from her house."

"St. Paul is a small city."

"No, it's not."

We drank more bourbon. Anne nestled against my chest. I tightened my grip on her shoulder.

"I was single when we first met," Anne said. "At the time, though, you were married to Laura. You became single after Laura was killed, only by then I was married to my first husband and had three kids. When I finally became free of him, you were in a committed relationship with Cynthia. Now that you're not with her, I'm married again. It seems we've never been able to get it right."

"So now we're getting it wrong."

"Do you want me to leave?"

"No."

Anne took both my glass and hers and set them on the table.

"I didn't think so," she said.

CHAPTER FOUR

St. Paul is a city of neighborhoods—many dozens of neighborhoods—and a man could easily spend a lifetime trying to sort them out. Even then he'd get an argument. I personally had no idea what was the difference between the West End and the West Side. I only know the people that resided there were happy to fight over it.

I lived in a four-story brown-brick building of studio, one-bedroom, and two-bedroom apartments in Crocus Hill, an eclectic, upper-income neighborhood of Victorian manors, carriage houses, and converted mansions that harkened back to the days of F. Scott Fitzgerald and bootleg booze. Some people—real estate agents mostly—insist that Crocus Hill is actually two neighborhoods subdivided by Summit Avenue, which just might have the longest stretch of mansions on a single road in the country. The "for sale or rent" listings refer to the area north of the avenue as Cathedral Hill because the houses are built around St. Paul's Cathedral. South of the avenue the area is labeled Summit Hill. I don't know why. It's the same damn hill.

I liked to jog the neighborhood before the kids lined up to catch their school buses, going east toward the edge of the hill looking out toward downtown St. Paul, cutting north across Summit, east again toward the cathedral, and then a slow southwest circle back to my place.

I had measured the route at exactly three-point-four miles. It also took me past the house where Cynthia Grey lived.

It was old and big—twelve rooms including a huge dining room that was perfect for entertaining. Cynthia had agreed to buy it before even setting foot in the place based solely on the recommendation of a real estate agent she had hired to scout properties. She hired another woman to furnish it—the cousin, if I'm not mistaken, of the woman she paid to clothes-shop for her, presenting her with a selection of the latest fashions in the spring and the fall. I promised myself I would never look for her as I passed, yet I nearly always did. Afterward, I'd ask myself the same question—"What the hell is wrong with you?"

Eight-fifteen A.M. and I knocked on Alexandra Campbell's front door, hoping she had already eaten her breakfast. She opened the door as if she were both surprised and dismayed that someone would interrupt her morning routine. She glanced at her watch after I identified myself.

"I have time for you, but not much," Campbell said.

She ushered me into her home and settled me on a sofa. Coffee was offered, and I accepted gratefully, not because I craved it but because I didn't want her to suspect I was there merely to catch her in a lie or trick her into making contradictory statements. She gave me what was left in the pot and sat across from me.

I was hoping she'd be a bimbo. I was hoping she'd have tats and piercings and speak with the vague uncertainty of someone who was well acquainted with pharmaceuticals—ya know. Instead, Campbell was a well-groomed forty-four-year-old tenured professor in the Department of Horticultural Science at the University of Minnesota. She was attractive but not flashy, intelligent without appearing condescending, and answered questions with the engaging demeanor of a woman who was unafraid of revealing embarrassing details about herself. She didn't even wear glasses. That, at least, would have been something.

"Professor Campbell, I'd like to ask a few questions," I said.

"About what I saw that night."

"About what you told the police and the county attorney."

"Happy to help. You have to call me Alex, though. You're too old to call me Professor."

She clamped her hand over her mouth and laughed into it.

"I'm sorry," she said. "That did not come out the way I meant. What I meant, only students and secretaries call me Professor."

I was torn. On one hand, I liked her. On the other, I knew she was going to be a very tough witness to discredit, and that basically was my job—to discredit her.

I gave her my card and told her to call me Taylor.

She accepted the card and gave her watch another glance.

"I'm not teaching this morning," Campbell said. "However, I like to maintain my scheduled office hours, especially this time of year. It's finals week, and panic is widespread. If we can proceed . . ."

"You live across the street from the house where Emily Denys lives."

"Lived, past tense. I'm sorry. That was rude of me."

"But true. Past tense."

"Terrible thing."

"Yes."

"I saw it."

"That's what you told the police. What you told the county attorney's office."

"Yes."

"Did you know Emily?"

"Yes."

"Did you speak to her?"

"Yes."

"How many times?"

"Are you asking for an exact number? A dozen times in the past year."

"So you recognized her?"

"Of course."

"Even at a distance?"

"Even at a distance."

"Would you say you knew her well?"

"Not at all. Our conversations were superficial and usually confined mostly to the weather. 'Will it ever stop snowing?' She asked me where I was from and what I did for a living, and I told her. I asked the same questions, and she replied that she worked for a bookstore, that she grew up in Albert Lea, and that she attended the University of Iowa. I told her not to let my students hear her say that, and she asked why, which I found odd. You'd think a UI grad would know that Gophers and Hawkeyes are not on speaking terms."

"You said you saw the killing."

Campbell paused before answering.

"I saw it," she said.

"What time was it?"

I was hoping she'd give an imprecise answer. She didn't.

"Nine fifty P.M.," Campbell said. "I like to watch the news before I go to bed, and I was keeping track of the time." She chuckled at the thought. "That's such a Minnesota thing—watch the ten P.M. news before going to bed."

"What did you see?" I asked.

"I saw Emily park her car in front of the duplex. I saw her walk toward the front door. A moment later, another car stopped behind hers. A woman got out and walked up behind Emily. The way she approached, I thought she was a friend and that she had followed Emily home. I saw Emily unlocking her door. I saw the woman raise up her hand. I didn't realize she held a gun until I saw the muzzle flash and heard the report. Emily fell. The woman walked back to her car."

"Walked?"

"Yes."

"She didn't run?"

"No. She didn't run."

"Professor Campbell," I said, "why did you wait so long before coming forward?"

"What do you mean?"

"Why didn't you tell all this to the police the night it happened?"

"I did."

"My understanding is that you didn't speak to the police until yesterday."

"I identified the woman who shot Emily yesterday. However, I spoke to the police the evening the shooting took place. I'm the one who called 911."

"Tell me about that."

"I called the police. Well, the 911 operator. I told her what happened. She notified the authorities, and then kept me on the line until the police arrived. I spoke to a detective named Casper—I still have his card. Yesterday, he returned, accompanied by another investigator who worked for the county attorney's office; a man named Martin McGaney. I have his card as well. They presented what they referred to as a photo array consisting of photographs of six different women and asked if I could identify any of them. I told them that the woman with strawberry-blond hair was one I saw kill Emily."

"Eleanor Barrington."

"I didn't know her name until after I picked her out."

"Had you ever seen her before?"

"No."

"Are you sure?"

"Yes."

"Did any other of the women in the photo array have strawberry hair?"

"No, but that made no difference."

A jury might disagree, I told myself. She must have known what I was thinking because he added, "The woman in the photo was the woman I saw shoot the gun."

"It was dark out at nine fifty, Professor Campbell."

"There was a full moon."

"Aside from the moon, was there any other light?"

"*Mr.* Taylor—since you refuse to call me Alex as I requested—come with me."

Campbell rose from her seat and went to her front door. I followed, because what else was I going to do? She stopped on her front steps and pointed to a garden beneath the picture window of her house. Most of the plants were just beginning to grow; tiny signs identified each species.

"I had just finished watering my plants," she said. "It's better at night. Illinois advises early morning watering—just before or after sunrise— to provide plants with sufficient water for the hotter and more stressful part of the day. Clemson, on the other hand, recommends nighttime because the maximum water is retained due to lower temperatures and wind speeds."

"Professor . . ."

"The point is I was standing right where I'm standing now when the murder took place. See there, there, and there?"

She pointed at three separate streetlights.

"They were all on," Campbell said. "Also, the light above Emily's front door was on. It's always on at night; it's wired to a timer. So, you see, I could see quite plainly. If you challenge my word, I suggest you return tonight, any night, stand where I'm standing, and look for yourself. The detective did."

"Still, it's what, seventy-five, eighty yards between here and there?"

"I wasn't close enough to see the color of the woman's eyes, if that's what you're asking."

"That's what I'm asking."

"Is there anything else, *Mr.* Taylor?"

"The vehicle that the killer drove . . ."

"I have no knowledge of cars. All I can tell you is what I told the other investigators—it was black, a very shiny black the way the light reflected off of it. And small. A coupe, I believe they call it. It had two doors."

I went at her a little more after that, soliciting specific details, repeating questions, challenging her memory of the events. There was nothing even remotely spurious in her responses or defensive in her manner. I expected that Helin would be considerably rougher in his questioning than I had been; yet I doubted he'd have any more success in jarring her testimony. No doubt he'd invite a judge to dismiss

Professor Campbell's statements on their merits, because that's what criminal lawyers do. I also knew the motion would be flatly denied.

It made me angry to think about it. Unlike Helin, I wasn't entirely sure Mrs. Barrington was innocent, but I was working for her, and I hate it when my team gets its ass kicked.

CHAPTER FIVE

North Oaks is nothing like the city where you live. For one thing, it owns no property. There isn't even a city hall; the mayor and city council meet once a month in the community room of a local bank. Police, fire, building inspections, trash and recycling, even legal services, are all provided by people and organizations that reside outside the city limits. A homeowners' association operates the parks. The streets are privately owned and maintained by the city's seventeen hundred residents and reserved solely for themselves and their guests. Believe me, they can afford it. The place can trace its origins directly to railroad tycoon James J. Hill and from his time till now North Oaks residents have always had one of the highest per capita incomes in the country. It used to have a gate manned by security guards, but that was abandoned some time ago. After all, it is Minnesota.

Mrs. Barrington's mansion, manor, plantation, estate, castle, palace—you decide what to call it—was located on Pleasant Lake. There was a long driveway leading up to it. I found what I had hoped I wouldn't find even before I stopped my car—a black, two-door BMW 640i coupe parked in front of a four-car garage. What's more, I was forced to agree with Professor Campbell. The way the sun glistened off the paint, it was a "very shiny black."

I went to the front door and rang the bell. I couldn't hear what it sounded like through the thick door. I waited long enough to wonder if it was even working when the door opened. An African American woman dressed in a maid's uniform stood on the other side; the kind of girl that Freddie used to chase, with a big chest and narrow hips. She seemed surprised to see me standing there, but it wasn't personal. I doubt even Girl Scouts were allowed to go door-to-door in North Oaks.

"May I help you?" she asked.

I introduced myself and added, "I'd like to speak to Mr. Barrington."

"I'll see if he's available to visitors."

"Is there a reason why he wouldn't be?"

"Hey, man—I only work here."

She closed the door, and I waited some more. I spent the time looking out over the grounds. It would have made a nice golf course if there hadn't been so many trees.

The door opened again, and the maid waved me inside. I stepped into a well-appointed foyer with a stone floor. To my right was an arched doorway that led to . . . I wanted to say a living room except it was so brilliant and well furnished, I didn't think anyone actually lived there. To my left was an identical archway that led to a dining room with a table large enough to skate on. In front of me was a spiraling staircase. There was a table next to the staircase. A silver plate rested on top of it, and I was reminded that there was a time when gentlemen callers would drop their cards on a tray to be delivered by servants to the lady of the house, who would then either grant or refuse admittance. Or maybe that only happened in the movies. Still, I would have paid money to open the drawer of the table to see how many cards were in there.

"Mr. Barrington will see you in the library," the woman said.

How cool is that, I thought. I decided the next time anyone came to visit me I was going to tell them *I'll see you in the library*, too. 'Course in my case, the library was also my living room, dining room, TV room, music room, rabbit pen, and computer hutch.

To reach the library, the maid led me past the staircase to a short corridor. Joel Barrington was standing in the center of the room when

I entered. He said nothing until the maid announced, "Mr. Taylor," and left the room, carefully closing the door behind her. Afterward, the words came out in a flurry.

"What the fuck do you want, you sonuvabitch?"

Given what I now do for a living and did before that as a cop, you'd think I'd be used to obscenities. Believe me, I heard them all in countless variations. Yet in that room, surrounded by several thousand hardcover books and comfy reading chairs and lamps, I was taken aback to the point where I actually took a step back. Joel must have taken that as a sign of weakness because he strode toward me, his fists clenched, his nostrils flaring.

"Why are you here, asshole?"

"Your mother—"

"Fuck my mother."

As soon as I was in range, he threw a punch.

I was shocked, yet not so shocked that I didn't get my left forearm up to block it. I was talking to myself—*This is crazy*—even as I slid my left hand up and grabbed Joel by the sleeve. I stepped inside, seized his right shoulder, and pivoted counterclockwise. *There's no reason for any of this.* At the same time, I set the inside of my right knee against his right leg, pulled with my left hand, pushed with my right, and lifted him off the floor. Yet I did not throw him as I was taught. *Be careful. He's the son of your client.* Instead, I pulled him over my leg and rested him gently on the floor without causing any of the bodily harm he so richly deserved. My sensei at Dragons, the dojo in Minneapolis where I work out at least a few times a month, would have been proud.

"When hand go out, withdraw anger," he liked to say. "When anger go out, withdraw hand."

Still . . .

"Do that again and I'll break your back," I said.

I stared down at him. Joel's face was twisted in pain as if I actually had thrown him across the room. His eyes were bloodshot, his face unshaved, and his hair was in need of a wash and comb. He shook his head back and forth as he spoke.

"You killed her, you killed Emily."

"No."

"You and my mother. You killed her."

"It's not true."

"It is. The paper said . . ."

The paper said what the CA wanted it to say, and I silently cursed Haukass for her irresponsible leaks. There wasn't a whole lot I could do about it, though, except perhaps give Joel something else to think about.

"Emily was hiding from someone," I said. "That's why she changed her name. She was hiding, and as soon as we learn who she was and who she was hiding from, we'll know who really killed her."

He stopped shaking his head and looked up at me as if the thought hadn't occurred to him before. Truth was, it hadn't occurred to me, either. I had been so intent on evaluating the mounting evidence against Mrs. Barrington that I had ignored until that moment what many lawyers call Plan B—blame someone else.

"No, it was my mother," Joel said. Yet the words weren't hurled with the same velocity.

I offered him my hand. He slapped it away, rolled to all fours, and stood on unsteady feet. He moved to a stuffed chair and sat; an old man at age twenty-four.

"I'm sorry for your loss," I said. "I know that you loved her. Emily wasn't the woman she claimed to be, though. You can see that, can't you?"

"She was kind. She loved me as much as I loved her. That's all I can see."

"Did she ever tell you her real name?"

"Emily was her real name. I don't care what you say."

"How did you meet?"

"How'd we meet, how'd we meet—you sound like my fucking mother. Where does she come from? Who are her people? Where did she go to school? She went to the fucking University of Iowa, goddammit."

What is with this family and its swearing, I wondered.

"No one by the name Emily Denys has ever been enrolled at Iowa," I said. "I checked."

"Bullshit."

"Mr. Barrington—"

"My mother killed her, and you helped."

"You say that as if you want it to be true."

"It is true. My mother knew I loved Em and that I wanted to marry her. Only she couldn't stand to see me happy with another woman. She couldn't stand to see me leave her house, leave her bed."

"Her bed?"

"Didn't my mother tell you? We've been sleeping together for six years."

"Are you serious?"

"It started nearly a year after my father was killed in a plane crash with his mistress. My mother came to my bedroom—it was the night of my eighteenth birthday party. She came to my bedroom and said she needed the comfort of a man's arms. That's what she told me—a man's arms. So I comforted her. It was my first time and I was happy to comfort her, comfort my mother. Only it didn't end there. My mother asked me to comfort her again the next night and the night after that. It became a regular occurrence. She'd come to me and say I was the only real man she knew and that she couldn't bear to spend the night without a real man and we'd comfort each other. Except that wasn't enough for her. Oh, no. She deliberately sabotaged every relationship I've ever had, chased away every girl I cared about because she needed her comfort. Because she didn't want me to leave her. That's why she killed Emily— to keep me to herself. I loved her so much. She was kind. She was good . . ."

Shock and anger and revulsion jolted me like well-aimed body blows. I tried not to let it show, but probably I did. Mrs. Barrington engaging in such a terrible thing—it felt worse than murder, somehow. I could have forgiven her for that. As for Joel—at what point during six long years of having sex with your mother do you stop being a victim and start becoming a co-conspirator? He certainly didn't sound as if he had been defenseless, unable to resist. Not at his age. The thought of them together, mother and child . . .

I fought the shock, though. I fought the anger and revulsion. I had spent a lot of years working for the cops, four of them in homicide. You're taught from the get-go to suppress your feelings, to take what comes. Otherwise your judgment becomes clouded; you make decisions based on emotion instead of facts. You can blow a case doing that. You can lose your life doing that. And if you suffered feelings of anxiety and stress later, along with unsettling memories and disturbing dreams, well, that was part of the job, too.

"Did you look for the gun, your mother's nine-millimeter Ruger, like we asked?" I said.

I didn't really care about the gun. I just wanted to think about something else for a moment.

"Yes, we looked," Joel said. "We couldn't find it because my mother ditched it after she killed Em."

There were a lot of other people who thought that, too, I reminded myself.

"The BMW in your driveway," I said. "Is that yours?"

"It belongs to my mother. She said it made her look young. Do you fucking believe that? She never wanted to be my mother. She wanted to be my fucking girlfriend. No more. No fucking more."

"Joel—"

"Do you hear me?"

"What you just told me, about you and your mother—did you tell the police?"

"Yes, I told them. I told them everything. Why wouldn't I? It's the truth. I hope the bitch goes to prison forever."

"Mr. Barrington—"

"Get out, Taylor. Get out of here before I kill you."

For a moment I wanted to see him try, so I could beat his brains in. I wasn't upset so much at Joel. I just wanted to hit somebody, anybody. Fortunately, cooler heads prevailed. Or was it my training again?

I retreated to the library door and yanked it open. A woman was standing behind it, an expression of abject terror etched across her young face. I didn't know if it was because I caught her eavesdropping or because of what she must have heard.

I glanced over my shoulder, making sure that Joel didn't see her, and

closed the door gently behind me. The woman was wearing blue jogging shorts and a sweatshirt with the sleeves pushed up; the name Har-
vard was stitched across the chest, although she was clearly too young
to be enrolled there. Her hair was strawberry like her mother's and tied
back in a ponytail. Her eyes were the color of blueberries and so clear
I thought I could see my reflection in them.

"Ms. . . ."

She wasn't interested in hearing anything I had to say. Instead, she
spun about and half ran across the corridor to the second-floor staircase. She padded up the stairs, reached the halfway point, stopped,
turned, and descended slowly. She paused four steps from the bottom
and leaned against the railing. I was forced to look up at her.

"You're Taylor," she said.

"Yes."

"I'm Devon."

"I know."

"I heard what . . . what my brother said. It's not true. Not a word of
it. I would know. He's just . . . he blames Mom for what happened to
Emily. He wants to hurt her for what happened to Emily, punish her.
That's why he's saying those lies. They are lies, Mr. Taylor. I promise
you they are. My mother didn't, she never . . . she didn't shoot Em,
either. It's all . . . it's crazy."

"How old are you?"

"Seventeen. Almost seventeen."

"I wish I could tell you something that would make all this better."

"Maybe I can tell you."

"What do you mean?"

"I can tell you about Emily. Joel won't."

I was desperate to hear what she had to say. The fact that she was a
minor frightened me, though.

"Your mother might not approve," I said.

"I don't care."

"You should talk to her or to her attorney."

"No. I'll talk to you. In private."

"Not in private," I said. "Not here. Meet me—" For a moment the only places I could think of were bars. "There's a coffeehouse off Highway 96 between here and the Shoreview Public Library."

"Caribou. On Village Center Drive before you get to the sushi place. I've been there. I know where it is. In two hours?"

"It would be better if you didn't come alone," I said.

She didn't say if she agreed or not, merely turned and climbed the stairs.

CHAPTER SIX

Stanislav, Kennedy, Helin, and DuBois was a litigation practice. It provided all the services you'd expect from a serious Top Ten law firm, yet its specialty was kicking ass and taking names. Every one of the fifty-seven attorneys on its roster had trial experience. Helin once told me that class ranking was low on the firm's list of prerequisites when interviewing potential associates. Mostly what the partners wanted to know was, Can you take a client's suit and beat someone over the head with it?

Some people might find such behavior appalling and point at SKH&D as an example of what's wrong in our sue-happy legal system. Can't we all just get along, they'd say. On the other hand, it's been responsible for a third of Freddie's income and mine over the past five years. Not to mention the best Christmas party of the season.

Which was one reason why I was always happy to walk the three blocks from my office to the Wells Fargo Center on Sixth and Marquette. The law offices were located on both the forty-first and forty-second floors, but the reception area was on forty-two, so that's where I stopped the elevator car. The doors slid open and I found Ramsey County Attorney Marianne Haukass glaring at me.

"Taylor." She spoke as if she had actually expected to see me there. "Talk to your friend."

She pushed past me as I stepped out of the elevator. Martin McGaney was with her. We had to perform a little dance before we could get around each other.

"Hey, Martin," I said. "How's it going?"

"Same old, same old. You?"

"Can't complain. See much of Scalasi these days?"

"Nah, man. The air she breathin' since they put stars on her shoulders is way too thin for us mere mortals. You?"

"Not since she married the architect."

"I hear he's a prick."

"McGaney," Haukass said.

McGaney stepped into the car.

"You know, boss, it doesn't always have to be a thing," he said.

The elevator doors closed before I heard her reply.

The receptionist recognized me and pressed a phone to her ear as I approached. She hung up just as I reached the desk and waved toward my right.

"He said to meet him in his office," she said.

"Thank you."

Helin started talking as I passed through the door.

"I was just about to call you," he said. "I'm taking Mrs. Barrington out of the adult detention center. Five o'clock. I'd like to do it later. Midnight. That way we'd miss the six and ten P.M. news cycles. The county deputies running the jail are acting all large and emphatic about it, though, insisting that inmates be released directly to the lobby no later than five P.M., which is bullshit, which makes me think Haukass is up to something. Anyway, I want you to be there. All right?"

"Sure."

"I'm trying to keep it secret, so there shouldn't be any cameras. But you never know."

"I'll be there."

"Good. Now tell me what you're doing here."

I don't know why I didn't just come out with it. Instead, I told him about my meeting with Professor Campbell, identifying a coupe similar to the one she described in Mrs. Barrington's driveway, and the fact her children had been unable to produce the gun.

"You could have told me that over the phone," Helin said.

"I bumped into the CA at the elevator."

"She came all the way across the river to offer me a deal, do you believe that?"

I wasn't surprised. The American justice system is dependent on deals; it's a rare case that actually sees the inside of a courtroom. That's because, unlike in the legal dramas you see on TV where the accused is nearly always innocent and usually saved by the heroic efforts of a brilliant, eccentric, and oh-so-sexy attorney who plays by his or her own set of rules, the vast majority of criminal defendants are guilty as hell. At the same time . . .

"This early in the proceedings?" I said. "Isn't that—"

"Bullshit."

"Premature? Especially if they can't produce the murder weapon?"

"Like I said before, she knows something I don't."

"Yeah, about that . . ."

I explained it all. Helin didn't speak for a long time, and I didn't interrupt him.

"Do you believe it's true?" he asked.

"The daughter says no. I have a meeting scheduled with her for later."

"Do you believe it, Taylor? You spoke to the man."

"Does it matter? How do you refute something like that?"

"You don't."

"It's so prejudicial—can the CA even get it into evidence?"

"She'll argue that it goes to motive, and once the words are spoken out loud in court—incest, mother-son incest—that's all the jury's going to hear. It's all they're going to think about. Maybe we should let Mrs. Barrington stay in jail a little while longer."

"I have a thought."

"Please."

"Joel is adamant that his mother killed Emily. I don't want for a second to tell you how to make your case, but to get his cooperation, I suggested that Emily was hiding from someone and that as soon as we learn who she was and who she was hiding from, we'll know who killed her."

"Plan B—it had crossed my mind. We know that the St. Paul Police Department ran her fingerprints through the FBI's fingerprint identification system and came up empty, which means Ms. Denys was never arrested anywhere for anything. Beyond that—it's possible the reason the cops haven't ID'd her yet is because they haven't been trying very hard. It's possible the CA doesn't want them to. Why complicate what looks like a slam dunk? Certainly, if we could argue Emily was hiding from someone—even if all we have is a person or persons unknown—that would provide a big complication."

"That's why I get the big bucks, to complicate things."

"You said you have an appointment with Devon Barrington? Go easy with her, Taylor. Kid-gloves treatment. She's underage."

"Plan B?" Freddie asked.

"Mrs. Barrington is going to need it."

I told him why.

"That is totally fucked up," Freddie said. "A mother sleeping with her son—I can't think of anything more fucked up than that."

"A father sleeping with his daughter?"

"How is that worse?"

"It just feels worse, maybe because I had a daughter."

"You know what I'm feeling? I'm feeling you might've been onto something before. I'm feeling this is one we really should walk away from."

"Nah, Freddie, you were right the first time. We can't quit. It'd be bad for business. Bad all around."

"Okay, so Plan B, then. You go talk to the little girl. I'll work on gettin' Emily's Social Security number; start there, see where it leads. I'm guessing the po-lice ain't gonna give us what they have."

"Sooner or later Haukass will have to turn over all pertinent information gathered in the case to Helin, but it's going to be later, as in the last possible moment."

"S'kay. I'm on it."

"Whoa, whoa. What about the prenup investigation we promised what's-his-name, you know, the gay guy who wanted us to check out his partner before he put a ring on it?"

"Tom Averback? A little overtime never hurt anyone."

"I don't want Echo to be upset with you."

"After I get done explaining, she's gonna be pissed at you, not me, don't worry about that."

"Who'd have thought you'd be the responsible one."

"Marriage and fatherhood does that."

"Yeah, I remember."

CHAPTER SEVEN

I'm not a coffeehouse guy. I don't think I've ever been in one except to meet a client who, for whatever reason, didn't want to be seen in my office. I have to admit, though—the café mocha Caribou served up was pretty good. Plus, the first link in its nationwide chain was forged in Edina, a self-satisfied suburb of Minneapolis, and I'm always one to support what's local.

I took the mocha to a table near the window. From there I was able to follow the progress of a black BMW 640i as it rolled down Village Center Drive, turned in to the parking lot, and maneuvered until it found an empty space. Both car doors opened, and I was pleased to see the maid step out on the passenger side. She had discarded her maid outfit for a pair of jeans and a tight T-shirt. Devon Barrington had changed clothes as well and was now dressed as if she were attending a business meeting—black jacket and skirt, white silk blouse, her hair down around her shoulders. She looked a full decade older than her "almost seventeen," and I thought it was dangerous for her to look like that at her age. Apparently the maid agreed, based on the scowl she gave me when she entered the coffeehouse, the one that said, "Don't even think about it."

Devon found me sitting against the glass and moved in my direction. The maid grabbed her elbow and pulled her back. Words were exchanged, although there was nothing angry about them. Devon continued to where I was sitting while the maid placed an order. I stood to greet her.

"Ms. Barrington," I said.

"Mr. Taylor."

She offered her hand and I shook it. It was very soft. I motioned at a chair and she sat, back straight and hands neatly folded on the table before us.

"The weather has been very pleasant," she said. "Don't you agree? Especially after that brutal winter."

"I do agree," I said. I was thinking that she was trying too hard to appear grown-up. I couldn't have that.

"Is school out for the summer?" I asked.

Devon's shoulders sagged almost imperceptibly as she answered.

"Last week," she said. "I'm already bored."

Given the maelstrom besetting her family, I found that to be a remarkable statement yet let it pass. By then the maid had appeared. She set a cardboard container of coffee on the table in front of the young woman.

"Thank you," Devon said.

"I'll be sitting over there. I'll be watching."

She meant it, too. The maid found an empty seat three tables away, and from that moment until she left the coffeehouse, she never took her eyes off me. I admired the way she was looking out for Devon. At the same time, it was very disconcerting.

"How well did you know Emily?" I asked.

Devon was deliberate in the way she took a sip of her beverage and set the cup down.

"I wish to discuss my brother first."

"Please do."

"He's a momma's boy. I know that sounds"—she searched for a word and found "silly. Especially considering what was said earlier. He's a full seven years older, yet he always seemed to demand more of Mother's attention than I did. My concern is that he might have fabricated some rather awkward adolescent sexual fantasies involving her that he has now twisted for purposes of revenge. Unfounded fantasies, I hasten to add."

"That's a lot of psychology for someone so young and well presented, too."

"I'm not so young, Mr. Taylor. Given our unfettered access to on-line content, I believe you'll find that my generation has grown much older much more quickly than previous generations."

"Let's talk about Emily Denys."

Devon took another sip of coffee before responding.

"My mother did not kill her," she said. "I know this for a fact."

"Do you?"

"For one thing, my mother would never commit such a crime. She is scrupulously law-abiding."

"No one is scrupulously law-abiding."

"My mother is. When she was nine years old, she told the police that her parents were growing pot in the wooded area behind their house. She knew what they were doing was wrong, you see."

"What did your grandparents think about that?"

"I don't know. I've never met them. My point—she would never have committed the act of which she stands accused."

"Why did your mother turn in her own parents? Did she ever tell you?"

"It was because they smoked marijuana daily and the smoke made her sick and she was afraid her dog would become sick, too."

"If she did that for her dog, imagine what she might do for her children."

"I can prove she didn't kill Em."

"How?"

"She . . . she was with me when the crime was committed."

I liked the way Devon was standing up for her family. It made me want to squeeze her hand and hug her shoulder. I did neither. Instead, I said, "Don't do that. Don't lie to protect your mother."

"I'm not lying."

"It's not on you to fix your family's mistakes. Whatever happened—and we still haven't sorted it out—it's not your fault or your responsibility."

"What's the phrase—last man standing? That's me. I'm the only adult left. If it wasn't for Ophira, I'd probably have a breakdown, too—just like Joel."

"Who's Ophira?"

"Our housekeeper. My friend."

I found the maid's eyes and raised my coffee in salute. She just kept staring.

"Devon, it's all right to be almost seventeen," I said. "In fact, I highly recommend it. I would hope that you stay almost seventeen for as long as humanly possible."

Her eyes narrowed as if she were concentrating on a single point far off in the distance.

"You don't seem to understand," Devon said. "Mr. Taylor, my father was killed under circumstances that brought scandal and embarrassment to my family. My mother is now in jail, accused of murdering my brother's girlfriend. My brother, who up until a few days ago was a smart, funny, caring, and gentle man, has become a raving lunatic accusing my mom of unimaginable crimes. Almost seventeen is no longer an option for me."

Poor sad little rich girl, I told myself. Make a Lifetime movie about her and we can all have a good cry, including me. Only it wasn't my job to feel sorry for her. I needed information.

"I don't know if you've been told," I said. "The plan is to bring your mother home tonight. You should have a long talk with her."

"I will."

"In the meantime . . ."

"You want to know about Emily. I liked her very much. Joel and I have always had a really solid big-brother–little-sister relationship. I can't remember a time when he wasn't looking out for me, you know? So when he started bringing Em around, I figured she was just being nice to me because of him, which is what the other girls he dated did. Pretend to like me. Only, Em, she really did. Like me, I mean. She was way nicer to me than she needed to be, taking me shopping and stuff even when Joel wasn't around. Not once did she ever begin a sentence by saying 'When I was your age' or 'When I was in high school' or 'When I was dating boys.' She was just so cool."

I believed her, too. The way Devon's blueberry eyes glistened as she described her friend, the way her language became more representative of her age, I decided Emily must have been very cool indeed.

"Did she ever talk about herself?"

"I never gave it any thought until we found out later that she wasn't . . . that her name wasn't Emily. But you know what? She never did speak about her own family or her friends or where she grew up or anything like that. It's only now, looking back, that I realize how lonely she must have been. She was the most profoundly lonely person I'd ever known. Funny how I didn't see that at the time."

"Maybe it was because when she was with you, she didn't feel lonely."

"You think? That would be . . . I hope that was true. I really do."

"How did she and your brother meet?"

"They met in a bookstore. I suppose you can blame me, because it was Christmas, going to be Christmas, and Joel didn't know what books to buy, didn't know what his sixteen-year-old sister wanted to read, so he asked Emily, and she was so pretty. Don't you think she was pretty, Taylor?"

"I wouldn't know."

Devon fished her smartphone from her bag and pulled up several photographs. She leaned across the table and angled the cell so we both could see them. I leaned in, too, but the look in Ophira's eyes caused me to pull back.

There were shots of Emily at the Mall of America, the Walker Art Center, a Minnesota Wild game, and what looked like someone's backyard. In many she was alone. Most were selfies, though, of her and Devon taken at arm's length. The girl was right—Emily was very pretty indeed, with luminous green eyes and short black hair.

I asked if I could take some of the photos, and Devon agreed, sending half a dozen shots to my smartphone.

"Anyway," she said. "Joel didn't know what to buy me, and he asked

Emily for recommendations. She said he should just get me a gift card and let me choose, only Joel thought that was lame, so between the two of them they selected sixteen books, one for each year. They should have given me the gift card because I read like three of them. But it gave Joel an excuse to spend hours with her, and then he asked her to coffee and then dinner and then drinks, and then they became an item, and then they became much more than that. So he got what he wanted, a girl-friend, and I got . . . what I really wanted was a car."

"From your pics, you seem to have spent a lot of time with Emily."

"I had to go to school, and she worked, and then Joel didn't want me hanging around with them like every minute, but yeah, I guess."

"Did Emily ever seem nervous or anxious to you? Did she ever seem out of sorts?"

"No, I don't think so. She was always calm . . . Except for that one time."

"What one time?"

"It was at the office. It was the day . . . it was the day before, before . . ."

Devon stared up and to her right as if she were conjuring the scene from her memory. Her eyes closed. When she opened them again, they were wet and shiny.

"The office?" I said.

"My mother has a suite of offices in downtown Minneapolis. That's where our accountants work, the people who run our businesses. It was my last day of school. We had a half day, which doesn't make sense to me. Why make us go to school for a half day on the last day? What's the point? We had nothing to do; our lockers were already cleared out. Anyway, Emily came to get me because she and Joel were going to take me to lunch at someplace really nice. We went downtown to meet him. Only the receptionist told us Joel was in a conference that had gone on longer than anyone had expected.

"We decided to camp out in the reception area and wait. After a while, Em said she was going to give Joel a wave, let him know that we were there. This wasn't as disruptive as it sounds because the confer-ence room, the whole room, was surrounded by glass walls, so she could just walk past and he would see her. She didn't even have to knock on the door or anything.

"Then she comes back and she's just . . . agitated. She walks right out the door. I'm like—what? And she says, 'I'm tired of waiting. Are you coming or not?' And she leaves and I follow her. We had lunch and she took me home, and the next day . . .'"

Tears formed in Devon's eyes that she wiped away with her knuckles.

"I don't want to cry," she said. "I've been trying so hard not to cry. You have to believe me, Taylor. My mother didn't do this."

"I do believe you." I didn't tell her why, though. "Do me a favor, honey. Do yourself a favor. Go home and cry your eyes out."

"What good would that do?" She turned her head and took a deep breath. "Good-bye, Taylor." She stood and rushed out the coffeehouse door.

Ophira stood, too, and made to follow her, pausing only long enough to glare at me as if she had seen Devon's tears, blamed me for them, and was now contemplating an appropriate punishment.

"Apparently you do more than just work there," I said.

"I don't know what you're talking about."

"So much craziness going on—keep an eye out for her, would you?"

"Someone needs to."

CHAPTER EIGHT

The receptionist who directed traffic at Mrs. Barrington's offices didn't know if she should talk to me. It wasn't that she had been sworn to secrecy. It was that she was loyal to her employer and wasn't sure if answering my questions would help her or hurt. Admitting to the cops that she heard Mrs. Barrington threaten to kill Emily Denys, she was sure that had hurt.

I had heard the threats as well since I had been standing there when they were made, the neatly printed results of Emily's background investigation in my hand. Yet I assured the receptionist that I was on Mrs. Barrington's side, too. I dropped the name of her attorney in case she wanted to check. To her credit, she did. You'd be surprised how many people would have simply taken my word for it.

Once Helin confirmed my identity, the receptionist started answering questions I hadn't even asked.

"You'll want to know about Joel," she said. "More and more he had been getting involved in day-to-day operations. Yet he's so young—younger than I am, even. It's hard to take him seriously, especially since he's always running to his mother for advice."

"That's what mothers are for."

"He wants desperately to be taken seriously, though; prove he's the man of the house, if you know what I mean."

"I know."

"Now, Devon Barrington—what a sweetheart. Always polite, always respectful, always smiling; never acts like she owns the place. When she talks to people, it's Mr. This or Ms. That. She refuses to call anyone by his or her first name. She says it's presumptuous. I love her to death. Everyone does."

"I'm interested in the meeting . . ."

"The meeting you asked about. Let's see."

The receptionist consulted the appointment calendar on her computer.

"Here it is—eleven A.M. to eleven forty-five A.M. U.S. Sand. Richard Kaufman. Allen Palo. They brought a secretary with them, too. Young woman. I don't have her name."

I transcribed the names she did have into my notebook and asked, "What was the meeting about?"

"I don't know. Something about digging up fracking sand, I guess. That's what U.S. Sand does. Operates fracking sand mines."

I dropped a few bars in the elevator car, yet the signal was strong enough that I could use my smartphone. It rang twice before Freddie answered.

"Fredericks and Taylor Private Investigations," he said.

"I still say we should have done best two out of three when we decided on our name."

"Quit your whining. You're the one who said tails never fails."

"Say, I've got a quick research job for you."

I told him what I wanted.

"How quick?" Freddie asked.

"Tomorrow morning is soon enough, I think. I need to run down to the jail and work crowd control while Helin springs Mrs. Barrington."

"Is there going to be a crowd?"

"Depends on the county attorney, I guess."

"Should I tell you what I discovered about the Denys girl or wait until tomorrow?"

"Tell me now."

By then I had escaped the elevator and was passing through the building's opulent lobby.

"I checked with the bookstore where she worked," Freddie said. "They might not have talked to me except the po-lice had already been there, so now they figured it was okay. What they told me, their employment process starts with an online application. If they like what they see, they bring the applicant in for an interview. If that goes well, the applicant gets a second interview. Somewhere along the line, the applicant must produce a photo ID. In Denys's case, she used a Minnesota driver's license. The store also conducts criminal background checks, something they do for every employee. Don't want no coke-heads, no embezzlers. 'Course, if that's all they do—"

"They're only checking the name the applicant supplied against police arrest reports. If the name is false, nothing will show up."

"Exactly, so she gets the job. Now, the Denys girl has to fill out a W-2 form listing her Social Security number, which she does, but after thirteen months of employment, of paying taxes to the man, of actually filing a return and getting a refund check, there ain't a single hiccup."

"Which means the number is probably legit. How is that possible?"

"What I'm saying, Taylor—the woman was ghosting. She did the cemetery thing, strolling among the headstones till she found someone who died who woulda been roughly the same age that she was, and stole her name. She obtained the dead person's birth certificate and used it to create a new identity—Social Security number, driver's license, what else?"

"Ghosting, Freddie, is based on the premise that government agencies don't share information, and maybe that worked fine before computers, when birth certificates were stored in one room and death certificates were stored in another down at the ol' county courthouse. Now, though, it's relatively easy for a clerk to use a search engine to see if a death certificate had ever been issued to the person listed on a birth certificate. Besides, a ghoster who applies for a replacement of a Social Security card issued to someone who died ten years ago, who claims to be that individual—the government is going to ask why she hadn't filed a tax return in all that time, why she didn't report any wages."

"Are you done? Because seriously, you're embarrassing me."

"Explain it, then."

"It's lots easier for a woman to take over a dead person's identity than it is for a man. You know that, Taylor, c'mon. What she does, she steals the ID of a dead female who was *married* and used her husband's name. That way the birth certificate and the death certificate will have two different surnames, which makes detection tougher, okay? Plus, the gaps in the ghost's employment history are gonna cause less suspicion because the ghost can claim that she spent those years workin' as a housewife, as a stay-at-home mom who made no wages."

"I like it."

"'Course you do."

"Except—"

"Here it comes."

"Ghosting only works if no one asks questions. Once you start looking like I did . . .'"

"That's the thing. No one was looking. The cops, you say they ran the Denys girl's fingers through the FBI's Integrated Automated Fingerprint Identification System, which means she's never been arrested. A search through the National Crime Information Center's missing persons files and the Minnesota Missing and Unidentified Persons Clearinghouse must have proved inconclusive, too."

"Which tells us what?"

"There was no drama. She didn't just disappear, making people wonder what happened to her, if she was kidnapped or murdered or hiding from an abusive husband or what. She was never declared a missing person; no one called the cops, said 'Find the girl.' She must not have left any debts behind, either, leastwise not big ones, cuz you know those guys, debt collectors, they never stop looking, and our girl wasn't that clever she couldn't have been found out by now."

"What you're saying, Emily was ghosting behind a new name and a new identity, even though no one seemed to be looking for her."

"What I'm saying."

"So why was she hiding?"

By then I was standing at a street corner with a dozen other pedestrians waiting for the light to change.

"I don't know," Freddie said. "But she *was* hiding, there ain't no doubt of that, is there?"

"I'll talk to you tomorrow."

"By the way, we're running low on K-Cups."

"Okay."

"Get the ones with cinnamon."

I was expecting a classic media frenzy like the kind you see on television. Certainly the CA had worked hard to create one. She must have informed every local TV station, news radio outlet, and newspaper, not to mention a couple of online news sites, of the exact time Eleanor Barrington was to be released from the Ramsey County Adult Detention Center, because each had representatives waiting in the lobby. Still, this was Minnesota, after all, and what I found more accurately resembled guppies nipping at the food flakes you sprinkle on the top of a fish tank than a shark attack.

The representatives stood politely along the walls, trying hard not to impede the progress of people who came and went through the front doors. They spoke quietly to themselves; there was laughter, but it was muted. The scene reminded me of visitors to an art museum who were having a wonderful time yet didn't want to disturb the patrons around them.

A long-legged blonde who looked better on TV than she did in person thought she recognized me and whispered, "Are you Holland Taylor?"

"I'm sorry, who?"

"The detective?"

I acted as if I had never heard the word before. At the same time, I thought: I don't have any plans for tonight . . .

"Never mind," she said.

Oh, well.

Finally, Eleanor Barrington stepped out of the elevator clad in a conservative business suit and holding the hand of her attorney. Film lights flicked on and camera flashes went off as if she were stepping onto the red carpet at a Hollywood premiere. The TV and radio reporters surged forward, microphones leading the way. I moved to insert myself between them and Mrs. Barrington. The print reporters hung back, probably out of courtesy to their broadcast brethren. The TV and radio reporters shouted. They wanted to have tape of themselves asking their questions for the ninety-second news holes they would fill later. Nobody actually expected Mrs. Barrington to answer the questions, though, which is why they were as surprised as I was when she slowed to address the reporters, walking at about ten feet per minute and speaking in a clear, almost melancholy voice.

"I adored that young lady. I wish this was over so I could mourn her death properly.

"No, I most emphatically did not kill her.

"Yes, I made that stupid remark. It was a turn of phrase taken out of context. I'm sure you're all guilty of saying the same thing at one time or another.

"It haunts me. I wish I could take it back.

"My son is heartbroken as are we all.

"Locked in jail for a crime I didn't commit—no, I don't feel justice is being served."

David Helin pulled on her hand, which served as a signal for Mrs. Barrington to stop speaking and pick up the pace.

"I'm sorry," she said. "It's been a terrible ordeal, and I just can't answer any more questions."

I pushed forward, creating a path to the front door. I expected resistance. There was none. The reporters seemed more than happy to step aside. It was a little disappointing. I would have been happy to accidentally nudge the long-legged blonde into a wall and then later apologize and offer to make it up to her.

The reporters kept asking questions.

Mrs. Barrington kept saying, "I'm sorry, I'm sorry."

I reached the door and yanked it open. Mrs. Barrington and Helin stepped past me. The door closed behind us. The reporters did not follow; I couldn't tell you why.

Helin was parked in the first row of the parking lot. He led us to his car, unlocked it with a remote, and opened the passenger door for Mrs. Barrington. She slid inside.

"I have questions, too," I said.

The expression on her face suggested that she wanted to hear them. Helin shut the door.

"Tomorrow," he said. He rounded the car and opened the driver's side door. "We'll talk tomorrow."

Helin started up the car and drove off as I walked to my own vehicle. He paused at the exit, his turn signal blinking, while a second car drove past him into the parking lot. I recognized the driver and watched the car as it moved quickly along the big curve and came to a sudden stop in front of the entrance to the detention center. County Attorney Marianne Haukass opened the passenger door and was stepping out even as the car rocked to a halt. She walked toward the building as if she were late for a very important date.

Then I understood—the reporters had remained inside the lobby so they could record the CA's promised rebuttal to Barrington's remarks, no doubt using the federal, state, and county flags as a backdrop.

Martin McGaney had been driving the car. He slipped out, leaned against the body, and settled in to wait for the CA. I called to him.

"Don't you just love politics?" I said.

"Marianne said I'm not to socialize with you anymore," he said. "You're the enemy, she said, and don't you forget it. And yes, I just love politics."

I lived about ten miles from the detention center, yet because of the rush hour traffic, it took me nearly thirty minutes to get home. I used a security code to get inside the building and a key to enter my second-floor apartment. I stood behind the closed door and contemplated the immediate future. I had a well-stocked refrigerator but didn't feel like cooking. So I left the apartment and ordered takeout from Dixie's down on Grand Avenue, brought it back, and ate it. Amanda Wede-meyer didn't knock on the door asking to play with Ogilvy. Anne Scalasi didn't drop by in search of stress relief. The phone didn't ring.

The Twins were playing the White Sox, and I watched a couple of innings. I turned the game off when I realized I didn't care if they won or lost. I used to *love* baseball. I found a book and started reading. Cynthia had always been amazed by the size of my library, literally thousands of hardcovers and paperbacks in bookcases and stacked on the floor. She asked me once if I had read them all, and I answered, "Why would anyone want a library filled only with books they've already read?" Yet it took me only twenty pages before I realized I *had* read the book before. I set it down and searched for another. I couldn't find any that didn't sound like something I had already read twice. I thought about heading for a bookstore to restock. Only I couldn't think of any titles or authors that I just had to have.

I opened a bottle of Maker's Mark, filled a tall glass, and turned on the TV again. Between the bourbon and a couple of sitcoms, I was numb in no time.

CHAPTER NINE

I was usually the first to arrive at the office in the morning, mostly because I couldn't think of a reason not to be. I brewed a K-Cup, the Cinnamon Sugar Cookie from Cameron's Coffee that Freddie liked so much, and watched as downtown Minneapolis came alive outside the window. Freddie had mentioned more than once that we should find new digs once our lease expired, somewhere that provided easier access for walk-in clients and where, as my mom would say, you don't have to pay a man twenty dollars to park your car. I was hesitant. Partly because we would be further removed from the law firms that provided so much of our income. And partly because I would miss the hustle and bustle of the city; I would miss the view. Who wanted to stare out the window at the parking lot of some crappy corporate office complex in the suburbs?

Freddie arrived and called my name. I called his back, which was how we greeted each other.

"Anything on the agenda I should know about?" I asked.

"Sackett called right after we talked yesterday. Company might be expanding."

"Good for them."

"They want to set up a time next week to talk about investigating the guys they're buyin' out, make sure they're on the up-and-up. They're also talking about maybe forty employee background checks, investigate every one of their new employees."

"Sounds lucrative."

"What I was thinking. About the frackin' guys—wait. I gotta tell you first. I mighta laid it on a little thick when I got home late last night, so if'n Echo seems a little icy next time you see her, that's on me."

"Swell."

"Just sayin'."

"What about the fracking guys?"

"U.S. Sand. It's based in Chicago with fifteen offices scattered around the country and Canada. It specializes in mining and processing silica sand. It used to be silica sand was like the main ingredient in making glass. 'Course now it's all about fracking. They pump this shit into the ground to open cracks and fissures that let the natural gas and oil flow out."

"Which is controversial."

"Which is *way* controversial. Week or so ago, thirty folks were arrested in Winona for protesting against frackin' on land owned by U.S. Sand. Which is probably why the website doesn't list names of the executive board members. They don't want people camping outside their mansions with protest signs. 'Course, they're not hard to find, you know? Just takes a couple of extra steps. These two guys—Richard Kaufman and Allen Palo—they're both directors of development, what they call themselves. They work out of an office near the state capitol building in St. Paul. Want to be close by so they can lobby them legislators."

"Why were they talking to the Barrington family, I wonder?"

"You know what we don't do that we should do? We don't give out bonuses. Cuz seriously, I deserve a bonus for this."

"For what?"

"U.S. Sand has a major operation going in a town called Arona in western Wisconsin. Lots of fireworks going on over there. Anyway, the Barrington family owns two hundred and fifty-four acres of land along the Trempealeau River just outside of Arona. I'm guessing U.S. Sand wants to buy or lease some of it."

"How do you know?"

"I accessed the county's property tax records."

"My God, you're getting good at this."

"About that bonus . . ."

"I bought the cinnamon K-Cups you wanted."

"Wow. That's all I got t' say to you. Wow."

"Emily sees Joel negotiating with U.S. Sand, and it upsets her enough that she bolts from the office."

"Could be she was a die-hard environmentalist," Freddie said. "These sand frackers, they strip the land, turning it into, well, a giant sandbox. So when she sees the boyfriend and them it pisses her off."

"Okay so far."

"She confronts Joel, calls him a few dirty names. Joel loses it and shoots her with the old lady's gun and decides to let her take the rap, piling on with this incest shit to make sure she goes down hard, leaving him to inherit the estate."

"Sounds like an episode of *Law and Order*."

"If you don't like that—you said the receptionist told you that Joel wants to be big man on campus. Okay, how 'bout he's hot for the deal with the sand frackers, but Mom's against it, so him and the frackers knock off the girl and frame Mom so Joel can take over and make the deal."

"Why kill Emily? Why not just pop the old lady?"

"Because then the cops will be all over Joel. This way Joel and the sand frackers are in the clear."

"That's awfully thin, too."

"My understanding, Plan B ain't about proving Mrs. Barrington is innocent, it's about throwing enough shit at the jury to create whatcha-call reasonable doubt."

"Yeah, but I doubt if Mom will let us throw her son under the bus like that."

"Why not? He's doing it to her."

"Still . . ."

"Okay, I got another theory. What if it ain't about the fracking company at all but the fracking guys themselves that made her run? They're from Chicago. Could be the Denys girl was from Chicago, maybe a prostitute in a previous life and they were her johns, something like that."

"She recognized them—"

"Or they recognized her—"

"Could you—"

"I'm on it."

A dark blue Chrysler 300 picked me up as I turned off Highway 96 onto West Pleasant Lake Road and followed at a respectful distance as I maneuvered through the North Oaks Golf Club to the lane that lead to Mrs. Barrington's palatial estate. It closed the distance, coming to within a car's length of my rear bumper when I drove up the long, meandering driveway, and I half expected to hear sirens and see flashing lights. When they didn't come, I figured it was because the driver didn't wish to disturb the neighborhood over a guy whose sole crime was driving an eight-year-old Toyota Camry in the land of milk and honey.

I parked it at the top of the driveway. I demonstrated my disdain for the tail by completely ignoring him as I walked to Mrs. Barrington's massive front door and rang the bell. The African American maid appeared moments later.

"Hello, Ophira," I said.

"It's you."

I threw a thumb over my shoulder in the general direction of the Chrysler.

"Friend of yours?" I asked.

"No friend of mine. He's a CSO—community service officer. Likes to roam the streets looking for trouble. He used to follow me all the time when I first started working here."

"That's because you're such a dangerous-looking young lady."

"I'm sure that was it."

Ophira opened the door wide, and I stepped past her. She blew a kiss at the officer before closing the door.

"Mrs. Barrington said you'd be around this morning. She said to put you in the library."

"Nice."

Ophira looked at me like I was nuts.

"How's Devon?" I asked.

"Much better."

I was two strides past her when I noticed she had stopped walking. I turned to meet her gaze.

"What did you say to her?" Ophira asked.

"I told her that none of what was going on was her responsibility."

"There had to be more to it than that."

"I also told her to have a good cry."

She stared at me as if she thought I was putting her on.

"May I ask you a couple of questions?" I said.

"Not about her."

"About Devon's brother."

"What 'bout him?"

"And his girlfriend."

"What 'bout him?"

"Were they together the night she was killed?"

"If you want to call it that."

"What would you call it?"

"Her running out of the house and him chasing, saying, 'Let me explain, let me explain'—that ain't together. That's coming apart."

"What were they fighting about?"

"I can't say."

"You can't say because you don't know or can't say because something is keeping you from speaking out?"

Ophira jabbed a finger toward an open door.

"In there," she said. "Don't touch anything."

I stepped inside the library. A grandfather's clock beat a steady rhythm. Beyond that, I heard no sound. I browsed the shelves. There didn't seem to be any strategy to how the books were displayed, fiction mixed with nonfiction, some novels in French and some in Italian, and

I wondered how the owners found anything. Or did they even bother to look? It could be, I told myself, the books were bought strictly for display.

"Good morning, Taylor."

The greeting caused me to pivot away from the shelves toward the door. Eleanor Barrington swept into the room the way you'd expect a 1940s movie star to enter—think Katharine Hepburn in *The Philadelphia Story*. She was wearing a summer dress with a revealing neckline and a full skirt that flowed like waves at sea.

"Good morning," I said.

She walked straight up to me and hugged my shoulders as if we were besties too long apart.

"It's good to be free," she said.

"You did well with the media last night. I was very impressed."

"That's kind of you to say."

"You behaved as if you actually did care what happened to Emily."

"David Helin prepared me for the questions I would be asked, and we rehearsed how to answer them."

"I guessed."

"So . . ." Mrs. Barrington stepped into the center of the room. "What do you think?"

"About what?"

"My ensemble, silly."

She spun in a circle, the smile never leaving her face.

"Very nice," I said.

"I wanted to look like a woman. After spending all that time in jail with those . . . people—it was important to me that I look like a woman. Do you think I look like a woman, Taylor?"

"That sounds like a trick question."

"And you don't miss a trick, do you?"

Mrs. Barrington laughed, although I had no idea what she thought was so funny. She moved to a cabinet and opened the doors, revealing a cache of alcohol.

"Is it too early for you to drink?" she asked.

"It's too early for anyone to drink."

Mrs. Barrington filled a squat glass with thirty-year-old Macallan, drank some, replaced what she drank from the bottle, and took another sip.

"Fuck, I needed that," she said. "Three days in jail."

"The Ramsey County Detention Center isn't exactly Devil's Island, and you're not Dreyfus released after five years of false imprisonment."

"My, but you do speak your mind, don't you? I used to like that about you. Now I don't."

"Ahh."

"I don't like you poking around my life. You questioned my son yesterday. My daughter, too. That makes me angry. Very angry."

"Actually, Devon wanted to talk to me and I let her. I concede your point, though. It won't happen again."

"It better not. I told Helin it fucking better not."

"Is there anything else?"

"Mr. Taylor, you wanted to speak to me, remember?"

"Yes. I have a few questions."

"You can ask me anything you like. Me. Not my children."

"U.S. Sand—"

"Assholes." Mrs. Barrington took another sip of her Scotch. "Are you sure I can't get you anything?"

"Why are they assholes?"

"They want to turn western Wisconsin into one massive silica sand mine. They've been buying property around Arona for some time now. Last year they made an offer on half of the land I own along the Trempealeau River. I turned them down, partly because I don't approve of their shitty methods. They preach environmental responsibility, claim to be eco-friendly. If you go to where they've been, you'll see that it isn't true. Mostly, though, it was because the property has provided my family, my husband's family, a refuge for many decades, and it's just too dear to give up."

"Your son met with representatives of U.S. Sand the day before Emily Denys was killed."

"That's true."

"Emily became very upset when she learned of the meeting."

"I can't imagine why."

"Why was there a meeting at all if you had already turned them down?"

"U.S. Sand didn't go away just because I told them to. They've continued to acquire property, continued to expand their operations in Arona. During the thirteen months since we last spoke, they've obtained nearly a thousand acres. Mines are being developed all over the place. It's not going to stop, either. The demand for silica sand for use in fracking is insatiable. An estimated ten thousand tons is needed for a single well. That's thirty to forty million metric tons a year, Taylor. It's going to get worse, too. You can be sure there will be more mines and more and more. In both Wisconsin and Minnesota.

"If that's not enough, water usage is intensive. The average mine requires as much as a half-million gallons each working day, and most of the mines work seven days a week. To get it, they're draining the watershed; they're taking it from the river. They are, in essence, creating what amounts to a man-made drought. And don't get me started about runoff.

"The point is—my property has an estimated market value of about three-quarters of a million dollars today, and it's dropping because of the effect sand mining is having on the community—the dust, the noise, the unending convoy of trucks. U. S. Sand is offering one-point-five million. Of course I'm going to listen."

"Did Emily know this?"

"If she did, I didn't tell her."

"Did your son?"

"I have no idea what they found to talk about. Taylor, there's nothing criminal about any of this. There's no conspiracy, nothing to hide, nothing to kill anyone over. It's strictly business. A multibillion-dollar business as it turns out."

"Okay."

"Is that it?"

"For now."

"Aren't you going to ask me? I know you want to."

"I'm sure we'll chat more as the case proceeds."

"Go ahead and ask. I won't be upset."

"Your son is prepared to testify against you."

"He'll change his mind."

"He's already made allegations that can be used in court."

Mrs. Barrington finished her Scotch, went to the cabinet, and re-filled her glass. She drank half of it and pressed the glass against her forehead.

"Ask me," she said.

"I'm not your lawyer."

"You want to know."

"It won't make any difference to how I do my job."

"It's true. Everything my son said is true."

"Okay."

"Okay? What's that supposed to mean?"

"Who else knows about you and Joel?"

"No one."

"Devon?"

"No one."

"Emily?"

"No. One."

"The night she died, she was upset about something."

"I don't know anything about that."

"Okay."

"Okay, okay. Admit it, Taylor—you hate me."

"Honestly, Eleanor"—it was the first time I used her given name—"I don't hate you. I don't hate anyone anymore. I used to. The list of people I hated was long and not particularly well organized. Yet over the years . . . Probably it's a product of seeing so many good people doing so many awful things for reasons that seem valid at the time. You can't hate that many people without becoming hateful yourself. It just drains you, too, the hate. Now—I'm like most people. I make it up as I go along. Mostly, I guess, it's a matter of what I can live with, and more and more I find that I can live with just about anything."

"Then I guess I'll have to hate myself."

"Feel free."

Mrs. Barrington fixed her eyes on me. For a moment, I thought she was going to speak. Instead, she took another long pull of the expensive Scotch and turned her back.

I said good-bye and left the room.

CHAPTER TEN

Helin had parked his car next to mine in the driveway, a Lexus GS. No one followed him, I noticed. He was walking toward the Barringtons' front door as I left the house. We met halfway.

"Do you want to know what I have so far or would you rather wait until I can put it in writing?" I asked.

"What I want, Taylor—no more conversations with anyone in the Barrington family unless I'm present."

"So I've been informed."

"I had a long discussion with Mrs. Barrington last night and . . . Listen, it's not you. You're the best investigator I've ever worked with, believe that. It's all on them. What a mess."

"Don't worry about it."

"I've had more likable clients than this one, that's for sure. Remember Judith Marie Strobel? What a joy she was."

"Too bad she poisoned her husband."

"What can you do? Sometimes the people we like really are criminals. This woman, though. She is so . . . so . . ."

"Screwed up?"

"We need to keep her out of a courtroom. The minute she steps into a courtroom . . . Find out about the girl, Taylor. Please. Hope she ripped

off a Mexican drug cartel, because right now that's the only chance
Mrs. Barrington's got."

"I'll do my best."

"You know, after Eleanor admitted that what her son said was true,
I came this close to walking away."

"Freddie and I were tempted to do the same thing."

"Why didn't you?" Helin asked.

"Why didn't *you*?"

"Professional pride, I suppose. Besides, despite everything, I still
don't believe she's guilty."

"At least not of the crime of murder."

I pulled out of Mrs. Barrington's driveway. The Chrysler 300 was
waiting for me. I spoke to its reflection in my rearview mirror as I ne-
gotiated the residential streets.

"C'mon, man. Don't you have anything better to do?"

I kept driving. He kept following. I had a thought. I pulled off the
street where Pleasant Lake Road intersected Highway 96 and parked
the Camry next to what used to be North Oak's security gate. The 300
pulled up behind me. I left the Camry and walked toward the driver.
He seemed anxious, so I showed him my empty hands. He powered
down the driver's side window, and I felt a blast of cold air. It was
seventy-three degrees in early June in Minnesota, and he had his air con-
ditioner on. What a putz.

"Officer," I said, "I'm going to reach for my credentials."

He watched intently as I slid my right hand under my sports jacket
and retrieved my wallet from an inside pocket. I showed him a photo-
stat of my license.

"I'm a licensed private investigator," I told him in case he couldn't
read. "I work for Mrs. Barrington."

He nodded like he knew it all along.

"May I have a moment?" I asked.

I backed away. He thought about it for a few beats before opening the door and sliding out of the Chrysler. He was a head taller than I was and dressed in full uniform. He pressed his fists against his hips and scowled at me.

"Well?" he said.

I admit I liked him better when he was sitting down.

"You're a community service officer," I said. "You work the mean streets of North Oaks."

I didn't mean to sound sarcastic, which turned out to be okay because apparently he didn't notice.

"I keep an eye on things," the officer said.

"You picked me up almost immediately when I crossed the city line."

"What of it?"

"Do you keep track of all the cars that come and go?"

"I try to pay attention."

"You know which vehicles belong to the residents and which are driven by interlopers." I liked the sound of the word so much I repeated it. "Interlopers."

"I know who's who."

"Four days ago, in the evening, did you happen to see a black, two-door BMW 640i coupe leave the city?"

The question wasn't as outrageous as it sounded. There were only three places an outsider could gain access to North Oaks, one off Highway 96 and the others off the less-traveled Hodgson and Centerville Roads.

The officer grinned at me.

"I saw nothing," he said.

"More to the point, did you happen to see a black, two-door BMW 640i coupe return to the city sometime after ten P.M.?"

"It didn't happen."

"Are you sure?"

"I'm sure," he said.

"It didn't sneak past you—going out, coming in?"

"Not on my watch."

He was being a good soldier, I decided, looking out for the welfare of his employers.

"You're willing to swear to that?" I asked.

"I am."

"In a court of law with a jury, prosecutor, and judge hanging on your every word?"

He thought about it and slowly shook his head.

That's what I was afraid of.

CHAPTER ELEVEN

The suite leased by the representatives of U.S. Sand was located in an office tower within sight of the Minnesota state capitol building. Except for a couple of dentists and an accounting firm, it mostly housed lobbyists representing everyone and everything from artists, farmers, auto dealers, beer wholesalers, and timber producers to cable providers, energy firms, insurance companies, healthcare organizations, and bowling proprietors, including something called the Minnesota Podiatry Association. The fact the building faced the *back* door of the capitol didn't surprise me a bit.

The suite was located on the third floor. I knocked and tried the door. It opened onto three rooms, two offices with windows facing the street and an interior reception area with no natural light. A young woman sat behind the desk. ESTHER TIBBITS was printed on a nameplate in front of her. Both her hair and her eyes were the color of Hershey Kisses; her breasts strained the buttons of her shirt. I tried hard to ignore them—the buttons, I mean.

"May I help you?" she asked.

I flashed my ID because it impresses some people and said, "I'd like to speak to Misters Kaufman and Palo."

"May I ask what this is pertaining to?"

I pulled my smartphone from my pocket and called up one of the pics Devon Barrington had sent me.

"Did you accompany Kaufman and Palo to a meeting held in the offices of Mrs. Barrington a few days ago?"

Esther hesitated before answering. "Yes."

I showed her Emily Denys's pic.

"Do you remember seeing this young woman?"

We were interrupted before she could reply.

"What's going on here?"

A man was standing in the doorway of the first office. He was nearly as wide as he was tall; the expensive suit he wore was cut to conceal his girth, but there's only so much even the most gifted tailor can do.

"Richard—Mr. Kaufman—this is Mr. Taylor," Esther said. "He's a private investigator."

"What do you want?" he asked.

"I'm investigating a murder," I said.

"Murder?" Esther said. "The girl in the pic, was she the one who was killed?"

"Yes."

"Oh, I am so sorry for that."

The way she lowered herself into her chair and hung her head, I believed her.

"Murder?" asked a second man. "Who said murder?"

He was taller than Kaufman and thinner. Together they reminded me a little of Abbott and Costello, although neither was even remotely as endearing.

"He said murder," Kaufman said.

"You're Allen Palo?" I asked.

"Yes."

"Gentlemen, if you would kindly give me a moment . . ."

"No," Kaufman said. "Hell no. We have nothing to do with any murder. Get out of here right now."

"Gentlemen—"

"Get out or we'll call the police."

"Fine. Go ahead."

Neither of them had anything to say to that. Nor did Esther, who was now watching the scene unfold with keen interest.

"Talk to me and it's kept quiet," I said. "Talk to the cops and it becomes a matter of public record. Your call. Or you can contact your employers in Chicago and let them decide. It's all the same to me."

The tall skinny guy grabbed the arm of the short fat man and they huddled up, turning their backs to me because they thought that was enough to keep me from listening. I did listen, though, and kept listening until I heard the phrase "bad publicity." I turned back to the receptionist.

"What happened to her?" Esther asked. "The girl in the picture?"

"She was shot," I said.

"That's awful."

Again I was impressed by what seemed to be her genuine concern, and I wondered if it came from some kind of kinship—pretty girls united—that caused her to empathize with a woman she had never met.

"Why are you here?" Kaufman asked. "Why do you want to talk to us?"

"It's common practice, when someone is killed, to speak to those who saw the victim last."

"What?" Palo said.

"You met with Joel Barrington five days ago in his office in downtown Minneapolis." It was a statement, not a question—I wanted them to think I knew more than I actually did. "You discussed buying property belonging to the Barrington family along the Trempealeau River outside of Arona in western Wisconsin."

"What of it?"

I showed him the pic of Emily Denys.

"Do you recall seeing this woman?" I asked.

"No."

I handed over my smartphone.

"Take a good look, both of you."

They shared the cell for a long moment and handed it back.

"I never saw her before," Kaufman said.

"Neither have I," Palo said.

"Yet you both did," I told them. "There's video evidence to prove it."

"That's crazy."

Palo might've had a point, I decided. I never asked if Mrs. Barrington's office had security cameras. Probably I should have.

"I don't remember seeing her," Kaufman said. "That's the honest truth."

"Taylor. Mr. Taylor." Palo's voice was consolatory. It was as if he suddenly remembered what he did for a living. "We wish to cooperate as best we can in this matter. Let us help you. Tell us who this woman was."

"Emily Denys."

"That was her name?" the receptionist asked.

"Yes. She was in Mrs. Barrington's offices when you were. She became aware of your negotiations and became very upset."

"Ill will hangs on us," Palo said. "We appreciate that we have enemies. What we do, helping to develop new energy sources to answer the growing demands of the American people, making our country less dependent on volatile Middle Eastern oil suppliers, is often and sometimes purposely misunderstood. Special interest groups spread their propaganda, confusing the issues, enraging citizens that more often than not hear only one side of this important story. We hope and pray that this unfortunate incident, this terrible, terrible killing of an innocent girl, is not related to these issues. If it is, you need to know that it does not involve us as individuals or U.S. Sand as a whole. Neither Mr. Kaufman nor I recall meeting Ms. Denys. Certainly we had nothing to do with her tragic demise. What's more, we deeply resent any suggestion to the contrary. So much so that U.S. Sand is willing to take all necessary legal action to protect our reputation from any sort of slander."

"Wow." The more time I spend with Freddie, the more I pick up his vocabulary. "Wow. That was impressive. It actually gave me chills listening to it. Did you just make it up, or is it part of an all-purpose speech?"

"Good day, Mr. Taylor," Kaufman said.

I actually expected him to repeat the phrase like Gene Wilder in *Willy Wonka and the Chocolate Factory*—"I said good day."

"Mr. Taylor," the receptionist said, "I remember the girl."

"Ms. Tibbits," Palo said.

I turned my back on him and approached the desk.

"We were in the conference room," Esther said. "The room was surrounded by glass walls. I guess it had curtains that you could close, but they weren't closed, so you could see people walking by. I was watching Mr. Barrington. He kind of smiled and gave a little wave, and I turned in my chair to see what he was looking at, and that's . . . that's when I saw her. The girl who was killed. She didn't do anything. She just turned around and walked away. I don't know if she even knew that I saw her."

"Did you ever see her before that?" I asked.

"No, sir. Never."

"What did Barrington do?"

"Nothing. The meeting just kept going on and on."

"Does that satisfy you, Mr. Taylor?" Kaufman asked.

"It answers my question."

"Then, sir . . ."

"Yes, I know. Good day."

I leaned back in my chair, my legs crossed at the ankles, my feet propped on top of my desk.

"Looks like a dead end," I told Freddie. "Mrs. Barrington was aware of the meeting. There's no grand conspiracy. U.S. Sand does seem a bit discombobulated, but that's probably just corporate paranoia."

"Speaking of dead ends—there are no missing persons reports matching Denys, no bulletins issued by the Chicago PD or Cook County."

"We're gonna have to find out who Emily really was, and we're gonna have to do it the hard way."

"Good luck with that."

"What do you mean?"

"Sackett called again while you were out. He wants to move up the meeting, get us going on investigating his acquisition right away."

"Define right away."

"He's buyin' me lunch at Manny's."

"Why you?"

"What can I say? I was the one what answered the phone. Besides, I'm better at this sort of thing than you are. You lack . . . What's the word? Subtlety."

"Subtlety? You used to carry a Colt Commander into church, for God's sake."

"What I'm saying, I'm better with computers than you are. You're a people person."

"That's so untrue."

"You used to be, before you got all morose on me. Look at the time. I gotta scoot."

"I don't know, Freddie. Manny's is a pretty high-class joint. They might not let you in dressed like that."

"What's wrong with the way I'm—?"

Freddie looked down at himself and then stopped. Ever since his marriage he'd been dressing like a jazz musician playing an after-hours gig.

"I remember when you used to be funny, too," he said.

"I remember when you didn't care what you looked like."

"We all adults now, partner."

CHAPTER TWELVE

The cops had sealed Emily Denys's front door with bright yellow tape. Apparently they had decided the entire place was a crime scene even though she had been killed outside. That was okay with me because I was interested in the door next to hers, the one leading to the second apartment in the duplex. There was no answer when I knocked. I knocked again and got the same reply. Probably the resident was at work. It was early afternoon on a weekday, after all. I made a note of it in the pad I carry and drifted back toward my car.

The Camry was parked at the curb. I stood on the passenger side and stared over the roof at the woman who lived across the street. Professor Alexandra Campbell was kneeling on a strip of foam rubber at the edge of her garden and gripping a three-prong hand rake. She was watching me watching her. She brushed hair out off her forehead and waved the rake, which I took as an invitation.

The professor spoke as I approached.

"Still asking questions, I see," she said.

"Trying to."

Campbell stood and offered her hand. I shook it. My gaze started low and moved upward. The rubber strip was in the maroon and gold colors of the University of Minnesota and cut to resemble a hand with a single finger announcing "We're No. 1." Campbell was wearing ratty sneakers. Her legs were long and athletic as if she actually used them for running. Her shorts hugged a slim waist. A flannel shirt with the sleeves removed revealed muscled arms and a graceful neck. Auburn hair with just enough gray to suggest that she didn't worry about it was tied back. Her eyes—when I first met her, I thought they were light brown, yet in the bright sunlight I realized that there was plenty of green in them, too. They were the kind of eyes that looked cheerful even when the rest of her face was trying hard to appear grim, like now.

"If you're looking for the roommates, Lisa Carrell left for work a half hour before you arrived. Mickie Umland is a flight attendant. God knows where she is."

I pulled out my notebook and wrote down the names.

"Neither of them were home when Emily was shot," Campbell added. "Mickie was in Chicago, I think she said when I saw her last. Lisa—she's a young woman. I suppose she went out with her friends after she closed up shop."

"Where does she work?"

"Grand Gourmet. She owns it along with a partner. Her partner opens the store at ten A.M. Lisa closes it at nine P.M."

"You seem to know an awful lot about your neighbors."

"We form a village, I suppose, don't we? Especially here in St. Paul. A kind of subculture built around a park or a church or a school. Don't you know your neighbors?"

It occurred to me that I knew Amanda and her mother, but just barely—her father had been arrested? Yet I didn't know the names of anyone else in the building where I lived or in the houses and apartments around me. My neighbors were merely faces to nod at, and it was probably my fault. I had become antisocial just like my mom said.

"No, I don't know my neighbors," I said.

"I make a point of knowing them."

"Good for you." I didn't mean for it to sound like a rebuke, yet I knew that it did.

"Like I said, Lisa wasn't home when Emily was shot," Campbell told me. "She didn't arrive until much later, until after the coroner or medical examiner or whoever it was removed the body."

"Medical examiner," I said. "In Ramsey County the medical examiner decides when a body is removed from a crime scene."

"It's always a good day when you learn something new."

"I suppose that depends on what you learn."

"Are you really this cynical, or is it just me that you don't like?"

The question was like a slap across the face, and I found myself recoiling to the point where I took several steps backward.

"No," I said. "I like you fine. I mean I'm not . . . it's because . . . my friends, I actually do have a couple friends, they'd tell you that I'm just going through a bad patch."

Her eyes seemed to contain a hidden smile.

"Really?" she asked. "How long has it lasted, this bad patch?"

"A couple of years."

"Get over it."

As coincidence would have it, Grand Gourmet was located on Grand Avenue about a half mile from my apartment. Given the parking issues along the street, I might have been better off driving to my place and walking there.

The tinkling of a bell greeted me as I passed through the front door, followed by the aroma of dozens of exotic spices all fighting for attention. The spices were set out on wire shelves, along with jars, bags, and boxes of cheeses, flavored vinegars, mustards, assorted sugars, salsa, a myriad of snack foods that I had never heard of, and an astounding amount of fine chocolate, all selling at heart-stopping prices. A young woman—at least she was younger than I was—stood behind a glass counter next to a stack of thick pamphlets with the title *Fancy Food Creations*. She was short and plump, with a smile as bright as the store's art deco lights.

"May I help you?" she asked.

"I'm looking for Ms. Carrell."

"I'm Lisa Carrell."

I flashed my ID at her and added my name.

"I'm investigating the murder of Emily Denys," I said.

The smile faded as she glanced around the shop.

"I don't want to bother my customers with this," she said. Satisfied that we were alone, she added, "I can't leave because my partner is on her lunch break."

"I'll try not to be an imposition."

"Besides, I don't know what I can tell you that I haven't already told the other cops."

Other cops. It's against the law to pretend to be a police officer. 'Course, I never actually said I was, did I?

"I know you weren't present when the shooting took place," I said.

"I was with friends. You can call them."

"What I was hoping is that you could tell me about Emily. Did you spend much time with her?"

"Not a lot. I usually work the night shift, and she worked days, so . . . Sometimes, though, on the weekends when neither of us had anything going on, we'd get together and drink wine and binge-watch *Buffy the Vampire Slayer*. Sometimes Mickie would join us, when she was in town, that is. That's my roommate, Mickie Umland. Emily tried to get me to go to the gym with her"—Lisa gave me the name, and I wrote it down—"but honestly, I don't have the time."

"What did you talk about?"

"This and that. When is the funeral, do you know? I've been looking for a listing . . ."

"There's some question as to her identity. Until he knows who Emily was for sure, the medical examiner probably won't release the body."

"I don't get it. She was from Albert Lea. She had people there."

"Have you met any of them? Do you know their names?"

"No. I just, I guess I just assumed from what Em told me."

"Did she ever tell you any stories about her family, about growing up in Albert Lea?"

"Not Albert Lea, I guess. She did tell me about going to the Upper Peninsula of Michigan once when Lake Superior was like bathwater; that it was so warm that year you could just walk into it, which astounded everybody."

"What was she doing there?"

"I dunno. Vacation, I guess."

"With her family?"

"With her dad. I got the impression that Emily didn't have a mother growing up. She never said anything specific, just the impression I got. I don't know if she died or abandoned her or what."

"Do you remember the conversation?"

"I was upset at my mother. She's such a . . . My partner and I have been running this business . . . Our fourth anniversary is in September, okay? Every year has been better than the previous year. We're doing really well. Yet my mother keeps waiting for it to collapse. She kept telling us what a stupid idea it was to start a business in a down economy, and now she's praying for it to go bust so she can say she told us so. Four years this has been going on. One day I just lost it and said I'd pay real money to put her in the ground, and Emily said she was surprised by how many women she knew hated their mothers and it made her feel left out. I asked if she actually liked her mother, but she didn't answer."

"Did she mention her father's name?"

"Dad. She called him Dad and sometimes the old man, but mostly Dad."

"Do you know what he did for a living?"

"I got the impression that he worked for the government."

"Why?"

"Emily said he really hated the government, and for some reason I thought that was because he worked for it."

"City, state, federal?"

"Sorry."

It went on like that for another ten minutes. Lisa had very little specific information to offer, only impressions.

"What about your roommate?" I asked.

"Mickie's a flight attendant, and she's home only ten or eleven days out of the month and rarely more than two days in a row, which makes her a perfect roommate, if you know what I mean. When she's home it's usually all day, so . . . I don't know what she and Em talked about or if they talked much at all. You can ask her."

"Where is she now?"

"I don't know. I can never keep track of her schedule. I don't know how she keeps track. Mickie's on reserve, so she doesn't always know what her schedule is, where she's flying to or when. Sometimes they call her two hours before the plane is scheduled to take off. She should be home tomorrow, though, if you want to drop by the duplex."

I thanked her, gave her my card, told her to contact me if any other impressions came to mind, and thanked her again. Lisa called out as I went to the door.

"One thing I know for sure. Emily was a Packer Backer. She loved the Green Bay Packers. I told her that it was sacrilege, a Minnesota girl rooting for any Wisconsin team. She said something about how you could have her Aaron Rodgers jersey when you pulled it from her cold, dead fingers."

I requested Emily Denys's complete employment history at the mega-bookstore, with emphasis on those days when she didn't report to work. Her supervisor wasn't sure she should give it up.

"What do you want it for?" she asked.

"Because it's important that we have all the information correct for the trial," I said. It sounds absurd, I know, yet it worked. It usually does. Most of the time when you begin an explanation with the word "because," people stop listening. They hear the word, which they translate to mean "there's a good reason to do this, go ahead," and tune out the rest. If you don't believe me, try it sometime.

Unfortunately, all I learned was that Emily was a particularly conscientious and resourceful employee who never missed a day, who was well regarded by customers and co-workers alike, who was quick to cover for fellow sales clerks that needed a break, who performed all the tasks assigned to her with a smile, who was on the bullet train to promotion.

"You get the impression that she actually enjoyed her job," I said.

"A lot of people do," the supervisor said. "Believe it or not."

I asked if I could interview Emily's co-workers. The supervisor granted permission, yet only after I promised not to be disruptive. It was a promise I couldn't keep because Em's friends all seemed to have an emotional investment in the girl. Some laughed while recalling her kindness and generosity. Others wept. They told me Emily remembered everyone's birthday and work anniversary with a small token—flowers, chocolates, homemade cookies, or tiny stuffed animals, depending on the temperament of the recipient. She drank white wine at the bar across the mall when her fellow employees gathered after work, but only a glass or two, and she never shirked when it came her turn to buy a round. Those who knew of her relationship with Joel Barrington, and it turned out to be nearly everyone, approved wholeheartedly.

"You should have seen his eyes light up when he saw her," one person said.

"You should have seen her eyes light up when she saw him," said another.

I suggested that Emily was a gold digger who was only interested in Barrington's money. No one believed me. A few of her friends—both men and women—were ready to take it outside to defend Emily's honor. I was impressed and more than a little embarrassed. In a short thirteen months, Emily had filled her life with friends, and lots of them—people who were literally ready to fight for her. I, on the other hand, was virtually friendless.

After my wife and daughter were killed I shed my friends the way you would change from a summer wardrobe to winter, a little at a time—quitting the cops to work in a one-man office, retiring from various softball and hockey teams, ignoring my family, passing on invitations to parties and barbecues until they stopped coming, spending my days solving the problems of strangers so I didn't have to deal with my own. That had changed when Cynthia came into my life, but only for a time. Now I was partnered with Freddie, who was no friend when we first started. While Emily seemed desperate to connect with other people in her new life, I was actively disconnecting, keeping them at a distance.

You can't go on like this, I told myself. Yet that was only the amateur psychologist talking, and by the time I reached my car my mind was focused on other matters.

The trainer who kept an eye on Emily when she worked out liked her as much as her co-workers.

"She was always smiling," he said. "Some people, they march into a gym like it's community service, like a judge is forcing them to either work out or go to jail. They never last, either. You get the New Year's resolution crowd, more than seventy percent won't use their memberships more than a couple of times, if ever. Sure, they want to lose weight, get in shape, but if they don't see results right away, they go back to Ol' McDonald's or his friends Taco and Bell.

"Emily, though, she joined in August, and you could tell right away she was dedicated. Not like she wanted to be a bodybuilder, no, no, no. She just liked to exercise, liked to run. On odd days, she hit the weights. On even days, she did a couple miles on the oval. She told me she'd been into it, running, ever since she ran track and field back in high school."

"What high school?"

"She didn't say. She did say she finished first in the 800-meters at state, though."

"Which state? What year?"

"I thought this state. The year—man, I don't know where you come from, but around here you never ask a woman her age, especially in a gym."

Freddie had left the office before I arrived. Or maybe he had never returned after his sojourn to Manny's. We had worked with Sackett before, and the man has been known to stretch his lunch meetings through the afternoon. The last time I had to take a cab home.

I fired up the computer and searched the websites of the Minnesota High School League, the Wisconsin Interscholastic Athletic Association, and the Illinois High School Association, taking down the names, schools, and locations of every winner of the girl's 800-meter run during a six-year period when I figured Emily must have competed. There were a lot of names. Minnesota had divided its high schools into two separate classes, and Wisconsin and Illinois had three each.

Afterward, I cross-checked the names against Facebook, Twitter, LinkedIn, and every other social site I could think of. People are outraged that the federal government and various internet companies have been actively compiling information about them, as well they should be. Yet they upload a terrifying amount of personal intel every day—especially the so-called millennials—that can be accessed by just about anyone, from prospective employers to the guy with a telescope that lives down the street. It took hours, but eventually I satisfied myself that forty-three of the forty-eight girls I had originally identified had not disappeared during the past thirteen months (half were still in college). That left five names, one in Minnesota, one in Wisconsin, and three in Illinois.

I used sites like the White Pages to find phone numbers; in some cases there were more than a dozen numbers for each spelling. I called the numbers one at a time, asking whoever answered if they had finished first in the 800-meter run at the state high school finals. Two women said they had. The sister of a third said the girl had taken a job teaching English in Beijing six months earlier. A mother in Minnesota told me her daughter was serving with the 101st Airborne. A man in Wisconsin said, "My daughter's not in right now, may I take a message?" Which I took as confirmation that she was alive and well.

I shouted at the ceiling above my desk.

"Sonuvabitch."

CHAPTER THIRTEEN

The sun had already set by the time I reached the apartment. I was unlocking my door when the door across the landing opened. Amanda stood inside the frame, still dressed in her private-school uniform.

"Hey, kid," I said. "How's it going?"

"Okay."

"Is your mother home?"

"No. She had to work late. Again."

"Want to hang out?"

"Can I?"

"Sure."

"Just a sec."

Amanda disappeared from view. When she returned she was carrying a carrot.

"You know, you don't have to bring food when you come over," I said.

"But what would Ogilvy say?"

I propped open the door like I always did when Amanda came to visit. She stepped inside. She didn't need to call for the rabbit; he was already waiting for her. Amanda sat down on the floor, as was her habit, and Ogilvy climbed into her lap, as was his. She hugged him for a long time.

I offered food and drink. Amanda turned me down.

"I'm sure your mother told you not to, but you're welcome to mooch off me as much as you like," I said. "Since you're always feeding my rabbit, the least I can do is feed you."

"I'm not hungry."

"Sure?"

"Do you have any"—she spoke the words as if she were naming a Schedule II narcotic—"root beer?"

"Coming right up."

I found a can of A&W, opened it, and poured some over ice in a tall glass. I gave it to the girl.

"I'd be happy to throw some ice cream in there, if you like," I said.

"Before dinner? My mom would freak."

"Your mom's a good person. She works so very, very hard."

"I know."

"You need to cut her some slack."

"It's not me. I can take care of me. I just want her to have some time for herself."

"You're a good kid, Mandy."

I thought about how much I'd like a shot or two of bourbon, yet decided not to in front of the child. So I drank root beer, too, while I asked about her day. I surprised myself by actually listening to what she had to say.

Eventually her mother appeared. Claire leaned against the door frame, the heavy bag pulling on her shoulder.

"Mommy," Amanda said.

She brushed the rabbit off her lap and moved to the woman. Claire sank to her knees and hugged her daughter.

"I missed you," Amanda said.

"I'm so sorry I'm late. I tried to get away . . ."

"It's okay. Don't be sad."

"Did you eat? Are you hungry?"

"I'm okay."

Mother continued to hug daughter. She saw me standing there.

"I keep apologizing to you," Claire said. "I keep thanking you."

"And yet you don't need to do either."

"You're a good friend."

What an odd thing to say, I thought. At the same time, I felt like the Grinch in the Christmas story. I could feel my heart suddenly growing larger.

"You look tired," I said.

"Don't get me started."

"You're staying for dinner."

"No, we can't."

"Yes, you can."

"What are we having?" Amanda asked.

"Mandy," her mother said.

"Spaghetti and meatballs," I said. "And salad."

"Salad?"

"You want to grow up to be big and strong like Ogilvy, don't you?"

"Oh, Taylor, don't be silly. He's a rabbit."

"Taylor, please . . . ," Claire said.

"What kind of friend are you that you'd make me eat alone?"

She nodded as if I had just offered to pay her medical bills. It was spaghetti, for God's sake. It wasn't like I was making the sauce from scratch. While I set the water to boil for the pasta, I thawed some Simek's meatballs in the microwave and tossed them into the store-bought sauce that was simmering on the stove. The salad was merely a mix of baby spinach and romaine lettuce from a plastic bag I picked up at a supermarket and a choice of creamy French, Italian, and honey-mustard dressing in plastic bottles.

While the food was cooking, I filled a long-stem glass with Merlot and gave it to Claire. She savored it as if it were something she enjoyed very much yet hadn't tasted in a long time. I gave Amanda an identical glass filled with root beer. She thought it was "very cool."

I closed my front door—the first time I had done that while the two women were in my apartment.

We ate at my small table. Amanda practically drowned her spaghetti in Parmesan cheese. She didn't talk much, but I figured that was because she didn't want to draw attention while she slipped leaves of lettuce out of her bowl and fed Ogilvy beneath the table. Her mother didn't seem to notice, and I certainly wasn't going to bust her. Yet after the third leaf, Claire calmly said, "The salad is for you, young lady. Not the rabbit."

"Sorry, Ogilvy," Amanda said.

After we finished, Claire announced that it was time for Amanda to go home, take a bath, and get ready for bed.

"Did you do your homework?" she asked.

"Yep."

"I want to check it."

"You always do that."

"Go."

Amanda hopped off her chair and did something completely unexpected. She hugged me.

"Good night, Taylor," she said. "Good night, Ogilvy."

Then she was gone. Claire watched me as she fingered her wineglass.

"Mandy wants to adopt you," she said.

"Seems that way."

"There are things you should know."

"You don't need to tell me anything."

"My husband is in prison for embezzlement. My ex-husband. I wish I could say he stole for Mandy and me. He did it to support his gambling addiction. I tried to help him. For years I tried to help, even after he bankrupted us, even after our home was foreclosed on. Finally, he was arrested. I divorced him after the first six months he was in prison. His family, most of my family, they said I quit on him. They keep saying it. It's not true. I didn't give up. I was beaten. There's a difference."

"Yes, there is."

"I want you to know because I want to adopt you, too."

I shook my head as if it were the worst idea I had ever heard.

"No, you don't," I said.

"You're lonely. As lonely as I am. I can see it in your eyes."

"That might be true. You and Amanda, you're among the few bright spots in my life right now. But . . ."

"But what? Are you going to recite that old line—don't get involved with me, honey, I'm trouble?"

"Hardly."

"What, then?"

"I'm coming off a difficult relationship, and I don't want you to be the rebound girl. I'd hate for anyone I care about to be the rebound girl. A month, three months, six—I don't want to look across the hall and feel awkward. I don't want you to feel awkward. I don't want your little girl to stop knocking on my door."

"The policewoman—is she the rebound girl?"

"Anne is my friend. Probably my best friend."

"That doesn't answer my question."

"I said it before and I meant it, Claire—you're always welcome here." She finished her wine and rose from the table.

"I'm glad to hear that," she said. "Because I'm not giving up on you."

To prove it, she pressed her body against mine and kissed my cheek. A moment later, she was gone. I stared at the closed door. I spoke loud enough to spook my rabbit.

"Taylor, you're the most pathetic human being alive."

CHAPTER FOURTEEN

I waited until midmorning before returning to the duplex where the girl who was killed once lived because I wanted to give Mickie Umland plenty of time to eat her breakfast. I knocked, waited, and knocked some more. Even though I was expecting it, the door opened swiftly enough to give me a start. The woman standing on the other side seemed older than her roommate did by a couple of years and thinner by many pounds. She was wearing shorts and a tight tank top without a bra. Her feet were bare, and I wondered if I had roused her from bed. If so, she was one of those women who slept pretty.

"Ms. Umland?" I said.

"Are you with the airline?"

"I'm a private investigator."

"You've got to be kidding me. Working for the airline?"

"No, no. This has nothing to do with your airline."

"Yeah, right."

"My name is Taylor."

"Oh, oh, okay. Lisa mentioned you when I got in this morning. She just left to do some shopping. I'm sorry. My head is . . . Please come in."

Mickie stood aside and let me pass, closing the door after me. She led me into the living room and gestured at a chair even as she spoke.

"I'm expecting trouble from the airline, and I thought you might be it."

"Trouble?" I asked.

"I love my job. I love flying. I love going places. There are some serious downsides, though, and the biggest of them is pilots, some pilots, not all. There are serious protocols in place that're supposed to eliminate sexual harassment, yet you still get guys . . . The other day I got up at four A.M., drove to the airport, and was hit on by a pilot. He was relentless. The only time it stopped was when I was in the cabin. We landed, I got hit on some more; had to listen to his BS all the way to the hotel, had him follow me to my room, had him call me while I was in my room. Pilots are forbidden to drink, but he knew I could sure use one. Or two. Or three. To relieve the stress, he said. Finally, it's midnight, I'd been on my feet for close to twenty hours, the pilot knocks on my door and tells me he can't sleep and he's pretty sure that I can't either, if you know what I mean—he actually said that. The man is twenty years older than me and married, so I"—she feinted a jab from the shoulder—"punched him in the nose and slammed the door. I've been waiting for someone to punch me back ever since."

"Did he report you?"

"Wouldn't you?"

"Not if it meant I had to explain to HR what I was doing knocking on your hotel room door at midnight."

Mickie wagged her finger at me.

"I hadn't thought of that," she said. "He could be in more trouble than me. Well . . ." She sat on a stuffed chair across from me, her long legs curled neatly beneath her. "How can I help you?"

I asked Mickie to tell me everything she knew about Emily Denys, which turned out to be very little, now that she had time to think about it. Emily had asked her once about becoming a flight attendant, and Mickie said she would help as much as she could. Only it never went any further than just talk.

"She was certainly pretty enough," the flight attendant said. "That's not supposed to make any difference in hiring, not the way it used to, anyway. You'd be surprised how much it helps, though. Or maybe you wouldn't be. You meet as many people as I do every day and you get pretty good at reading them. Taylor, you don't look to me like someone who's surprised very often."

"Did Emily ever surprise you?"

"Not really. She liked to play the virginal innocent, the sweet little thing from small-town USA, but really, she was just like everyone else, looking out for herself."

"How did she look out for herself?"

"Well, first there was the psychologist fresh out of the U trying to get a job as a counselor in the St. Paul School District. He lasted until Em found out about the humongous student loans he was carrying. Then there was the investment banker who also just graduated who drove a ten-year-old Mercedes. He seemed like a keeper until Emily realized it would be awhile before he could afford to buy a new Mercedes. Next came Barrington. He was already where Emily wanted to be, so she played him."

"Played him?"

"A pretty girl manipulating a man with money? That comes as a surprise to you?"

"Doesn't fit what others have told me about her."

"I'm not saying she was a bad person. Not saying she didn't genuinely like the guy. I'm just saying the woman had goals, okay? And she knew how to reach them. What I mean—I have these very short shorts that only come to here." Mickie indicated a spot on her thighs that suggested her shorts weren't much longer than her panties. "I hardly ever wear them but this one time that I did, and Em kinda turned up her nose and said she didn't think they were appropriate for a good Christian girl. That surprised the hell outta me because in all the time I knew her, she never said or did anything to make me believe she was some kind of religious fanatic.

"Then later, the three of us were watching *Buffy*, and I asked her where the boyfriend was, and Em said he was with his mother, which seemed to annoy her. I asked if she and he had ever been intimate. She said no. She said that she was waiting for her wedding night. She was so very matter-of-fact about it. There was no preaching or anything. At the same time, it made me feel . . . It made me think I had given up a lot that I didn't need to give up. It made me wish I were more like her, okay?"

"Okay."

"But then I came home this one time. It was late, a hot summer night, Emily's front door was open, although the outside screen door was locked, and I could hear her, not shouting or anything, yet I could hear her saying, "Yeah, yeah, yeah, just like that," and I'm like, what the fuck? I look through the window and, well, there was Emily bent over the arm of a sofa taking it from behind, Joel feeding it to her, and you know what? It didn't look like this was a new experience for her, okay?"

"You're telling me Emily wasn't who she claimed to be."

"None of us are, but Taylor, I liked her even so. The woman who killed her, the boyfriend's mother—she makes me wish to God that Minnesota had capital punishment."

I asked more questions, but Mickie's answers weren't any more illuminating than her roommate's had been. I gave her my card, and she promised to call me if she thought of anything more. She walked me to the door, opened it, and gave me a hug. I don't think she was interested in me so much as she craved human contact, which seemed to prove that it isn't how many people you meet, it's how many you connect with that matters. At the same time, it caused me to remember the hug Claire had given me the evening before. It was all I could do to keep from hugging Mickie back.

The door was closed, and I stood outside the duplex, my back to the street. The yellow crime scene tape had been removed from Emily's door. I tried the handle. Locked. I gave it a shake, just the same. I had burglar tools, although it's illegal for me to possess them. It would have been easy to let myself inside. If I could have thought of a good enough reason to risk arrest, I probably would have. Only I doubted that there was anything I could see that the cops hadn't, so I let it go. Instead, I turned and started down the sidewalk.

I saw a man approaching at a right angle. He was in his early twenties with brown hair cut in the military style, and he was dressed in camouflage hunting clothes, which I thought was ridiculous. Not only were they warm—I could see sweat beading on his forehead—it was the middle of St. Paul, for God's sake. What was he stalking? Chipmunks?

Movement on my left caused me to turn my head. A second man, dressed in identical clothes, was advancing on me as well. He was the same age and had the same haircut, except that his hair was blond. He was speaking into his sleeve. While he spoke, the first man pressed his hand against his left ear.

They weren't wearing the same camo outfits because they were *Duck Dynasty* wannabees, I told myself. It was a uniform.

And they were closing in.

My fight-or-flight reflex activated. Most people, when that happens, they blow it off, tell themselves that they're behaving foolishly. So they get onto the elevator with the stranger, they stop to assist the driver whose car is stalled on the road; they continue walking across the dark and deserted parking lot. Time and experience had taught me to never do that.

When the hunters closed to within ten yards on either side of me, I dashed straight toward my Camry, moving as if a starter's pistol had sent me down the track. If I looked foolish, who cared?

The two hunters adjusted their routes and moved to intercept me. They might have managed it, too, if I had stopped to get inside the car. Instead, I continued across the street, running toward Professor Campbell's house.

Their hands reached under their shirts.

Guns were pulled.

Shots were fired.

"Wait," one of them shouted. If he was talking to me, he was wasting his breath.

There was a car parked across the street, and I dashed around it, using it for cover.

Bullets tore into it.

I kept running.

"Cease fire, cease fire."

"He's getting away."

Campbell opened her front door and stepped out, holding the door open. What an incredibly foolhardy thing to do, I thought. Did she not know what was happening?

"Taylor, in here," she said.

Apparently she did know.

I ran straight at her.

Behind me, a voice spoke.

"We were sent to ask questions, dammit."

I dove across Campbell's stoop, my arms wide. I hit her high in the chest and drove her back through the door into the house, a perfect flying tackle.

She went down hard. The back of her head hit the floor. I heard a moan.

I rolled onto my back and used my foot to slam the door shut.

My cell was in my hand and I was dialing 911. I didn't hear any more shooting, yet I kept low as I crawled to Campbell's picture window just the same. I peeked carefully over the ledge.

"911, where is your emergency?" the voice asked—where, not what.

"Shots fired," I said, and recited the address of the duplex.

I stood slowly and surveyed both ends of the street through the window. The two hunters had disappeared.

"Is anyone injured?" the operator asked.

I look down at Professor Campbell. She was gasping for the breath I had knocked out of her.

"Are you okay?" I asked.

"No, I'm not. Are you?"

I didn't answer because I didn't know how she'd react, but I felt fine. I felt exhilarated. I didn't tell the 911 operator that, either.

"I don't think we need medical attention," I said.

The operator told me to remain on the phone until help arrived.

I went to Campbell and helped her to her feet.

"That was incredibly brave," I told her. "Opening the door like that. My God, though. What were you thinking?"

"I was thinking that there was a neighbor who needed help."

I eased her into a chair.

"When you threw yourself on top of me, you were trying to protect me, too, weren't you?" Campbell said. "From the bullets, I mean."

"Honestly, Alex, I was just trying to knock some sense into you."

"At least we're on a first-name basis again."

It took ninety-seven seconds before the first officer appeared at the scene and only two and a half minutes before three other squad cars joined him. Seventeen minutes later, Detective Casper of the St. Paul Police Department arrived. He wanted to know if the shooting was connected to the murder of Emily Denys. Six minutes after that, Martin McGaney drove up. He wanted to know the same thing.

I said yes, of course it's connected.

"How do we know it's not about something else you're working on?" Casper asked.

"I heard one of them say they were sent to ask me questions. Apparently the other panicked when I took off and started throwing bullets around."

"Questions about what?"

"About the Denys killing."

"Did he say that?"

"Why else would they have been here? Obviously they had staked out the place."

"Obviously. You're way too smart to let someone tail you."

"That's right. I am."

"Puhleez."

"What can you give us besides the camouflage suits?" McGaney asked.

I gave him estimates of age, height, weight, and skin color.

"They had military-style haircuts, one brown, one blond," I said.

"Is that it?" McGaney threw a thumb in my direction. "He calls himself a trained investigator."

"I can't believe I used to work with this guy," Casper said.

"Did you?"

"For about six months, wasn't it, Taylor? Just before you pulled the pin?"

"Stop it," I said.

"'Course, that wasn't long after Scalasi was promoted over him."

"Sounds like jealousy to me," McGaney said.

"She is a woman, so . . ."

"Stop it," I repeated.

A door-to-door was conducted; neighbors were questioned. Apparently Mickie Umland had stepped into the shower immediately after I left her place and didn't see or hear a thing, although she did confirm that I had stopped by to ask questions. But no, she hadn't seen two camo-wearing hunters carrying handguns beneath their shirts lurking about. Neither, as it turned out, had anyone else within a several-block radius.

Meanwhile, Alexandra gave her statement—gave it several times without wavering. Most eyewitness testimony is unreliable, yet hers was shockingly accurate. It was the scientist in her, I figured. It also reminded me that her testimony against Mrs. Barrington would be formidable.

I asked her several times if she was all right, and so did the others. She said no the first time I inquired, of course, yet ever since Alex had kept insisting that she was fine.

"Shaken," she said finally, and smiled. "Not stirred."

That's what made me think she was hanging on by her fingernails. Why wouldn't she be? A running gunfight on the front lawn right after breakfast is not a common occurrence for most people.

"I'm sorry about your car," Casper told her.

"My car?"

"That's your vehicle parked on the street?"

It was stated as a question, yet Casper already knew the answer. He ran the plates before arranging to have the car towed to the impound lot so forensics could start pulling bullets out of the body.

"Yes, that's my car," Alex said.

"It's pretty badly shot up. If you have comprehensive, your insurance should cover it. Otherwise—"

"My car," she said. "My poor car." I knew she could have been just as easily talking about herself.

Alex sat down in the middle of her floor and pressed her limbs together until she was about the size of a beach ball. I sat next to her, wrapping my arms around her shoulders. She leaned her head against my chest.

"It could have been me," she said.

I made a lot of comforting sounds, and so did the officers, yet at the same time I told myself that this is what comes from opening your door to strangers in need.

We stayed like that for a long time while the officers went through the motions of an investigation. Finally Casper asked, "Professor Campbell, is there someone you can call to stay with you? A friend or relative?"

Alexandra patted my arms, indicating that it was time to let her go. I helped her to her feet.

"I have friends," she said. "You're leaving, too, aren't you, Taylor? To work your case?"

"It's what I do," I said.

The way she smiled sadly and shook her head, I think she took more meaning from my words than I meant to put there.

CHAPTER FIFTEEN

David Helin was delighted.

He was in a conference room when I arrived at the SKH&D offices, and the receptionist had no intention of interrupting until I explained my sense of urgency. A few moments later, he was practically jogging down the corridor toward where I sat, his arms wide and a happy grin on his face.

"They shot at you?" he said. "That's wonderful."

There were other people in the reception area, and they all stopped what they were doing. I noted the expressions of alarm on most of their faces.

"I'm sure he didn't mean it the way it sounds," I said.

Helin hustled me into his office.

"I don't have a lot of time for this," he said. "Specific details. Who is they?"

I explained, ending with what one of the shooters said—"We were sent to ask questions."

"The professor—"

"Alexandra Campbell," I said.

"She heard this?"

"She did. She might have saved my life."

"Is she willing to testify?"

"Yes."

"To what she heard?"

"Yes. Unfortunately, she's also willing to testify that she saw Mrs. Barrington shoot Emily."

"If it looks like a conspiracy and sounds like a conspiracy . . ."

"Whose conspiracy, though?"

"I don't care. Yes, I do. Unravel it, Taylor. Unravel it."

"I don't think we're going to get much help from the city and county cops."

"What did the CA say?"

"She wasn't at the scene. Her investigator, McGaney—he remains skeptical."

"Even better. A conspiracy and a cover-up."

"If you say so."

"The fact is they shot at you. In front of witnesses. I can do a lot with that. You've made my day, Taylor. I couldn't be more pleased."

He left his office, apparently in a hurry to return to his meeting. He called to me over his shoulder as he disappeared down the corridor.

"Keep up the good work."

I returned to the office. Freddie spoke to me without lifting his eyes from the computer screen.

"Taylor, hey," he said.

"Freddie."

I moved to the safe we keep between our desks. It was stacked with the coffeemaker and K-Cups, so he didn't know what I was doing until I knelt and started working the combination.

"So, how's it goin'?" he asked.

"I've been better."

I swung open the door of the safe, reached inside, and retrieved a nine-millimeter Beretta semiautomatic handgun. Freddie didn't react until I also pulled out two magazines.

"Two?" he said. "Really?"

"I want to make sure I have enough bullets to go around."

"Wanna talk about it?"

I slammed a mag into the butt of the handgun and jacked a round into the chamber while I explained.

"Whose cage did we rattle?" Freddie said.

"I don't know. Yet somewhere along the line someone became aware that we were attempting to learn Emily Denys's real identity, and they sent two trigger-happy thugs to ask about it."

Freddie set his index finger against his cheek and said, "Hmmm."

"What? What does 'hmmm' mean?"

"The whole point of Plan B is to muddy up the waters, create whatchacall reasonable doubt."

"I know what Plan B is."

"Except, what if Barrington really did pop the Denys girl for all the reasons we already know about? What if the Denys girl was on the run, hiding out from someone like we suppose? Now, what if, because we were asking about her, this someone just learned that Denys was dead, realized she was really whoever she was, and now is trying to find out what happened to her?"

"I've got a headache, Freddie."

He opened his desk drawer, found a small white bottle, and tossed it to me from across the room. I caught it with one hand, struggled with the childproof cap, finally opened it, and shook out two pills that I swallowed without water because that's how tough I am.

"What's the plan?" Freddie asked.

"Retrace my steps, including all the calls I made yesterday, and see what we find."

Which is what I did for the rest of the day and discovered—nothing.

I drove home with the Beretta muzzle down in the cup holder located directly behind the Camry's gearshift—not that I had suddenly become paranoid. The fact that I studied the face of every driver of every vehicle that passed me on the freeway or pulled next to my car at a stoplight—that was just me getting to know my neighbors.

The gun was in my hand, in my pocket, after I parked and moved to the entrance of my apartment building. I inputted the security code into the electronic keypad with my free hand and waited while an older couple strolled past on the sidewalk. The woman smiled.

"Beautiful evening, isn't it?" she said.

"Just swell."

My remark caused her smile to fade a bit, but then I sometimes have that effect on people.

I opened the door, slid inside the building, and made my way to the second-floor landing. I unlocked my apartment door, went inside, and froze. There was someone there. I could feel it. I could hear it. Light breathing coming from—where? If I hadn't been so jazzed with adrenaline, I might have missed it. As it was, my heart was pumping blood through my arteries like a fire hose.

It couldn't be the rabbit, I told myself as I eased the Beretta out of my pocket. There definitely was someone in the apartment.

I turned the switch. The overhead went on, flooding the apartment with light. In the movies, you always see the good guys wandering through dark houses looking for the bad guys with nothing but a flashlight. What a bunch of morons.

I gripped the Beretta with both hands, the right pushing out slightly and the left pulling in to steady it. My back was against the door as I swept the sights over the living room, down the corridor, and over to the kitchen area. Movement to my right caused me to retrain the gun there. I saw a hand reach up and grip the top of the sofa. A second hand joined the first. A woman pulled herself up. I saw the crown of her head followed by her face. I aimed the gun at her. She blinked as if I had just roused her from a nap.

"You're home late," she said.

I lowered the gun, pointing it at the floor.

"Geezus, Annie," I said.

Scalasi rolled off the sofa and moved to my side. I deactivated the Beretta and set it on the narrow table next to the door. She wrapped her arms around my waist and held tight, her forehead brushing my chin. I felt her badge against my stomach.

"I heard what happened," she said.

"Just another day in paradise."

"Sure."

I leaned down and kissed her lips.

"How are you?" I asked.

Her response was to press her mouth hard against mine. She was in uniform, crisp white shirt and tie, blue skirt. She had removed her shoes. Her matching jacket was folded and draped over a chair; I could see a single gold star pinned to each shoulder.

"I was frightened when I heard about the shooting," Anne said. "I tried not to show it because . . . because I'm always telling people that you're just a guy I used to know, a man I once worked with." She stepped away from me. "I had to lock myself in my office until I stopped trembling. Imagine having that reaction. It surprised me a little bit."

"We're friends. I'd be upset if someone shot at you, too."

Anne removed her tie.

"That's good to know," she said. "So, tell me, have you discovered who the woman is, yet—Emily Denys?"

"No."

She opened the top button of her shirt.

"If it makes you feel any better, the officers working the case don't have a name, either," Anne said. "They do have something that you don't, though."

"What's that?"

"They have the bullet."

From her expression, I knew Anne expected me to guess what she was talking about, so I worked the puzzle in my head. It was difficult, because while I was doing that, she kept opening buttons until her shirt fell open, revealing the powder-blue bra beneath it. The only breathing I could hear now was mine.

Think, Taylor, I told myself. The bullet taken from the back of Emily's skull . . .

"NIBIN," I said.

"The National Integrated Ballistic Information Network. My officers ran the bullet through the computer system. They got a match seven hours after they started. It took several days to work the bureaucracy—big surprise. First they had to acquire the bullet from the original source, which took a lot of official correspondence, not to mention UPS. Afterward, they had to bring the bullet to the BCA and order up their own ballistic tests, which took another day."

"What are you telling me?"

"I shouldn't be telling you anything. I promised myself I wouldn't."

"Annie?"

She unbuttoned her skirt, pulled down the zipper, and let it fall into a puddle at her feet.

"The bullet that killed Denys was fired from the same gun that was used in an unsolved homicide thirteen months ago."

"Where?"

Scalasi stepped out of the skirt.

"A small town called Arona in western Wisconsin," she said.

She turned and moved toward my bedroom. I could detect a hint of powder-blue panties beneath the tails of her shirt.

"Who was killed?" I asked.

"I'll tell you later."

I was on the phone ten minutes after Scalasi left my apartment. Helin wasn't as happy as I thought he would be when I explained the connection between the murder of Emily and Mayor Todd Franson in Arona. Not even when I added that he was killed in the same manner as the girl, a single shot to the back of the head while he was unlocking the door to his house, and that the killing occurred at about the same time Emily first appeared in the Cities. Instead of hopping up and down as he did after the shooting earlier, he became quiet.

"Up until now, I thought this was a good thing," I said.

"The Barrington family has property in Arona, a summer retreat of some sort, doesn't it?"

"Yes."

"In fact, from what you told me, it's the same the property U.S. Sand wants to turn into a silica sand mine."

"Yes."

"You can bet the CA will be working very, very hard to connect the killing of the mayor to Mrs. Barrington. If she does . . . Tell me that Eleanor didn't even know who he was, this Mayor Franson."

"Do you want me to ask her?"

"Hell no."

"Then you ask her," I said. "In the meantime, why don't I drive out there tomorrow morning and take a look around?"

"Why don't you?"

"At the very least I can flash Emily's pic and see if anyone can identify her."

"Keep in touch."

"Tell me, though—Haukass knew about the bullet yet kept it to herself. Can't she be cited for withholding evidence from the defense?"

"While the CA's obligated to turn over all evidence, discovery can unfold gradually, sometimes more gradually than what you might consider fair. Probably, though, she has no more idea if this is inculpatory evidence that proves Mrs. Barrington is guilty or exculpatory that proves she's innocent than we do, and she'll want to know before she gives it up."

"What if I'm the one who finds out if it's inculpatory or exculpatory?"

"Keep it to yourself. At least until you talk to me."

CHAPTER SIXTEEN

Arona was a two-hour drive from the Twin Cities if you obeyed the posted speed limits. It was the largest city in Kamin County in Wisconsin with just over three thousand residents, yet it wasn't the county seat. That honor belonged to Tintori Falls, about twenty-five miles east. Even though it was out of my way, that's where I drove first thing in the morning because that's where the sheriff lived.

I found the Kamin County Sheriff's Department a block off the main drag. It was located in one of those flat, ultramodern, energy-efficient, multipurpose brick buildings that somehow manage to always look like an elementary school. That impression changed quickly once I stepped inside, though, and approached a desk that was protected by a thick wall of bulletproof glass. I told the female officer I found there who I was and what I wanted. She directed me to a blue molded-plastic chair and told me to wait.

I expected a long wait. Instead, the officer was back in less than a minute. She pushed a hidden button, and I heard a loud buzzing sound. She waved me through a security door and led me down a brilliantly lit corridor to a spacious office. Directly behind a cluttered desk stood a large man with white hair and glasses and wearing a neatly pressed white shirt with a five-point star over his left pocket and an American flag sewn above his right. He made no attempt to shake my hand, so I didn't try to shake his.

"Mr. Taylor," he said. "I've been expecting you."

"You have?"

He jerked his head to his left. I followed the movement to a comfy-looking sofa against the wall. Martin McGaney was sitting on the sofa. He gave me a little finger wave. I didn't know if he was saying hello or tut-tut.

"'Morning, Martin," I said.

"Taylor."

"You're out and about bright and early today."

"So are you."

"You're here cuz of the bullet," the sheriff said. "Tell me I'm wrong."

I went into my spiel, explaining my presence and purpose in an out-of-state jurisdiction to the proper authorities just like the handbook suggests.

"Sheriff, I am a licensed private investigator from the state of Minnesota. I am investigating the murder of a woman who went by the name of Emily Denys in St. Paul. I have reason to believe that her murder is connected to the killing of a Kamin County resident some thirteen months ago. I am asking for your cooperation in this matter."

The sheriff smiled and turned to McGaney.

"I like 'im," he said. "A little formal for my taste."

"He's not a bad sort once you get past his attitude."

"Hell's bells, son, all them PIs got attitude."

"Tell me, Taylor," McGaney said. "How'd you know about the bullet? The BCA didn't even confirm a match until late yesterday."

He probably already guessed that Anne Scalasi told me, yet there was no way I was going to give her up.

"You might find this hard to believe, Martin," I said, "but there is a surprisingly large number of employees in the Ramsey County Attorney's Office who simply do not like their new boss."

"Actually, I don't find that hard to believe at all."

"A mite prickly in person, is she?" the sheriff asked. "Cuz over the phone she was charming as all get-out."

"Marianne Haukass is a politician," I said.

"They're all politicians, son. So am I when it comes down to it. That's why I'd like to see some closure in the Franson case before the next election. Which is also why I'm not gonna kick if you go down there. You're not going to get any cooperation, at least not from me or my office. You want to go pokin' around, though, you got my blessing. Who knows, might be you raise up some dust we missed. Right now we ain't got jack. Let me tell ya, that's embarrassing. A mayor—the goddamned mayor, mind you—catches a nine in the back of the head and we can't solve it? Embarrassing."

"Don't you have any suspects?"

"Problem is we have too many suspects. Half the town hated the prick. Well, anyway, forty-nine percent if you go by the last election."

"Can I see your field reports?"

"What part of you're not going to get any cooperation from me don't you understand? The skirt down in Arona might let you see hers, but not me."

"Skirt?"

"The police chief in Arona is a woman," McGaney said.

"Ahh."

Anne Scalasi had received a steady litany of insults when she joined the St. Paul Police Department and worked her way up the promotion ladder, yet I don't remember "skirt" being among them.

"Now, Mr. McGaney here—he and his boss have all my cooperation and copies of most of my records," the sheriff said. "Call it professional courtesy. Maybe they'll share with you."

I gave him a hopeful glance. After all, we were friends—sorta. McGaney waved his finger at me.

"Can you at least tell me if you identified Emily Denys?" I asked.

"When we do, I'm sure your lawyer friend will be the first to hear about it."

"I got a question for you, now," the sheriff said. "You carrying?"

"I have a permit for Minnesota," I said. "Not for Wisconsin, though, so no, I'm not armed."

The sheriff glanced at McGaney as if he were seeking confirmation.

"I'll bet real money he has a gun stashed in his car, probably the trunk, probably a Beretta. I believe that's his weapon of choice."

The sheriff was looking directly at me when he said, "As long as he keeps it in his trunk we ain't got no problems."

"Thank you for your time," I said.

I headed for the door. McGaney called after me.

"Haukass said if we ran into each other I should tell you—the tow truck operator who boosted all those vehicles, he copped a plea. Your testimony won't be required after all."

With that, whatever leverage I had with the woman was gone.

"It's always a pleasure, Martin," I said.

"Best to the assistant chief next time you see her."

Arona was one of those small towns that seemed to stretch forever. There was a McDonald's at one end of the main street, a Subway at the other, and in between just about everything you'd expect to find in a small town, plus several healthcare centers, one linked to the Mayo Clinic. North of town was a factory that manufactured furniture, and south was a facility where they processed chicken. West along the river, bait shops, boat rentals, resorts, and campgrounds catered to tourists. Surrounding it all were family farms stretching to the horizon.

Yet what I noticed most were the heavy trucks. At least a half dozen rumbled past while I stood at a gas pump filling my Camry, a cloud of yellow dust following each like the contrails of a high-flying jet.

"You believe this shit?" the owner of the service station said. "Been like this for over a year now. They say there are over nine thousand truckloads of frack sand leaving the state every day. I believe it, man. Just sitting here, if you don't see a truck driving past every ten minutes you think there's something wrong with your watch."

"Must get old in a hurry."

"People used to walk the streets, you know? Used to stroll down Main Street. That was a thing. Nobody does that anymore. Not with these monster trucks flying by all the time."

"You live here long?"

"My whole life."

"Working a service station, you must know everyone."

"Wouldn't say I know 'em, but there ain't but a couple of us pumping gas, so we pretty much *see* everybody at one time or another."

"Did you ever see this girl?"

I showed him a pic of Emily on my cell phone. He took the phone and studied the screen for a moment before passing it back.

"No, can't say I ever saw her before, and if I did, I'd think I'd remember. Not too many women hereabouts look as good as she does. What's it all about?"

"A missing girl I was asked to find."

"You one of them private eyes?"

"Something like that."

Another truck filled with silica sand rumbled down the street as he spoke.

"If she lives around here, I can't blame her for running away."

CHAPTER SEVENTEEN

Wisconsin had changed. I remembered when it was good-natured, with a healthy us-versus-them attitude, the same attitude that you'll find in Minnesota. Now it was us-against-us, with the population pretty much split along party lines. It started with the election of a polarizing governor and the rancorous recall election that followed. Over a million voters signed the recall petition. The governor survived the recall, and soon after the petition was uploaded to the internet. Now whenever anyone attempts to run for office, apply for a state job, or simply seek government assistance, the powers that be check the petition, and if your name is on it, you're screwed.

There just didn't seem to be much middle ground anymore, a fact that was emphasized when I checked into the Everheart Resort, Restaurant, and Bar nestled along the Trempealeau River. The owner was named William Everheart. He told me to call him Bill and added, "I don't want any trouble in my place."

"Are you expecting trouble?" I asked.

"I got sand miners staying here, and environmentalists, and tourists that came for the fishing and water and want to be left alone—three groups that hate each other so, yeah, I'm expecting some trouble. Not to mention the townspeople. The community—used to be we had names. Now we have labels—right wing, left wing, neoconservative, flaming liberal, obstructionist, reactionary, bleeding heart, fascist, so-cialist, pro-business, anti-government, tree hugger . . ."

"What about you?"

"I'm trying to keep an open mind."

"That makes you an endangered species, doesn't it?"

"I'm a local businessman, emphasis on local. Sure, I cater to out-of-towners that want to stay in my rooms or occupy a spot at my camp-ground down the road. They rent my boats, buy my bait, and work the river and streams for trout. Lots of the customers who eat in my res-taurant, drink in my bar, and sing karaoke on weekends, though, they're local. Some of them work the sand. It doesn't pay for me to be one thing or the other."

"You're not worried about the mines affecting your business?"

"'Course I'm worried. On a good weekend, I'll draw five hundred people, and that goes right up through hunting season. The silica sand facility they're proposing, it's less than a mile away. If it pollutes the river and streams, killing the trout; if it pollutes the air, turning the forest yellow with blowing sand; if it depletes and destroys what Mother Na-ture gave us here—I'm out of business."

"Why let the sand miners stay?"

"I'm hoping there'll be some adults among them, that they'll show some real responsibility."

"Have they so far?"

"There's going to be a town hall meeting at the high school audito-rium. I'll know better then. In the meantime . . ."

"You'll get no trouble from me."

"I'm going to hold you to that. I probably wouldn't even have said anything except you don't look like you're here to wet a line."

"I'm looking for a girl."

I pulled up Emily's pic on my smartphone and handed it to the re-sort owner.

"Well, if you're looking for a girl, that one there's worth finding," he said.

"Have you seen her?"

"No, I don't think so."

Everheart swiped the screen with his finger. Another pic appeared and then another. I reached for the phone, annoyed at his rudeness. You don't swipe someone else's phone, c'mon. But he stopped me.

"Wait," Everheart said. "I know her."

"Who?"

He held up the pic for me to see. It was a selfie of Emily and Devon.

"That's the Barrington girl, isn't it? Sure. She used to come in all the time, mostly with her brother. They'd shoot pool in the bar. Haven't seen her for . . . it must be a year at least."

"What do you know about her?"

"Not a lot. She seems like a nice kid. Always polite. Can sing, too. Most people who do karaoke, they make you want to dive under the table. Devon has a nice voice, kind of sweet. 'Course, she was always sober. This is a family place and we let kids run around, but it's also a bar. Her older brother, on the other hand . . . Meh, Joel's all right, I guess. He always looked to me like he was counting his money, though. Devon's old lady—don't get me started. I doubt Eleanor Barrington could string five words together without complaining about something."

"Did the Barringtons come here often?"

"Often enough. There aren't that many options 'round abouts if you want to get out of the house, although the Barrington house . . . The family has a place down on the river a couple miles north of here. Very nice. They call it Mereshack, if you can believe it. I'd hate to see 'em sell it off."

"Why would they?"

"Last I heard U.S. Sand wanted to build a four-hundred-acre facility that includes some of the land the house is sitting on."

"Last I heard, Mrs. Barrington turned them down."

"That was a year ago, before all that shit about the mayor came out. Who knows what the woman is thinking now?"

"What shit about the mayor?"

"You don't know?"

"What can I say? I'm new here."

"He was trying to work a deal, get the city to condemn the property, the four hundred acres U.S. Sand wants for its facility, condemn it through eminent domain. Someone shot him before it could happen. Anyway, Mrs. Barrington's property, that was part of the deal, and I haven't seen any of them around here since. Which is my point. The Barringtons have been a part of Arona for over a hundred years. The park—have you seen our park, where Main Street splits around it, creating a kind of island? The grandfather gave the city both the park and the fountain. The son gave us the amphitheater. The grandson, when we had a drive to build the new library, he matched all the funds everyone else donated; this was right before his plane went down. Now, after all that, for the mayor to try something sneaky like he did, Eleanor could easily decide to say screw it, sell the land to the miners, and go somewhere else. Which would be too bad. You have me curious, though, the questions you're asking. Are you some kind of detective?"

"Some kind," I said. "The girl"—I showed him the original pic on my smartphone again—"is a friend of the family, and she's gone missing. I was asked to find her."

"Is she from around here?"

"That was my impression."

"Sorry I can't help you."

"Don't be so sure."

"What do you mean?"

"Can you direct me to the public library?"

The library was located across the street from the Arona City Park. I walked through the park to reach it. It was called, simply, the Arona City Public Library. I didn't see the Barrington name anywhere, not even on a plaque, at the library or the park. I liked the family for that. Usually, when someone donates money to a public cause, they demand naming rights in return.

I found a sign outside the library door—NO FIREARMS OR WEAPONS ARE ALLOWED ON LIBRARY PROPERTY. It made me pause long enough to remember that my Beretta was still in the spare tire compartment in the trunk of my car before stepping inside. There were metal detectors at the door, and I didn't know if they were there to catch gunrunners or keep preteens from skipping out with copies of *Fifty Shades of Grey* tucked in their backpacks.

I found the main desk. The woman sitting behind it greeted me like we were old friends and asked if I agreed with her that it was a beautiful day. I did agree and received her prediction for the weather through the coming week, which I also agreed with. Eventually she asked what I wanted, and I told her. She led me exactly to where I needed to be and, after promising more assistance should I need it, left me alone. I thanked her. As soon as her back was turned, I removed the last ten Arona High School yearbooks from the shelf and carried them to a table. I searched through them one at a time.

I couldn't find a photograph of Emily Denys or anyone who resembled her.

I did come across two photographs in the Graduating Seniors sections of consecutive yearbooks that I recognized, however.

The first was Esther Tibbits, the well-endowed young woman who worked for U.S. Sand, the one who seemed so upset that Emily had been killed.

The second was one of the young men dressed in camo that ambushed me outside Emily's duplex, the kid with the short blond hair.

His name was Eric Tibbits.

CHAPTER EIGHTEEN

There was a cluster of businesses near the center of Arona that could be compared to Grand Avenue in St. Paul or Uptown in Minneapolis if you were being exceedingly generous. I found antiques, jewelry, ski and bike supplies, candy, a bakery, a couple of cafés and coffeehouses, a wine bar, a wildlife art gallery and supplies, a glassworks, a florist, designer clothes, and something called Legend of the Celts.

At the end of the street was a one-story building built of redwood that somehow reminded me of a Royal Canadian Mounted Police outpost even though it had an American flag flying in front. A sign read CITY HALL and listed in much smaller type offices for the mayor, city council members, planning and zoning, public finance, parks and rec, public works, building inspection, and storm water management. The police had their own entrance around the corner. The door was unlocked; there wasn't even a bell to announce when visitors entered. I parked myself in front of a desk reserved for the receptionist/secretary/dispatcher. The desk was unoccupied. On the wall next to it hung the names and photographs of the chief of police, three officers, and two dispatchers.

I leaned against the desk and watched a woman sitting at a blue-metal desk at the far end of the room and reading a newspaper. I recognized her from the photographs on the wall. It could have been a college library it was so quiet; my voice was like a roar of thunder even though I spoke softly.

"Good afternoon, Chief," I said.

The woman dropped the newspaper and leapt to her feet. Her hand went to her heart, not her gun, which, believe it or not, disappointed me. If it had been Scalasi, she would have pumped two rounds into me by now.

"You startled me," she said.

"I apologize for that, but honestly, this place is about as secure as a box of cornflakes. Even the public library has better security."

The chief quickly crossed the room. She was wearing sneakers, black Dockers, and a blue short-sleeve knit shirt. Except for the nine-millimeter Glock and badge attached to her belt, she looked like a playground monitor.

"We're kind of informal around here," she said.

"Sure."

Yet I didn't approve. Too many cops get shot these days for them to be careless over security. Probably, because they lived in a small town, the Arona officers thought they were safe. They weren't.

She offered her hand.

"I'm Chief Maureen McMahan. I bet you're Holland Taylor."

I shook her hand.

"How did you guess?"

"We don't get many men wearing sport coats in Arona. Besides, the sheriff called. Said, 'Honey'—he likes to call me honey. 'Honey,' he said, 'I'd take it as a personal favor if you help Taylor out, except not too much.' He was particularly keen that I not let you read the paper we generated on the mayor's murder. Taylor, there's something you should know."

"What's that?"

"I hate being called honey."

The door behind me opened, and a woman entered the station house who was as casually dressed as the chief. She was sucking a soft drink through a straw and carrying a bag from the Subway down the street.

"I'm back," she said in case we hadn't noticed.

"I'm going to step out," the chief said. "Let me know if anything happens."

"Of course."

"Taylor, walk with me."

We followed a sidewalk in the opposite direction of the retail cluster to a well-worn path that led to a clearing in the woods with a park bench. From the bench, we could watch the sparse traffic churning through the town.

"I'm not going to let you look at our records, and not just because the sheriff asked me not to," the chief said. "I'd be happy to tell you what's in them, though, as long as you keep it to yourself."

"I appreciate that."

"What do you want to know?"

I pulled the smartphone from my pocket, pulled up Emily's pic, and showed it to her.

"Do you know this woman?" I asked.

The chief studied it for a moment.

"No, I don't," she said.

"Do you have any missing person reports resembling her."

"I don't have any missing person reports at all. Who is the girl?"

I explained.

"Why do you think she was from around here?" the chief asked.

Although neither the sheriff nor McGaney had mentioned it, I knew they would be mighty displeased if I told anyone about the matching nine-millimeter slugs. If Emily Denys's killer was from Arona and heard about it, he'd be a complete moron if he didn't ditch the gun immediately. 'Course, you could argue that he was a complete moron for not getting rid of it in the first place. The question was—how much could I trust Chief McMahan? I had no doubt that she was honest, yet she didn't strike me as being particularly professional. On the other hand, if I didn't answer her questions, it was unlikely that she would answer mine.

"It's complicated," I said.

"I'm listening."

I proceeded to tell her about my involvement with Mrs. Barrington, adding nothing that she couldn't learn for herself by reading the articles posted on the website of the St. Paul *Pioneer Press*. I concluded with a question.

"Do you know Esther Tibbits?"

"What does she have to do with your killing?" the chief asked.

"I'm not saying she has anything to do with it."

"Last I heard, Esther was working as a secretary, community liaison, whatever you want to call it, for a team of U.S. Sand executives who are negotiating to open a silica sand mine and processing plant near the river."

I explained about Emily's reaction to her encounter with the lobbyists, ending with my meeting them and Esther in their offices.

"The next day I was ambushed by a couple of kids dressed in camouflage," I said. "I identified one of them as being Eric Tibbits."

"Esther's brother?"

"I'm not sure if he was the one who was shooting or not. I was moving pretty fast."

"Does the sheriff know this?"

"I didn't even know it until a half hour ago."

The chief stood, but she wasn't going anywhere. She was just one of those people who liked to move around when she was thinking.

"What do you want me to do about it?" she asked.

"Nothing at all."

"I could arrest him. I could hold him for Ramsey County."

For a brief moment, I wondered if it would be worthwhile to bust Eric Tibbits. You'd be amazed what some people say while they're trying to talk themselves out of trouble.

"Maybe later," I said.

Chief McMahan stretched her arms, her back, and continued to move to and fro.

"I don't know what I should tell you," she said.

I didn't know how to respond to that, so I said nothing. Instead, I sat there and watched as she paced back and forth in front of me. Finally she stopped.

"What do you know about the murder of Mayor Franson?" she asked.

"Almost nothing," I said. The information I had gleaned from the internet was sketchy at best.

"No one realized what a thoroughly corrupt individual he was until after he was killed. The things he did . . ."

The chief paused and shook her head as if after thirteen months she still couldn't believe it.

"Taylor," she said, "before she went to work for U.S. Sand, Esther Tibbits worked as the mayor's secretary. She claims she didn't know what was going on. I don't believe her. The fact that U.S. Sand hired her so soon after the mayor was shot only reinforces my opinion."

"What was it that Esther pretended she didn't know?"

"As it turned out, Franson knew that U.S. Sand was negotiating with individual property owners to buy or lease land that they could convert into silica sand mines. He purposely kept it a secret from the rest of us until after he had arranged for the company to buy property owned by both his mother and brother. Permits, everything was put in place. They were actually digging when the mayor made the announcement, and he only did it because the story got into the paper. Later, we discovered . . . The newspaper printed a story the day after he was killed that accused Mayor Franson of working in secret with the city planner and the city attorney to have Arona annex four hundred acres and make it available to U.S. Sand."

"The four hundred acres the company wants for its new facility?"

"He was going to seize the property and have the city sell it to U.S. Sand. How much Arona would make on the deal, no one knows. How much he was going to get paid under the table, him and the others—no one knows that, either. Or at least they aren't saying. U.S. Sand and Esther aren't saying."

"This included Mrs. Barrington's property?"

"Eleanor Barrington? I think so, some of it anyway. Nothing came of it, though. That's because someone shot the mayor in the back of his head while he was unlocking the door to his house, shot him before he could make it happen. People around here call it 'the Conspiracy.' There were so many suspects at the time that we didn't even consider the militia."

"What militia?"

"They call themselves the Red Stone Patriots. Their politics are somewhere far right of the Tea Party; preaching the anti-government gospel, all rights to the individual, that sort of thing. They've never been a problem, at least not until . . . If Esther told her brother what Mayor Franson was doing and he told the militia, he's a member, you see . . . These guys, they believe that private property is sacrosanct. If they thought . . . I need to make a few phone calls."

"Chief . . . ?"

"Call me tomorrow. We'll talk more tomorrow."

Chief McMahan moved briskly down the path, to the sidewalk, and back to City Hall. I followed at a more sedate pace, so she reached the building long before I did. I circled City Hall, heading for my car. I stopped when I came across a parking space with a sign that read ACT-ING MAYOR. The space was filled with an SUV badly in need of a wash and wax. I flashed on Richard III systematically eliminating his rivals for the English throne. Or was that Kevin Spacey? The thought caused me to smirk. At the same time I told myself, that's what homicide cops do, what I used to do—question suspects who might have benefited by the victim's untimely demise, including acting mayors. Besides, what's the worst he could do? Throw me out?

Apparently, City Hall employees took security more seriously than the chief of police, because I had to get past three of them before I could get anywhere near the acting mayor. Along the way, I learned that he was a she—Dawn Gischler, a woman with silver hair, a puffy figure, and piercing blue eyes. She was wearing a peasant shirt, flared jeans with a wide belt, and sandals when I found her leaning on her desk, a bundle of white typing paper between her hands. She was staring at the bundle as if she were trying to set it on fire with her heat vision. I knocked on the door.

"Are you a reporter?" she asked.

"No."

"What do you want? If it's about U.S. Sand, the town hall meeting is scheduled to start at seven P.M. at the school auditorium. You can make your statement then."

"None of the above."

"Well . . . ?"

"My name is Taylor. I'm a private investigator."

"Oh, God. Now what?"

"I'm investigating a murder that took place last week in St. Paul, Minnesota."

"What does that have to do with Arona, Wisconsin?"

"Probably nothing. On the other hand, it might be connected to the murder of your mayor."

"I need this today. I really do. Oh-kay." The acting mayor gestured at a chair in front of her desk. "Sit."

I sat.

"What's your name again?" Gischler asked.

I gave her a look at my license.

"Holland Taylor," she said. "I thought Holland was a gal's name."

"A lot of the guys I grew up with will tell you the same thing."

"What brings you here, Mr. Taylor?"

"As I explained to the chief—"

"That nit?" Gischler waved a hand. "Sorry. Talking out of school. Go on."

"My killing might be connected to the Red Stone Patriots, and the Patriots might be connected—"

"Is that what Maureen told you? The county sheriff investigated the killing from here to Sunday, and he didn't find a connection to the militia. She's just trying to prove her worth to the community now that her job is up for review. Do you know how she got her job?"

I had no intention of answering the acting mayor's question. I had no intention of saying anything at all. She was upset and in a mood to vent. So I let her.

"Maureen was a dispatcher, for God's sake. The way she got her job—the mayor, Mayor Franson, hated the police department. We had a chief named Philipps. Good man. Used to work as an officer in Chicago. He was a sergeant, I think.

"One day he gets a call about a dog running loose on the property next to Franson's place. The mayor made the call. He wanted the owner cited. Instead, Philipps gave the dog owner a warning. The mayor was upset. He said, this was in Philipps's report, he said, 'We've got two hundred and fifteen ordinances, and if these people'—his neighbors—'if they breathe wrong I want them cited.'

"The next day, the mayor calls Philipps again, saying he wanted his neighbor cited for blowing grass clippings into the street. The chief sent the mayor a letter stating that the Arona Police Department would not become a tool in Mayor Franson's personal vendetta against his neighbors. He sent copies of the letter to the city council and to the city attorney. The city attorney backed Philipps, and so did we.

"Next thing we know, the mayor is ordering Philipps to use city police officers as crossing guards near the school. In retaliation, Philipps gave Franson a ticket for parking in a police-only spot right here at City Hall. The mayor ordered him to tear it up. Philipps refused.

"Finally, Mayor Franson proposed at our regular Thursday meeting that the city disband the police department. The resolution caught us all completely by surprise. According to Wisconsin state law—our attorney made this clear to us—state law requires that any municipality large enough to be classified as a city must have a police department. Franson wanted to disband our police department anyway, and worry about the consequences later, meaning let's fight this thing in court, and while we're at it, leave Arona without police protection for what—a year? Two?

"Obviously something had to be done, and that something was replacing Chief Philipps. Who did the mayor have in mind for a replacement? Maureen McMahan, who had a law enforcement degree, who was certified to be a Wisconsin police officer, yet who didn't have a single day of experience. Somehow, he got the votes and Maureen was in.

"You have to give her credit, though, because one of the first things she did was to investigate the mayor for misconduct in office for making the city pay for all of his personal expenses during a trip he took to

Washington. Franson went ballistic. He claimed that the investigation was retaliation because he took someone else to D.C. with him instead of Maureen. He told me that the chief was trying to get revenge because he was now sleeping with someone else instead of her.

"What is wrong with people? The man was married. Maureen was married. I'm begging him, don't do this in an open city council meeting. Franson wouldn't listen. He said he was tired of being punished for being the mayor. That was on a Monday. By Tuesday he was dead. On Thursday they made me acting mayor until the election in November because I was the senior city council member. Isn't life grand?"

"It worked out for you," I said.

"You think so? Look at this." Gischler took the sheaf of papers she had been staring at when I arrived and shook it at me. "It's a petition started by the Red Stone Patriots demanding that the city council vote to make English the official language of Arona. I'd ignore it except that ten percent of the city voters signed the damn thing, which means I have to bring it before the council, which means all hell is going to break loose, never mind the potential legal ramifications if we adopt it. This on top of the controversy over the silica sand mines. I hate this job. I just hate it. There's no way I'm running in the election."

"The story you told me about Chief McMahan sleeping with the mayor, does the county sheriff know?"

"Ask him."

"We're not on speaking terms."

"Guess you're out of luck. Taylor, you'll have to excuse me. I need to get ready for that damn meeting tonight. It's going to be a nightmare, a real nightmare."

"Are you planning a vote of some kind?"

"No. That comes in two weeks. Tonight we're just giving everyone a chance to have their say. Democracy at work. God . . . God, I hate this job."

CHAPTER NINETEEN

The publisher slash editor slash news reporter slash chief cook and bottle washer locked his fingers behind his head, leaned back in his chair, propped his feet on his desk, and repeated the question I had just asked him. "Who do I think killed the mayor?"

I wasn't surprised that everything in Arona was close to everything else, but I had driven only two hundred yards from City Hall before I spied a sign above a jewelry store.

KAMIN COUNTY RECORD
PUBLISHED EVERY WEDNESDAY

I parked on the street and climbed the stairs. For the second time that day, I was mistaken for a reporter.

"It's the sports jacket," the newsman told me. "I used to wear one, too, when I was with *The Des Moines Register*."

His name was Skip Zetzman, and he took over the *Record* after accepting a buyout from the struggling Iowa newspaper nearly ten years earlier.

"These people never heard of investigative reporting until I got here," Zetzman said. "It was all 'Arona resident teaches Hawaiian dance at hula school' and 'Heart disease is on the rise: what you need to know.'

Most newspapers are in financial trouble. Yet I've managed to both maintain our circulation and actually increase advertising revenue. It helps that there's been a lot to investigate."

I started by showing him the smartphone pic of Emily, which he didn't recognize, explained that I was investigating her death, and suggested there was an outside chance it was linked to the silica sand mining in Arona. I figured that would get him talking, and I was correct. I had never met a reporter who wasn't delighted to tell you how much they knew that you didn't.

"Who do I think killed the mayor?" Zetzman asked. "I think it was the enviros."

"Environmental extremists have committed God knows how many acts of vandalism and harassment," I said. "To my knowledge, though, they've never actually killed or injured anyone, unlike say, the nut jobs in the pro-life and animal rights movements."

"There's always a first time."

He had me there.

"What about the Red Stone Patriots?" I asked.

"The neighborhood bad boys? There's always been some dispute over the meaning of the word 'Wisconsin.' Some people think it means 'red stone,' and that's where their name comes from but, man, they don't care about the environment. If they were in charge there would be no EPA. Besides, they've been all talk and no action since starting up a half-dozen years ago. They have a compound a few miles out of town where they practice shooting automatic weapons in case black helicopters should descend upon us. Other than that, we usually don't hear much from them unless it's an election year."

"Like this year."

"Yeah, but I'm still betting on the enviros. The place has been crawling with them ever since they discovered that Mayor Franson was trying to sell the place to U.S. Sand. We even have our own group of activists. KICASS, short for Kamin Independent Citizens Against Silica Sand. Catchy, huh? These guys, they compare what the mayor was doing to Benedict Arnold attempting to surrender West Point to the British."

"If I'm not mistaken, you broke that story—"

"You heard about that, huh?"

"The day *after* the mayor was killed."

"Yeah, but I knew about it a couple of weeks earlier. I needed to get someone to confirm on the record what my original source told me off the record before going to press. This isn't an online media operation, all right? It isn't Fox News. I'm trying to be responsible here. It was a good story, too. What Franson was doing . . . The legal process of eminent domain is called condemnation. What happens, once the local government decides it wants a parcel of land or a building, it contacts the owner to negotiate a selling price. One, the owner can take the offer, which they almost never do. Two, the parties kick it around until they decide what the fair price is, and then they make a deal. Or three, the government files a court action, claims it tried to negotiate a sale in good faith, appoints an appraiser to establish fair market value, condemns the property, pays off the owner, and tosses him on the street. Franson was going straight to option three. He didn't even contact the property owners. They had no idea what he was up to. Getting killed when he did, that was just unfortunate. Believe me. Kicking the mayor around every week was going to be pure pleasure. 'Course, now I've got Bob Barcott, and he's almost as good."

Zetzman rapped twice on the top of his desk for luck.

"Bob Barcott?" I asked.

"He's in charge of planning and zoning for Arona, and he is a pro-sand fanatic. Complaints have been rolling in about him threatening to tear down the homes and cabins of people who speak out against the mines and slapping frack opponents with bogus zoning violations. He told one homeowner who complained about the noise that zoning codes require houses to be one thousand feet from a mine and that he was twenty feet shy of compliance. He told the homeowner that he had ten days to bring the house into compliance or the house would be removed. Except the code prohibits mine owners from opening a mine within one thousand feet of a house, not the other way 'round. I have no doubt that Franson was in the pocket of U.S. Sand. Now that he's gone, it looks like they got someone else to do their dirty work. God, I love Bob Barcott. He's gonna sell a lot of papers."

"The story you broke about Mayor Franson—who told you what the mayor was up to?"

"Now, now, Taylor. A journalist never reveals his sources."

"Was it Esther Tibbits?"

"Ahh, Esther. That's what brought you to Arona. Esther Tibbits, who was the mayor's new sex toy and who now works for U.S. Sand."

Anne Scalasi would be appalled, I told myself. She would never have made that mistake, asking a question that told a suspect more than his answer would have revealed to her. No wonder she was promoted over me.

"New sex toy?" I asked.

"The one he played with after discarding his old sex toy."

"Who would that be?"

Zetzman lifted his hand and let it fall as if he had no way of knowing. I didn't believe the gesture.

"Chief McMahan?" I said.

"You do know a thing or two, don't you? No, it wasn't Maureen. It was the woman who came after Maureen, no pun intended."

"The woman he took to Washington, D.C.?"

"There you go."

"The acting mayor told me—"

"Dawn? What did our resident hippie have to say?"

"That Mayor Franson said he was going to reveal his relationship with both Maureen and the woman he took to D.C. at the council meeting right before he was shot."

"Did she name names?"

"No."

"It's possible she doesn't know the name."

"I bet you do."

"You're insisting that I say it, aren't you?"

"Say what?"

"It was my wife. Sheila. There. Are you happy? I thought she was visiting her family in Philadelphia. Surprise, surprise."

"I'm sorry. I had no idea."

"Neither did I until Maureen told me."

"The chief—"

"Apparently Franson and Sheila met at the airport in Minneapolis and flew out to D.C. together. Maureen discovered the truth when she investigated the expenses the mayor submitted to the city and thought I should know. That was kind of her, don't you think?"

"She's a peach."

"No big deal, though. It all worked out in the end."

"Did you and your wife reconcile?"

"Hell, no. I divorced her on the spot, and she moved back to the East Coast. That's what she always wanted anyway. We met in school. I took her to Des Moines and then up here, and all the while Sheila yearned for the coast. I only hope she's happy at last."

I had a thought that I couldn't help but give voice.

"Your wife didn't leave until she exposed what Mayor Franson was up to," I said—a declarative statement, not a question.

Zetzman raised his hand and let it fall again; apparently it was a habit with him.

"What can I tell you?" he said. "The mayor liked to brag, and my ex felt she owed me one."

"What did his wife think about all this?"

"The mayor's wife? Bridgette? All I know is that she moved in with her brother-in-law, who's been living high, wide, and handsome ever since he sold most of his farm to U.S. Sand. For the record, she was the first person the county sheriff interrogated after Franson was killed."

"How did that work out?"

"She remains at large, as they say."

"With her brother-in-law?"

Zetzman lifted and dropped his hand.

It was starting to be a long day, and it was barely half over when I left the offices of the *Kamin County Record*. There was a café across the street, and I decided to try my luck. It wasn't just because I was hungry, either. I had learned long ago that small-town waitresses can be terrific sources of information. They always seemed to know when a farmer was having an off year, when a customer's balloon mortgage was coming due, when the weather was making people weird. They could tell you which customers were on the verge of divorce, who was escaping the kids for a cozy night out, who were dating for the first time. They always seemed aware of the emotions at the tables they served.

I stepped inside. A sign told me to wait until I was seated, so I did. While I waited, I scanned the room. I discovered five people crammed into a booth in the corner—Esther Tibbits, her employers Richard Kaufman and Allen Palo, Acting Mayor Dawn Gischler, and a man wearing dress slacks and a button-down shirt that I didn't know.

I found a copy of the *Record* at a stand just inside the door and pretended to read it, hoping that the party wouldn't notice me. Finally the hostess led me to a table for two. Along the way, I paused at the booth, lowered the paper, and said, "Hey, whaddaya know, everybody's here. Small world, isn't it?"

Call it a flair for the dramatic.

"You," Kaufman said.

"What are you doing here?" Palo asked.

"Investigating a murder," I said. "What are you guys doing here?"

Esther turned her head and looked out the window.

"Taylor," the acting mayor said. She seemed genuinely distraught that I had caught her with the sand miners. The unidentified man sitting next to her didn't seem to care one way or the other. "We were talking about the town hall meeting that we're all attending tonight."

"Please, don't let me interrupt. Esther . . ." She turned her head and glanced up at me. She was wearing a light blue shirt that emphasized her chest and a dark blue skirt that emphasized her shirt. "Tell your brother I'm looking forward to meeting him again."

"What's that supposed to mean?" Kaufman asked.

I could have answered, only the hostess seemed anxious that I continue following her to my table, so I did that instead. Once seated, I buried my head in the menu. I didn't look up until the waitress was filling my water glass. Her name tag read PATTY.

"I don't know what you said," she told me, "but it sure upset those folks over at Booth Number Four."

"It did?"

"They're using a lot of obscenities that a small-town girl like me doesn't hear very often."

I didn't believe that for a moment. It might be a small town, but they still get HBO.

"Are you sure they're upset at me?" I asked.

"Are you 'that goddamn fucking Taylor'?"

"'Fraid so."

She shrugged and said, "Would you like to order a beverage while you look at the menu?"

I wanted bourbon, but it wasn't that kind of place. I asked for a Coke. She told me they only served Pepsi.

"Okay," I said.

Patty tapped the menu.

"Today's special, the open-face turkey sandwich, is really good," she said.

"Then that's what I'll have. Say—"

"Yes?"

"Do you know the man sitting next to the acting mayor?"

Patty glanced at the booth and turned away.

"Bob Barcott," she said. "He's head of Arona's planning and zoning."

"Thank you."

Patty hurried away. I stole a glance back at Booth Number Four. The acting mayor and the two lobbyists were leaning toward each other and speaking earnestly. Barcott sat back. Esther looked bored nearly to tears. A moment later, the waitress returned with my drink. A man sitting at a nearby table with his wife spoke to her.

"Patty, can I get my check?" he said.

"Coming right up, hon."

Another man, this one sitting in a booth behind me, called to the first man.

"You got a lot of nerve, Paul," he said. "I gotta give that to ya."

I turned to look. There were two men sitting in the booth. I didn't know which one spoke, but Paul did.

"What are you talking about, Hank?" he asked.

"Coming into town with so many people ready to kill you."

"Nobody wants to kill me."

"Guess again."

"'Sides, this is my town. I live here."

"You put yourself above the town."

"What I did, it isn't any different than raising corn and soybeans," Paul said. "Silica sand is just another crop you're harvesting, 'cept it pays more than corn or beans ever did."

"Tell that to Lisa. Her asthma is so much worse."

"I'm sorry to hear that."

"Sure you are."

By then, Patty had returned with the tab. Paul paid it in cash and left with his wife. Hank shouted at him as he left the restaurant.

"You're ruining the fucking town."

A moment of silence followed. There wasn't a second outburst, however, and the diners settled back into their meals and conversations.

"You get a lot of that?" I asked.

Patty set a plate filled with turkey, dressing, mashed potatoes, corn, and gravy served over sliced white bread in front of me.

"Yeah, these days," she said. "Paul and Hank, they live next door to each other, used to be friends. The sand mines, I don't know."

"Who's Lisa?"

"Hank's little girl. Paul's goddaughter. People are upset because, well, a lot of them figure the sand miners are raping and pillaging the land. If you're Paul, though, what do you do? They were going to foreclose on his place. The lease he signed with the mining company paid him enough up front that he was able to pay off his debts. He claims the mining company says they're only going to dig up small areas at a time and then reclaim them quickly, so he'll still be able to farm most of his property. I don't know."

Patty left me alone with my meal. It reminded me a little of Thanksgiving, which reminded me that I blew off my brother's dinner invitation last year and spent the holiday alone in my apartment watching football games that I didn't care about.

Get out of your head, I told myself, a feat easier said than done. Fortunately, I had help. I was nearly finished with my meal when Kaufman appeared at my table. He took the chair opposite me without asking and sat down on it as if he were attempting to break it with his massive frame.

"What are you doing here, Taylor?" he wanted to know.

"I told you. I'm investigating a murder."

"You sonuvabitch."

"Don't call me names."

"I told you, we had nothing to do with that girl's death."

"I never said you did."

"If you think you're going to put that on us, make unsubstantiated allegations in front of the people at the town hall meeting, accuse us of murder—"

"I'm not that guy."

"We're supposed to take your word for that?"

"Why not?"

"You're working with the environmentalists, you bastard."

I pulled my fingers back on my right hand and tucked my thumb in, forming what the boys and girls at Dragons call *teisho*, meaning "palm heel." I hit Kaufman under the jaw. The force of the blow snapped his head back. Both he and the chair fell backward into a heap.

My first thought wasn't that this was *his* fault for calling me names even after I told him to stop.

Or that it was *my* fault for deliberately attempting to provoke him and his party when I stopped at their booth.

My first thought was that I should have accepted my brother's invitation to Thanksgiving dinner.

Kaufman began to sputter. He called me even more names. He said I attacked him. He said he was going to call the police. His partner joined in while he attempted to help Kaufman to his feet, which wasn't easy because he was so fat. Esther Tibbits remained seated in the booth. Acting Mayor Gischler and Bob Barcott left the restaurant.

"I don't know what you're talking about." I spoke loud enough for just about everyone in the place to hear. "I was just sitting here, minding my own business, eating my lunch, and you come over and threaten me if I interfere with your mining operations. What was I supposed to do?"

"That's a lie," Kaufman said.

"No it's not," Hank said. He was standing next to his booth, apparently happy to stick it to the sand miners. "I saw it all. He was sitting there like he said, and you came over—"

"And threatened me," I added.

"It's a lie," Kaufman said.

"Why did you come over to his table?" Patty asked.

"To tell him—"

"To tell me what?" I said.

He hesitated too long before answering. It was a mistake that doomed him to a guilty verdict and Kaufman was enough of a PR man to know it. Instead of attempting a plausible explanation, he hissed at me.

"We know how to deal with people like you."

"See what I mean," I said.

Disapproving murmurs followed Kaufman and Palo as they made their way to their booth. They searched for Gischler, threw money on the table when they realized she and Barcott were gone, and beat a retreat from the café. Esther trailed behind, paused at the exit, gave me a long, menacing stare, and followed them out.

"I don't know," Patty said.

CHAPTER TWENTY

I turned my attention to the remains of my lunch. Soon the other customers did the same. Just as I finished, Patty reappeared and offered
a dessert menu. I turned her down. She gently slapped my check on the
table and wished me a nice day. I glanced at the amount and debated
cash or credit card, even as I reminded myself to save the receipt. Stanislav, Kennedy, Helin, and DuBois were very keen about receipts.

I decided credit card because I liked to conserve my cash when I was
away from home. Before I could do anything about it, though, a hand
snatched the bill off the table. The hand belonged to a man who was
about fifty and tall and looked like he spent a lot of time outdoors.

"I've got this," he said.

"That's generous of you."

"Are you here for the big meeting?"

"No, actually. I'm not."

"Your friends from U.S. Sand seem to think so."

"I can't help what they think. And they're not my friends."

My response seemed to satisfy him in some way, because he grinned
and offered his hand.

"The enemy of my enemy is my friend," he said.

I shook his hand while thinking the enemy of my enemy might know
something I didn't.

"I'm Holland Taylor," I said.

"Doug Pinter."

I gestured at the chair across from me, and he sat. I noticed the chair wobble, and I wondered if it had been damaged when Kaufman fell out of it.

"I'm the executive director of KICASS," he said.

"Kamin Independent Citizens Against Silica Sand."

"You're familiar with us?"

"In a manner of speaking."

"Who do you represent?"

I could think of a couple of names, yet I didn't want to reveal any of them.

"I'm a private investigator," I said. "The name of my client is privileged."

Pinter nodded his head as if he understood perfectly.

"Not U.S. Sand?" he said.

"Oh, no. Certainly not."

"If you're not here for the meeting, then why are you here?"

"You could say I'm seeking enlightenment."

"About a girl who was killed? Forgive me, but I overheard what Kaufman said earlier."

I reached in my pocket for the ever-present smartphone, called up Emily's pic, and showed it to Pinter. He didn't recognize her either.

"Is U.S. Sand responsible for her death?"

"Are you responsible for the mayor's death?"

"I don't like your insinuation."

"I'm sure U.S. Sand wouldn't appreciate yours."

He stared at me for a few beats, the fingers of his hand drumming an impatient rhythm on the tabletop.

"I'm trying to figure this out," he said.

"No, you're trying to decide how to use it to your advantage. I don't blame you for that. Here's the skinny. The girl was killed about a week ago in St. Paul, Minnesota. I have reason to believe her death has something to do with what is going on in Arona. Our friends at U.S. Sand are convinced I'm going to blame them. The truth is, though, there's no evidence at all to suggest U.S. Sand was involved. Anyway, no more than there's evidence to suggest that you were involved."

"Me?"

"You. KICASS."

"If you think you can blame us—"

"See, now you're behaving exactly like U.S. Sand. Paranoia is a terrible thing, isn't it?"

"We've been unjustly accused of other crimes."

"The murder of Mayor Franson?"

"Among other things."

"Such as?"

"Such as vandalism, spray-painting buildings, sabotaging equipment, sending threatening emails to those responsible for environmental abuse and their families."

"Is any of that true?"

"Neither I nor anyone involved with KICASS is responsible for these things."

"Who is?"

"Radicals acting outside the law. We do not approve of their activities. Yet we understand. While we cannot condone violence in any form, the urgency of the current crisis facing us demands that we do everything within our power to try to prevent or mitigate the irreparable harm that is being done to the environment by both fracking and silica sand mining."

"Did you just make that up?"

"I think I prefer Kaufman and Palo. They're bastards, but at least I know where they stand."

"Tell me about the mayor."

"Todd Franson was a pig."

"I heard that."

"Never mind that he liked to use and abuse women, he sold his office to the sand miners."

"What women?"

"That's what you're interested in. The women he slept with?"

I raised my hand off the table and let it fall, just like Skip Zetzman had.

Pinter pointed his finger at me.

"Franson's crime," he said, "is that he opened the door to these people and invited them in. That's what's important. Arona has become ground zero for sand mining, and it's all because of him. I'm glad he's dead."

"Do you know who killed him?"

"No."

"Would you tell me if you did?"

"No."

"So much for not condoning violence."

Pinter was on his feet now.

"You're not our friend," he said.

"I don't have any friends."

He took my check, crushed it into a ball, and threw it on the table before stomping out of the café.

"So much for a free lunch," I said.

Before I left, I asked the waitress if she could tell me where the mayor used to live. She directed me to a large white house with an old-fashioned porch less than a mile away from the café and a good ten miles from Mrs. Barrington's home along the Trempealeau River. There were many houses nearby and lights lining the street. Despite that, Todd Franson's killer was able to park a vehicle, walk along the sidewalk, come up from behind him on his own porch, calmly put a bullet in the back of his head, and make good a getaway without being witnessed by anyone.

For a moment, I was a homicide cop again, working angles and testing theories. If I had my way, I would have interviewed each and every person who lived on the street. I would have reenacted the crime at night to see how much light the streetlamps threw, determine where someone could have hid in the shadows, and decide what the neighbors could have seen and what they couldn't have. I might even have brought out a K-9 unit. Yes, there were a lot of things I might have done to catch the killer if I had still been a homicide detective.

I was a private investigator, though. Catching killers was no longer my job.

An app on my smartphone directed me to a farm outside of Arona where Mayor Franson's brother lived. It wasn't hard to find. I took a corner and instead of forest, I found a long, flat field where nothing was growing. In the middle of the field, there was a huge gash in the raw earth. Two pyramids rose up on either side of the gash, one of rich topsoil and a second, much higher hill of yellow sand. They were both surrounded by heavy machines operated by men who were laboring mightily to make the gash deeper and the pyramids higher. The sight caught me by surprise. For some reason, I thought that silica sand mines were holes dug deep into the ground. This one was a straight-up strip mine, where they simply scraped away the soil close to the surface and processed the sand beneath it.

At the far end of the field there was a farmhouse and a barn. I followed an asphalt road around the field to the house. The road was covered with yellow dust; it scattered behind my Camry like snowflakes in a blizzard. I parked in the driveway, went to the front door, and rang the bell. There was no answer. I knocked. Still no response. I wondered if the residents could hear me above the noise of the heavy equipment in what amounted to their front yard.

I walked around the house toward the backyard. My shoes kicked up the dust as I went. I found an older woman pinning what looked like a small quilt to a clothesline. Her back was to me. As she pinned it, a man roughly the same age approached her from behind. He slid his hands around her waist and squeezed tight. The woman squealed. The man began kissing her neck and throat. She said, "You're driving me crazy." His hands moved up her waist and cupped her breasts. Her mouth fell open and she leaned her head back against him.

I turned my back and looked out toward the strip mine.

"Excuse me," I said.

"Who are you?" the man asked.

I spun around slowly. The man was now standing in a defensive posture, the woman behind him. Her hand rested on his shoulder.

"Good afternoon," I said. "My name is Taylor. I deeply apologize for interrupting you."

"You weren't interrupting," the man said.

The woman smiled and shoved his shoulder. They both started to giggle.

"I could come back at a more convenient time," I said.

The woman shoved the man again as she slipped past him.

"There's no time like the present," she said. "Are you with the mine?"

"No ma'am. Are you"—I nearly said the mayor's wife, yet caught myself in time to say—"Bridgette Franson?"

"Yes, I am."

"My name's Taylor, like I said. I'm a private investigator. I'm looking into the murder of a young woman in the Twin Cities that might be connected to the murder of your, of Mayor Franson."

Bridgette glanced over her shoulder at her companion. Some kind of signal was exchanged, and he came up in a hurry.

"I'm Mark Franson, Todd's brother," he said.

He thrust his hand at me. I don't think he wanted to shake so much as separate me from Bridgette. I pulled the smartphone from my pocket and called up Emily's pic.

"Can you tell me if either of you recognize this woman?" I asked.

I handed the phone to Bridgette, and she shared it with her brother-in-law.

"No," Bridgette said. "Sorry."

"No," Mark said.

Bridgette returned the phone.

"Is this the woman who was killed?" she asked.

"Yes."

"Who is she?"

"We're not entirely sure. She went by the name Emily Denys, only we think that was an alias."

"What makes you think her death was connected to my brother's?" Mark asked.

There was that question again.

"We believe she might have been involved with the sand mines," I said.

Mark turned his head and grimaced as if I had just made an off-color remark.

"Yeah, well, they've been the cause of a lot of misery," he said. "Look, you came here to speak with Bridgette, right? You don't need me."

"Mr. Franson—"

"I'll just get out of your way."

"Sir—"

Bridgette rested a hand on my wrist to keep me from speaking. We both stood in the yard and watched as Mark retreated to his farmhouse.

"He's still upset about it all," she told me.

"About the murder of his brother?"

"No. About making about a deal with U.S. Sand. He loved farming. He'll tell you now that he should never have listened to Todd."

"Why did he?"

"He wanted plenty of money so I would be comfortable when I left my husband to live with him."

The remark caught me so far off guard that I didn't know what to say, so I ending up saying, "Oh-kay."

Bridgette smiled at me and hooked her arm around mine. She led me to a low stone wall that had been built around a fire pit. There was yellow dust on the wall that she brushed away with the flat of her hand. We sat next to each other.

"We knew each other when we were kids; practically grew up together," Bridgette said. "Todd was the ambitious one. He always wanted to be somebody. Mark wanted to be a farmer like his parents. I married the wrong brother. I knew it right away, too. What can I say? It happens. I was going to stick with him, though, because that's what you do. That's what my generation was taught to do. I knew he was cheating on me, of course. That was okay, because I was cheating on him with

Mark. Only it became ridiculous, Todd's cheating. Maureen McMahan, the little girl he hired to be his secretary, Dawn Gischler—"

"The acting mayor?"

"Those are only a few of the women he dallied with, Taylor. This actual list is longer than the phone book. Well, if we still used phone books. It was okay when he was just a businessman. Except then he was elected mayor, for goodness sake, so you knew it was all going to come out, eventually. Instead of being a dark little secret, our infidelity was going to blow up, as the kids say. It was going to be a public embarrassment. That's when Mark made his deal with the sand company, so it would be easier for me to leave Todd when it hit the fan. I just wish he would've talked to me first, because I would have lived with him in a tar shack. You're probably wondering why I'm telling you all this."

"A little bit."

"After Todd was shot, do you know who the sheriff questioned first? It was me. He said Todd's cheating and my relationship with his brother gave me plenty of motive. He asked if I had an alibi. I told him that I was sleeping with Mark at the time. He didn't think that was very helpful. Oh, well. I expect that most people in town think I did it. Or Mark did it. Or, more likely, that we killed Todd together. Fortunately, there's a whole universe of other people to blame, too, which is why Mark and I weren't arrested. Don't you think?"

"Probably."

"I didn't do it, though. Neither did Mark. I just wanted to tell you that. I don't care if you believe me or not. Some do. Some don't. That's all right by me. It's kind of liberating, having some people think you're a murderer. I no longer have to worry about appearances. When I was married to Todd, I worried about it all the time."

"Who do you think killed your husband?"

"The sand miners."

"Why?"

"At the end of the day, they're businessmen. They don't want problems, they don't want headaches, they don't want controversy, and I think working with Todd, that's all he gave them. They didn't need the city to condemn any property. There are plenty of people around here who'd be happy to sell them the land they need. A year ago, there were seven mines in the county. Now there are eighteen. I think they found out what Todd was doing and decided to cut their losses. If the *Record* hadn't printed the story, no one would have even known what he was up to."

"Speaking of the *Record*—"

"You're wondering how Skip got the story? Probably from Sheila. I'm only guessing, though. Sheila. I was sorry to hear about her and my husband. I liked her."

"How did he manage it, so many women?"

"Todd found out what they wanted and he gave it to them. That was his way. Mousy Maureen wanted to be chief of police. The little Tibbits girl, she wanted to have an important job. The reporter's wife wanted to escape her dull country life."

"What did Dawn Gischler want?"

"Porn sex."

"Excuse me?"

"There are three kinds of sex, Taylor. Romantic sex, quickie sex, and porn sex. Dawn wanted to be tied to the bedposts, and Todd was happy to oblige."

"You're kidding?"

"I'm sixty—"

"You don't look it."

"Aren't you sweet? I'm sixty, but Dawn is much older. You'd think she'd be a little more . . . conservative."

"How do you know all this?"

"Todd. He kept very few secrets from me. It gave him a sense of power, and pride, I think, to brag about his conquests. I, of course, never told him a damn thing, especially about Mark and me. It wasn't just women, though. Take the city attorney. He did what he did, which, if it wasn't illegal was certainly unethical, because he wanted to keep his job. Todd had managed to get rid of Chief Philipps, and he told the attorney he could get rid of him, too. Probably he told Bob Barcott the same thing."

"Blackmail?"

"Are you asking me if Todd was above blackmail? Of course he wasn't. Except, if he did anything besides threatening to have someone fired, or whatever, those are the secrets that he *did* keep from me."

"Did you tell all this to the sheriff?"

"Not at first. I didn't want him to suspect that I had a hand in killing my husband. He figured most of it out on his own, though, and I ended up giving him the rest. Him and the chief. Maureen. She's over forty. You'd think she'd know better, too."

"What about Eleanor Barrington?" I said.

"What about her?"

"Did she and your husband ever cross paths?"

"Oh, I don't think so. Not in the way that you mean. That's the kind of thing Todd would have bragged about, bedding Mrs. Barrington. I met her a few times. A lot of people don't care for her. I like her, though. I like her kids, too. Maybe if Todd and I had children we wouldn't have turned out the way we did. Why? Do you think Mrs. Barrington is involved in this?"

"I have no idea."

"If there's anything more I can do to help . . ."

"You've been surprisingly forthcoming, as it is."

"That's because I no longer have anything to hide. All my secrets are public record."

I used the app on my smartphone again, this time to get directions to the Barrington estate. It was tucked along the Trempealeau River just northwest of Arona, as advertised. Only when I turned off the county blacktop onto the dirt road, an iron driveway gate stopped me. A sign read: MERESHACK. NO TRESPASSING. The trees on each side of the gate made it impossible to drive around, so I parked my Camry, circled the gate on foot, and continued down the road.

Poplar, birch, oak, maple, and fir trees formed a border on both sides, making the road feel more like a trench. A few of them had NO HUNTING and NO TRESPASSING signs attached. There was plenty of tall grass and shrubs, too. The vegetation gave off a kind of peaceful scent as though nothing bad could ever happen again in the world. The sun was on its downward arch, and shadows dappled the forest floor. The only noise came from light wind rustling leaves and the call of birds.

I followed the road for what seemed like a mile until I came to a clearing at the top of a hill. The Barrington estate lay below the hill between the river and me.

"This is what they call a shack?" I said aloud.

There was a barn that looked as if it had built by Amish carpenters two hundred years ago and a couple of small cottages that might have been used in one of those life-is-so-whimsical-in-the-English-countryside movies that you occasionally find on the Independent Film Channel. The main house had two floors and a lot of odd angles. Apparently it had indeed started as a shack and had been expanded a little at a time over the decades until it had an eccentric appearance. The house was surrounded on all sides by a wooden deck. Most of the furniture on the deck was located in the front, facing the river. The deck facing the forest had only a few tables and chairs, yet it also had a covered hot tub.

I followed the road down the hill. The grounds were well kept, and since the Barringtons hadn't been there for over a year, I assumed they had help taking care of it. I passed the barn, which I figured must also serve as a garage, passed one of the cottages, and stopped at the main house. I knocked on the door; no one answered. I tried the knob. The door was locked. I peered through windows. There was a living room, dining room, and massive kitchen on the main floor. I followed the deck. A sliding glass door led from the house to the area where the hot tub was located. When I put my face up against it, I could see a large bedroom. The furniture inside seemed elegant and without dust, and I had a thought—were there Merry Maids in Arona?

I left the house and made my way to the Trempealeau. A dock built with treated lumber ran about thirty feet along the river's edge. There was plenty of galvanized hardware where you could tie up to the dock, yet no boats that I could see and no boathouse to store them in, which made me go "Hmmm" the way Freddie does. Maybe the Barringtons didn't navigate the river. Maybe they just sat on their dock and watched it flow past.

I sat on a narrow bench made from the same wood as the dock. Along with the wind-swept trees and birds, I was now serenaded by the murmur of gently flowing water. It made me sigh with contentment. I found myself asking how anyone could turn this into a silica sand mine, permanently destroying the beauty of it all for the temporary comfort of money.

Ahh, money. That's the thing, isn't it? It is astonishing what people will do for money.

The ringing of my smartphone startled me. I was tempted to ignore it; the caller ID told me I probably shouldn't.

"Hey," I said.

"How you doin'?" Freddie asked.

"I didn't get a chance to ask before I left. How's it going with Sackett?"

"Man likes his gin martinis."

"So he does."

"Besides that, I think we're in for a nice payday. The company he wants to buy? Looks like the owners might have been inflatin' its actual value while at the same time siphonin' off its assets."

"Oh yeah?"

"By a lot, too. I want to bring in a forensic accountant, make sure we've got these guys nailed before I take it to the client."

"You have anyone in mind?"

"Steve Vandertop."

"You mean Sara?"

"I mean Steve, dammit. He can be Sara all he wants after hours. I can't believe I hit on that."

"Have you ever told Echo you were involved with a transvestite computer hacker?"

"We weren't involved, and you're not telling 'er, either."

"All right, all right."

"How's your case goin'?"

"Swear to God, Freddie, this town is about as screwed up as it can be. It's like civil war is about to break out. As it is, I've been here less than a day and I can already count at least ten suspects who might have killed this horndog mayor of theirs. Unfortunately, I can connect only one of them to the killing of Emily Denys."

"Mrs. Barrington?"

"I'm afraid so."

"I think we might be riding a losing horse in this one."

"It wouldn't be the first time."

"Yeah, well . . . Listen, I didn't call about any of that."

"Why did you call?"

"Cuz I got a call, we got a call; this woman you gave your card to."

"What woman?"

"Professor Alexandra Campbell. She said to tell you that she was feeling much better, but if you wanted to talk about the shooting yesterday, she'd be happy to listen."

"No kidding?"

"I looked her up. She has a pic on this U of M website for plants. Pretty damn hot for a woman her age."

"You mean a woman our age?"

"What I'm saying. You should, you know, seize the opportunity."

"I'm a little busy right now, Freddie."

"Taylor, give the lady a call."

"Freddie—"

"I'll tell Echo if you don't, and she'll give you hell."

"What's her number?"

I inputted it into my phone as he recited it to me.

"I'll call her later tonight," I said. "If I don't get shot between now and then."

"That's the spirit."

CHAPTER TWENTY-ONE

The lobby, bar, and restaurant seemed pretty congested for five P.M. when I returned to the Everheart Resort, and I asked the young man working the desk about it.

"It's happy hour," he said. "Plus, there's a lot of folks looking for a drink or quick meal before heading off to the big meeting. This is a small town, and there aren't that many places to gather."

"I get it."

"You should see the place on Friday nights before the high school football game, and then after the game, too. We always do good."

"Is Bill Everheart around?"

"I haven't seen him for a while. I can reach him on his cell."

"That's okay. Maybe you can help me?"

"That's what I'm here for."

"Is there a business, a service, in Arona that specializes in cleaning other people's cabins, that takes care of the cabins during the off-season when the owners aren't around?"

"Not really. There are people who do that, especially during the winter. Get paid to keep an eye on a place, plow out the driveways, that sort of thing, but not a business per se."

"What people? Can you give me some names?"

"Do you want to hire someone?"

"I'm trying to find out who takes care of the Barrington place when the family's not in residence."

"You're talking about Cheryl. Cheryl Turk. Yeah. She looks after Mereshack."

"Do you know her?"

"She works here."

"At the resort?"

"She's one of them that takes care of the rooms. She's probably taking care of your room."

"Where can I find her?"

The desk clerk glanced at his watch as if the answer to my question could be found there.

"I don't know for sure," he said. "She's around somewhere. Maybe the laundry."

"Is it possible you can find her for me? If she has time, I'd like to ask her a few questions."

"You're the detective guy, right?"

"Right."

"Where will you be?"

"In the bar."

The desk clerk grinned as if I had lived up to his stereotype—where else would a PI be if not the bar?

"I'm on it," he said.

"Good man."

The late Thanksgiving lunch I ate was still with me, so I passed on the happy hour appetizers and ordered bourbon. The waitress told me that all rail drinks were half price.

"We used to advertise 'em at two-for-one, but the MADD people thought we were promoting excessive drinking, so now it's half price," she told me. "You can still order two, though."

I ordered just the one.

I did a quick survey of the premises while the waitress went to get it. From my table, I was able to observe the bar, the restaurant, and much of the lobby. I was the only one sitting alone. That was okay. I admit I sometimes regretted quitting the cops and the sports teams. I'd chastise myself for neglecting to return the phone calls of my friends and refusing their invitations until they stopped issuing them. I'd regret being alone. Not often, though. For the most part, I liked being alone. I liked relying only on myself. It was so much easier.

The waitress returned with my drink, and I entertained myself with some serious people watching. The patrons seemed to separate into two camps. Those opposed to the sand mines gathered in the restaurant area, while supporters congregated in the bar. I amused myself by guessing who belonged where as the individual customers passed through the entrance. Sometimes it was easy. Many of the environmentalists wore T-shirts with slogans printed on them. On the other hand, I didn't see a single article of clothing that promoted sand mining, although an older, wider woman had the words JOBS JOBS AND MORE JOBS silkscreened onto her sweatshirt. She went with the miners.

Richard Kaufman and Allen Palo belonged with the miners, too, of course, although neither of them seemed to acknowledge their allies. Instead, they seated themselves at a table in the restaurant with a clear view of the front entrance. Palo flagged a waitress while Kaufman buried his head in a menu. I don't know what he ordered, but it seemed to take him a long time to do it.

"Mr. Taylor?"

I turned my attention to a woman who was dressed as if she had just finished cleaning her basement.

"Mr. Taylor? My name is Cheryl Turk. They said you wanted to see me?"

I stood, shook the woman's hand, and offered a chair.

"I hope I'm not taking you away from anything," I said.

"No, no. I was due for a break."

"Is there anything I can get you?"

"No, please. I'm fine. What is it you need?"

"I was told that you look after the Barrington place."

"I wouldn't say look after. It's not like I'm guarding it or anything. I just, you know, dust and vacuum, wash the windows, sweep the deck, make sure the grass gets cut and the snow gets plowed. It's a side job. I do the same for a couple of other places, although mostly in the winter. We get a lot of summer people—that's what we call 'em. They got their cabins, their lake homes, and they visit 'em for a couple of weeks or for three-day weekends, the Fourth of July. The rest of the time, they hire me to, you know, keep the place clean, keep the grass from getting out of hand, make sure the driveway is cleared in case there's a fire or something."

"You do this for the Barringtons?"

"Uh-huh, like I said, although they're year-round. They come down all the time. At least they used to."

"I was out there earlier this afternoon. You do a very nice job."

"Thank you, but—no one's supposed to be out there. Mrs. Barrington doesn't even want me to bring someone along when I clean the place."

"She wants to keep it all private."

"I don't blame her for that. Do you want people hanging around your place uninvited?"

Good point, I decided.

"Besides, they found some beer cans in the woods this one time above the hot tub. Do you know where the hot tub is?" Cheryl said. "On the back deck?"

"Yes."

"They found some beer cans, and the family, Mrs. Barrington, they've been worried about intruders ever since."

"When was this?"

"I don't know. A year ago. Longer."

"How long have you been working for the Barringtons?" I asked.

"Five years? Six? Even when she was here every other week, Mrs. B would have me come in to keep the place nice. She's not the kind to do much dusting herself, you know. What is it you want me to tell you, anyway?"

I retrieved my trusty smartphone, pulled up Emily's pic, and asked the same question I had asked everyone else.

"Nope," Cheryl said. "I've never seen her before."

"Are you sure?"

"Pretty sure."

"Never saw her at the Barrington place?"

"No. Why would I?"

"She used to date Joel Barrington."

"I don't know anything about that. I haven't seen her. I haven't seen Joel, either, for that matter. Not for a year or more. Not since they, the Barringtons, stopped coming down like they used to."

"When was that?"

"Like I said. A year or so."

"I meant specifically."

"You mean the actual day? How should I know?"

"Was it after Mayor Franson was killed?"

"It had to be after. At least, well, wait. I know they were here for the funeral. Everyone was at the funeral. It was kind of comical. Not him getting killed, what I mean . . . Everyone was trying to guess who did it, you know? My money was on the wife. Still is. Sleeping with the brother-in-law . . ." Cheryl shivered as if she found the idea frightening. Yet the word she used was "juicy."

"The Barringtons went to the funeral?" I asked.

"They wanted to pay their respects, I guess. I know they knew the mayor, can't say if they were friends or not. Devon, the girl, was there, and so was Joel. I don't remember Mrs. Barrington, though. I don't remember seeing her there."

"You say they knew Mayor Franson?"

"I guess. I'd seen 'em chatting, him and the Barringtons, once in a while."

"Where?"

"Here. Everybody comes here. It's the only really good place in town. The mayor, he was always cruisin' the place."

"Did he ever hit on you?"

"Sure. Everybody got a turn sooner or later. Wait. I did see him out at their place once."

"When?"

"I don't know. Before he was killed. What does it matter?"

"I'm trying to figure out some things."

"I don't know what I can tell you. I mean, I don't live there, at Mere-shack. I just clean the place once a week. Although . . ."

"What?"

"I keep a ledger. Mrs. Barrington is real particular. She doesn't worry about money so much, she just wants to know what I do and when I do it and how many hours it takes. Sometimes, she'll tell me to do something or not do something, and then she'll forget she told me because it'll be like a month or more without us talking, well, a year now, so I keep track of what she says and the date she says it in my ledger, and when I send her an invoice, I include all that. I could look. I don't know if it'll help, though."

"I'd appreciate it very much."

"You going to be around tomorrow?"

"In the morning, at least."

"I'll go look tonight, then."

"Thank you."

Cheryl rose from her chair.

"You really are a detective, aren't you?" she said.

"I really am."

"Cool."

"Sometimes it is."

Cheryl gave me a little wave and drifted out of the room. I turned my attention back to Kaufman and Palo. Palo was eating what looked like a Caesar salad from where I sat. Kaufman was attacking the first of two cheeseburgers and a plate of fries. They took turns glancing at their watches and watching the door as if they were expecting someone.

I studied my own watch for a moment. It was after normal business hours, yet I took a chance and made a call. I was relieved when the receptionist at Mrs. Barrington's office answered.

"This is Holland Taylor," I told her.

"The private investigator?"

"Yes."

"No one's here. I was just about to leave myself."

"I'm sorry I'm calling so late. I should have called earlier, but I didn't think of it until now."

"Think of what?"

"Could you do me one quick favor before you leave?"

She didn't answer.

"Please," I said.

"What?"

"You keep Mrs. Barrington's calendar."

"Her business calendar. I have no idea what the woman does on her own time."

"Can you check to see where she was about a year ago?"

"Yeah, I guess."

I gave her the exact date Mayor Franson was killed.

"I'm going to put you on hold. Just a sec."

My ear was immediately filled with the sound of Beethoven's "Ode to Joy." I watched Kaufman and Palo while I listened. Why they didn't see me seeing them I couldn't say. Palo must have seen something he did like, though. He stood abruptly and smiled. Kaufman turned in his chair and saw the same sight as his partner. He stood, too, clutching his napkin to his chest.

And Cynthia Grey walked into the restaurant.

"What the hell?" I said aloud.

The "Ode to Joy" was replaced by the receptionist's voice.

"Taylor," she said.

I didn't answer.

"Mr. Taylor, are you still there?"

I averted my eyes.

"Yes, yes, I'm here," I said. "Sorry."

"The date you gave me, Mrs. Barrington wasn't in the office the entire week, including that day."

"Where was she?"

"New York. She flew out early Monday morning and didn't return until Thursday night."

Mayor Franson was shot late Tuesday evening, I reminded myself.

"Are you sure?" I asked.

"As sure as I can be. It's not like she took me with her."

"Thank you. I appreciate it."

I ended the conversation and looked up. Cynthia Grey was sitting now at the table with the two lobbyists. She was smiling. They were grimacing as they spoke earnestly to her, as if they were describing a problem that they expected her to solve. I had the distinct impression the problem was me.

I made another call. This time Freddie answered.

"Have you called the professor yet?" he asked.

"No."

"What's keeping you?"

"Dammit, Freddie. Business first."

"What business?"

I told him that the receptionist in her office building said Mrs. Barrington was in New York when the mayor of Arona, Wisconsin, was shot and killed outside his house.

"What do you want me to do about it?" Freddie asked.

"Prove it."

"Do you want me to contact David Helin?"

"I don't give a damn who you call."

"What's with you all of a sudden?"

Apparently the boys knew I had been watching them after all, because they directed Cynthia's attention to my table. She looked me directly in the eye from across the room. And winked.

"You should have my problems, Freddie," I said. "You really should."

CHAPTER TWENTY-TWO

She was dressed in black with just a hint of white showing at her collar and sleeves. That was her uniform, what she always wore in the office or to court; it was what she was wearing when *Mpls St Paul Magazine* took her photograph outside the Federal Court Building for an article entitled "The Black and White World of Cynthia Grey."

She crossed the room, moving around and past the other tables with the self-assurance that money and limited celebrity can bring until she reached mine. She smiled—a perfect smile in a perfect face surrounded by perfect brown hair. Her perfect brown eyes glistened. She said, "Hi."

"Hi," I said.

"Fancy meeting you here."

"You're a long way from home yourself."

"You've frightened my clients."

"Your clients? I remember when you only represented underdogs. DWIs that you thought needed counseling instead of jail time, sexual harassment victims, employees fired because of age discrimination. Now you're working for the Man? You disappoint me."

"What? Again?"

I took a sip of my bourbon, wishing I had ordered two.

"Are you going to offer me a chair?" Cynthia asked.

I gestured at the one across from me, and she sat.

"You didn't really accuse my clients of murder, did you?" Cynthia asked.

"No, I didn't. In fact, I actually defended them when someone else accused them of murder. Imagine that."

"They seem to think otherwise. They seem to think you're here to defame them at the town hall meeting this evening."

"I can't imagine why."

"The fact that you assaulted Richard Kaufman in full view of a couple dozen witnesses during lunch—"

"Talk about your unsubstantiated allegations. Anyway, why do you care?"

"They have my law firm on retainer."

"No, I mean why you personally? Do these guys have enough juice that they can pick up a phone and have a senior partner come riding to the rescue?"

"The first call was to an associate. It got kicked up to a junior partner, who announced that we needed a presence in Arona to help U.S. Sand deal with a troublemaking private eye named Holland Taylor. I couldn't resist taking a look for myself. Actually, it worked out nicely. Kaufman and Palo are very impressed that the firm thought enough of them to send a partner; no doubt word will get back to the home office in Chicago. Besides, I get to see you again."

Just then my young waitress reappeared to take Cynthia's order.

"The lady will have an iced tea, unsweetened, with a wedge of lemon," I said. I pointed at my bourbon. "I'll have another one of these."

The waitress left.

"How are you, Holland?" Cynthia asked.

"Well. I'm quite well."

"I've seen you jogging past my house from time to time."

"I run several different routes. You're on my three-and-a-half-mile track."

"I've been tempted to meet you on the sidewalk with a towel and a bottle of water like they do in the marathons."

"You should."

The waitress returned with our drinks. Cynthia offered to pay—she was on an expense account. I said I'd pay, I had one, too. Yes, she said, but hers was going to be picked up by U.S. Sand. I let her get the check.

"How's Annie these days?" Cynthia asked. "Assistant Chief Anne Scalasi, I should say."

"Okay, I guess. Between the job and her new marriage, I don't see much of her anymore."

Cynthia nodded her head as if she believed me.

"How about you?" she asked. "Have you been seeing anyone?"

"No one seriously. A woman named Claire who lives in my building; a professor at the U named Alex Campbell. You?"

"Nobody."

"Hard to believe. You're such a beautiful woman."

"You've always been so kind. No. I don't have much time for a social life these days."

"What I said before, I was joking. I was very pleased when I read that you merged your law practice with the current outfit. Very proud. You've finally made it to the big time, just like you've always wanted, although"—I threw a thumb at Kaufman and Palo—"the riffraff you hang out with these days . . . I think I liked it better when you were defending addicts from draconian drug laws."

"It's not as different as you might think."

"That's telling."

"Who are you working for?"

"Didn't the riffraff tell you?"

"All they seem to know is that it involves the murder of Emily Denys—and maybe Eleanor Barrington."

"Ahh."

"You're not going to tell me, are you?"

"No, I don't think so."

"You seem to be in a mood."

"Yes, I have been for quite a while now."

"With the world in general or just me?"

I shrugged in reply.

"I want you to stay away from my clients," Cynthia said.

"I know."

"That's not an answer."

"You didn't ask a question."

"Taylor."

"Grey."

"I know all of your secrets, Holland."

"I know all of yours." I nearly added, "That's why we broke up," but let it pass.

Cynthia stared at me for a few beats while she slowly stirred her iced tea with a fingernail. She smiled and sucked the tea off her finger.

"I swear, you're enough to make a girl jump off the wagon," she said.

"Can't be as bad as all that."

Cynthia stood.

"Are you going to the town hall meeting?" she asked.

"I wasn't, but yeah, I wouldn't miss it now."

She glanced over her shoulder at Kaufman and Palo.

"Can I ask you for a favor?" she said.

"I'm not going to call 'em out, if that's what you want to know."

"Well, then I can safely tell them that I put the fear of God into you and you won't be a problem anymore."

"At least not until I've gathered more evidence."

"Can I see you afterward?"

"Afterward?"

"After the town hall."

"Sure."

"Where?"

I came *this*close to giving her my room number. Instead, I tapped the tabletop.

"Right here," I said.

CHAPTER TWENTY-THREE

Apparently they built Arona Area High School on the flattest piece of ground in the least picturesque part of town that they could find. It was a comparatively new building—the date 1992 was carved into a cornerstone—with a football field, baseball diamond, tennis court, and an asphalt parking lot big enough to accommodate the Mall of America. Beyond that, there were only empty fields and darkening blue sky.

I parked the Camry in the first empty slot I could find and followed the crowd to the school entrance. It was slow moving, and I couldn't figure out why until I saw Chief McMahan and her officers running handheld metal detectors over each visitor and inspecting the contents of every bag. A man about ten years older than me objected to the search. He was dressed in a camouflage outfit identical to the ones worn by the only other Red Stone Patriots I'd ever seen.

"I have a legal right to carry a concealed weapon anywhere I choose," he said.

"Not into a school," the chief told him.

"So you're saying no self-defense is permitted beyond this point. You're saying, 'I don't care if you or your family is in danger, I will not allow you to defend yourself.'"

The man was speaking loudly, and some of the visitors stopped to listen.

"The beauty of the concealed carry law, Chief of Police Maureen McMahan, is that only a handful of citizens need to be armed in order to protect the greater part of society from harm. That's because criminals are never really sure which of the law-abiding citizens around them may be carrying a weapon, and that deters their criminal activities. By insisting that no guns are allowed, you're inviting criminals to come into this very school and commit whatever mayhem they desire without fear of facing an armed citizen."

The chief stared at him for a long moment, and I was wondering if she was considering his argument. Finally she said, "Are you done, Curtis? Because you're holding up traffic."

Curtis stepped aside. Apparently he was unarmed. Yet he wasn't done. While the chief and her officers continued to search the other visitors, Curtis spoke to those whose attention he had attracted earlier.

"The most dangerous place in town right now is the parking lot of this school," he said. "Criminals know that every one of us leaving this place will be unarmed. We'll be easy pickings for robbers and rapists. I wonder how many criminals might be out there right now, burglarizing cars to harvest the guns that permit holders like me were forced to leave behind because Chief of Police Maureen McMahan wouldn't allow us to take them inside. Who's going to protect us from them?"

"Who's going to protect us from you?" one of the listeners asked.

"I'm not a criminal."

"We should take your word for it because you wear camouflage everywhere and carry concealed weapons?"

"I live here."

"You moved in thirteen months ago. That doesn't mean you live here."

Curtis stepped toward the listener; the listener stepped toward him. They stared menacingly at each other, like two boxers trying to hype a pay-per-view bout. If it were a playground, I'd expect someone to start chanting "Fight, fight, fight." Instead, Chief McMahan stepped between them.

"The meeting is going to start in a few minutes," she said. "If you want a seat up front . . ."

The two men separated slowly even as they sneered at each other, then went off in opposite directions. The chief moved back to the school entrance. I caught her eye as she did.

"Taylor," she said. "I want to talk to you later."

I nodded at her.

The floor of the high school auditorium had room for about two hundred people, and most of the seats were taken. I was up in the balcony, where there was space for one hundred more; most of the seats were empty. There were chairs arranged behind tables on the stage that were occupied by the acting mayor and other representatives of the city government, as well as Kaufman and Palo. Each of them had their own microphone. Probably they didn't need them. The auditorium had surprisingly good acoustics, and I could actually hear them speaking quietly to each other. Another mic was set on a stand in the center aisle a few rows back from the stage. A line had already formed behind it that included Curtis.

Skip Zetzman was seated near the mic. I didn't see a notebook, although he did have a digital camera and a leather bag filled with several different-sized lenses. There were also four video cameras scattered throughout the auditorium. They were manned by an older gentleman, an older woman, a young man, and a young woman. They could have been members of the same family by the way they looked and dressed. None of the cameras carried the logo of a local TV station. I guessed they were part of a public access operation, the Arona version of C-SPAN.

Esther Tibbits gave a bottle of designer water to both Kaufman and Palo. They thanked her before waving her away. She took a seat in the front row. Her dark blue skirt hiked up to there, yet she did nothing about it. By contrast, Cynthia Grey was next to her, a portrait of a lady sitting. She occupied only half of her seat, her legs crossed at the knee, her thighs touching, the hem of her black skirt pulled down, toes pointed toward the floor, her back straight, a notebook in her lap, and her hands folded over the notebook just as the etiquette instructor had taught her. I tried not to stare. It wasn't easy, and not only because she was so damn pretty. She had been one of the few women who had been able to help me chase away the alone feeling after Laura and Jenny were killed.

Finally Dawn Gischler opened the proceedings with a brief speech about decorum and common courtesy. I was surprised to see that she had exchanged her peasant shirt, jeans, and sandals for a pink business suit. She said she knew that many people in the auditorium wanted to be heard, and she hoped that the audience would be respectful of differing views. She also asked that they limit their remarks to three minutes or less so that everyone would have a chance to speak.

"We're on cable TV, so please watch your language," Gischler added.

While listening to her, I was reminded of what Bridgette Franson had said about the acting mayor and her lust for porn sex. I slapped my face twice to dislodge the image that formed in my head.

Doug Pinter was the first to address the audience and, as I expected, went well over the three-minute limit. He spoke about the environmental terrorism perpetrated by the hydraulic fracturing industry, the poisoning of water and land. "Fracking," he said, "poses an unacceptable risk to our drinking water, to our health, and to the future of our communities." He was quite eloquent and received a nice ovation when he finished.

What I didn't expect was Allen Palo's rebuttal.

"I agree with everything you said," he announced. "Americans shouldn't have to accept unsafe drinking water just because natural gas burns more cleanly than coal. I read that scientists at Stanford University have proven that some companies are fracking for oil and gas at far shallower depths than they're supposed to, sometimes through underground sources of drinking water. They get away with it because of weak safeguards and inadequate oversight. This is unacceptable. U.S. Sand is for anything that'll force these delinquent companies to play by the rules. It's important that you understand, though, that we are not involved in the hydraulic fracturing business. We sell sand. We hope our customers behave responsibly. But if they don't, there's not a lot we can do about it."

So it went. For every problem there was a solution; for every accusation, a counterargument. It was as if Kaufman and Palo knew every question before it was asked. I suppose they had been through enough of this kind of meeting that they did know. I had to give them props—they were very good at their jobs.

"According to the Occupational Safety and Health Administration, exposure to silica sand particles can cause lung cancer."

"If you follow the regulations, there is no threat to the environment, there is no threat to public health, and we follow the regulations. Our operations are well within EPA standards."

"I'm concerned that no one is monitoring the noise and the water."

"We placed a seismograph at a house where our neighbors complained about blastings. We tested the water at our expense of another neighbor who said that mining had altered his well. We're trying to do what's right out there."

"We're losing farms."

"Sand mining has created thousands of jobs."

"You aren't creating as many jobs as you want us to think. Besides, the benefits of sand mining aren't here in Arona. They flow to the pockets of the company owners who live in beautiful houses on the lake in Chicago, hundreds and hundreds of miles away from the noise and the trucks and the blowing sand."

"When Arona was forced to close its only nursing home, it was U.S. Sand that came to the rescue. We not only made sure that the facility stayed open and protected one hundred and fourteen quality jobs, we have also promised an additional one million dollars a year for other community commitments."

"The head of our zoning department is using his position to retaliate against any and all residents who speak out against the frac-sand mines."

Heads turned to find Bob Barcott, who was sitting in the audience, a notebook on his knee and a pen in his hand.

"I hope that is not true," Kaufman said. "In any case, we do not interfere with local government."

"We chose to live here because of the peace and the solitude, and the mining company has taken all that away."

"If we left town tonight, by tomorrow morning there would be someone to take our place, someone who doesn't share our commitment to the community or the environment. We're ranked number one in the industry. The next company that comes in won't be any higher than second place."

All the while, Curtis edged closer to the microphone, waiting for his turn to speak. Finally it came.

"I'm Curtis Blevins," he said. "You all know me. You know what I stand for. I'm an advocate of people's rights. I personally am opposed to sand mining in Arona. There are more suitable areas where mines and neighbors can better coexist. At the same time, landowners ought to be free to do what they wish with their land without fear of government or big business. I will oppose the annexation of property any way that I can."

He had more to say, except I didn't hear him. I was distracted by the muzzle of a handgun pressed against the back of my neck.

"Don't say a word," a voice said.

I didn't.

Nothing happened.

I guess he expected me to put up an argument.

I turned my head slightly. My peripheral vision caught the sight of a young man with blond hair dressed in camo.

"Good evening, Eric," I said. "Long time no see."

"You're coming with us."

"Okay."

"Get up. Slowly."

I did.

"We want to see your hands."

I held them away from my body.

"This way."

I let Eric lead me up the stairs to a door at the back of the balcony. Along the way, I recognized his companion, the one with short brown hair who had helped Eric attack me at Emily's duplex.

We reached the door, and Eric pushed me through it.

The corridor was brightly lit and empty. Metal lockers lined the walls on each side. The classroom doors were all closed. It made me wonder—where do the teachers in small-town schools go during the summer? What do they do? Probably it was an odd thought to have given the circumstances; still . . .

Eric stood in front of me. His companion remained behind. The companion moved quickly, clapping me into a full nelson. I didn't resist.

Eric chuckled, actually chuckled like a villain in a straight-to-video thriller. He held open his hand. There was a shotgun shell in his palm, what he had pressed against my neck.

"Sucker," he said.

"Imagine my embarrassment. Did your sister send you?"

"Leave Esther out of this."

"Out of what, Eric? What do you nitwits want?"

"You don't fucking call us names."

"I apologize. What can I do for you upstanding young men of the Red Stone Patriots?"

"You can stay out of our business."

"What business?"

"Fuck you."

He moved toward me and cocked his hand as if he wanted to punch my face.

I brought my hands up and pressed them against my forehead so the kid holding me in the full nelson couldn't bend my head forward.

As soon as Eric was in range, I jumped up and kicked him in the face. I was actually aiming for his jaw, only I missed. Eric fell back just the same.

I came back down. My attacker moved his legs apart while he struggled to hold me. I brought my own leg straight back and kicked him in the groin with my heel. He let go.

I bent forward, reached between my own legs, grabbed his ankle, and pulled upward. He fell backward onto the floor. I was still holding his leg. I pulled it up high, exposing his groin. I kicked him again.

He rolled on his side and cupped himself.

Eric had managed to get to his knees. He was holding his face with both hands. I managed to get a grip on his short hair. He brought his hands down and looked up at me.

"What?" he said.

I rammed his face into a locker door. My hand slipped off his scalp and hit the locker, too. I think I hurt myself more than I hurt him.

While we were both dealing with our injuries, I reached into my pocket, produced my smartphone, and pulled up Emily's pic. I took a better grip of Eric's hair and turned his face so he could get a good look at the screen.

"Who is this girl?" I asked.

"I don't know."

I shoved Eric's face into the locker again.

"What's her name?"

"I don't know."

I hit him again.

"What is her name?"

"I don't know."

I hit him a third time.

"He said he doesn't know."

I turned my head. Chief McMahan was standing in the corridor, her hand resting on the butt of her holstered nine-millimeter Glock, a gunfighter ready to throw down.

"Of course he knows," I said. "Why else would he and his friend attack me outside her duplex in St. Paul? Why else would they attack me again in the corridor?"

"Let him go. I mean it."

I released my grip on Eric's hair, and he slumped to the floor.

"Move away," the chief said.

I did.

"You don't get to hit him again. Or anyone else for that matter."

"Am I under arrest?"

The question seemed to slow her down.

"No, of course not. I saw what happened. They attacked you."

"You saw them?"

"It's a high school. There are cameras everywhere. I'm going to arrest them both and take them to our lockup. I won't have you taking the law into your own hands."

I looked down at my hand; my knuckles were scuffed and swollen. I flexed my fingers.

"Is that what I was doing?" I said.

"Are you all right?"

"You're asking me?" I looked down at Eric; his face was red and puffy. There were only a few small cuts, yet they were bleeding profusely. I glanced at his friend; he was still holding himself and moaning loudly. "Yeah, I'm fine."

"I'm going to take them both to the station. I need you to come down and make a statement."

"No, no, no, don't do that."

"Don't do what?"

"Arrest them. Let them go."

"What? Why?"

"Honestly? I might want to talk to them again later when you're not looking."

"This isn't funny."

"Not to them, anyway."

"Taylor, I don't think I like you."

"That's too bad, Chief, because I'm starting to like you more and more. By the way, what was it you wanted to talk to me about?"

"I wanted to warn you that Eric Tibbits and his friend were in the school."

CHAPTER TWENTY-FOUR

The line behind the microphone had grown considerably shorter by the time I returned to my seat. I searched for Curtis Blevins in the audience, and couldn't find him.

A woman stepped up to the mic. She was carrying what looked like a folded blanket. I didn't recognize her from where I sat until she stated her name.

"I'm Bridgette Franson."

That caused a stir in the audience and a few ohhs and ahhs, yet she didn't acknowledge it.

"I live near a sand mine. There's a layer of sand on my car every single day. I brush it off and the next day I come back and there's another layer, and I park in a garage. The same with my porch and sidewalk. The same with my windows and roof. I never open my windows anymore no matter how hot it is. The sand gets inside anyway. It covers my dishes in the cabinet; I have to wash them before I set the table. My clothes are full of it. So is my hair. I can feel it in my throat, in my nose. I'm not asking anyone to feel sorry for me. I'm asking you not to make the same mistake that we made by selling our property to these people.

"I've heard a lot of talk tonight about how prolonged exposure to airborne crystalline silica can cause cardiovascular disease and increase the risk of lung cancer. I compare it to secondhand smoke. These two will tell you that the problem doesn't exist, just like the tobacco companies claimed for how many years that cigarettes weren't addictive and that they didn't cause cancer. Believe me when I tell you that I have been around a great many liars in my time . . ."

I heard a hoot and a smattering of applause.

"These two are as accomplished in the art as anyone I've ever seen. This quilt was hanging on my line for only a couple of hours this afternoon."

Bridgette unrolled the quilt she was carrying and gripped one end with both hands. She waved it up and down frantically. A cloud of yellow dust formed and spread across the auditorium.

"My advice?" she said. "Don't believe a word these people say."

Bridgette turned and walked back up the aisle, trailing the quilt behind. Applause followed her; some people cheered. One of them was a woman dressed in jeans, a white dress shirt, and a blue sports jacket not unlike the one I wore. She sat down next to me.

"You go, girl," she shouted. I watched her as she applauded. In a softer voice she asked, "Are you having fun yet, Mr. Taylor?"

"Have we met?"

She reached into her pocket, withdrew a thin wallet, and handed it to me. I opened it slowly, as if it were a bomb. Instead, it was the lady's credentials. I read it aloud.

"Special Agent Rachel Colgin, Bureau of Alcohol, Tobacco, Firearms, and Explosives."

"Don't you just love the way that rolls off the tongue?" she said.

I handed the wallet back.

"You're a little young to be working for the Department of Justice, aren't you?" I said.

"Says the old man of forty-three."

"Forty-two. My birthday isn't until the end of the month."

"Happy birthday."

"Whenever I meet someone from the Justice Department I always ask the same question—what did I do?"

"It's not what you did. It's what you're going to do."

"What am I going to do?"

"Good, Taylor. You're going to do good."

"I already don't like the sound of this."

Colgin patted my knee the same way my father did just before telling me how much fun we were going to have putting new shingles on the house.

"Let me tell you a story," she said. "Once upon a time, there was a magical people called Yuppers that lived in a land called the Upper Peninsula in the kingdom of Michigan. Some of these Yuppers, about eighty-five hundred, resided in a city called Menominee. Menominee, Michigan, not to be confused with Menominee, Wisconsin. It's very pretty. You'd like it there.

"Now, Menominee, Michigan, is located across the Menominee River from its evil rival Marinette, Wisconsin. The river marks where the Upper Penninsula begins and Wisconsin ends. Both towns are also on the western shore of Lake Michigan. They like to call themselves inland seaports. Only Marinette has the edge in that regard. To keep up, Menominee decided to expand its harbor facilities. To do this, it needed to acquire the land immediately adjacent to the existing harbor. The city made what it considered a fair market offer. Except the owner of the property was a feisty anti-government sort named Curtis Blevins, and he refused to sell. The city instituted a complete taking of the land."

"Condemnation via eminent domain," I said.

"Look at you knowing how the government works. I bet you got nothing but A's in high school civics."

"The city took Blevins's property."

"Yes, it did. It paid him less than he would have received if he had accepted the original offer, too. Blevins was upset, to say the least, and who can blame him? He decided to depart the city by the inland sea and never return. Unfortunately, the night before he left, he indulged himself with a little domestic terrorism."

"What did he do?"

"He blew up Menominee's Welcome Center, the building the city used to greet visitors and promote commerce. Classic IED. Anhydrous hydrazine. Ammonium nitrate. Aluminum powder. Glass canning jar. Cell phone detonator. Ka-boom. You know what the ATF thinks of bombs."

"You don't like them."

"We don't like them."

"How do you know he did it?"

"I know."

"Why isn't he in custody?"

"There's knowing it and there's proving it. Seems the court demands evidence before locking up an American citizen and throwing away the key."

"How inconvenient."

"Too bad he's not a foreign national. Oh well. If wishes were horses, beggars would ride."

"What does this have to do with me?"

"He has refused on several occasions to converse with Special Agent Rachel Colgin of the Bureau of Alcohol, Tobacco, Firearms, and Explosives. Yet he might speak to you."

"Why would he do that?"

"Because you just beat up his nephew. I saw the fight, by the way. I was rooting for you."

"Blevins and Eric Tibbits are related?"

"Yeppers."

"That makes Esther Tibbits his niece."

"Raises a few questions, doesn't it?"

"Yes, it does."

"Is the apparent bombing by Curtis Blevins of a public building in Menominee, Michigan, over a dispute involving eminent domain related to the murder of Mayor Todd Franson, who was attempting to abuse the same power in Arona, Wisconsin, and is that somehow related to the murder of Emily Denys in St. Paul, Minnesota?"

"Do you always speak like this?"

"Whatever do you mean?"

"How do you know who I am and why I'm here?"

Colgin tapped her chest.

"Bureau of Alcohol, Tobacco, Firearms, and Explosives," she said. "Aren't you paying attention?"

Actually I wasn't, because at that moment I heard a voice that forced me to gaze back down at the auditorium floor. A woman with strawberry hair was now standing at the microphone.

"I'm Devon Barrington," she said. "First, I must apologize. My mother had hoped to be here tonight. Unfortunately, she was unable to attend."

"Not without violating the conditions of her bail agreement," Colgin said.

"Shhhh," I told her.

"Nor could my older brother be here," Devon said.

"I wonder what that's about," said Colgin.

"Would you please?" I said.

"So it falls to me to publicly address the representatives of the U.S. Sand Company, Acting Mayor Gischler, members of the Arona City Council, and the citizens of this fine community which my family has loved and supported for nearly a century. My statement is simple—our property is not for sale at any price."

I was surprised by the high volume of applause Devon received. She waited patiently until it receded.

"We are aware, of course, that steps have been taken in the past to acquire our property by hook or by crook, as my mother put it," she said. "Please, don't do that. If you persist . . . My mother gave me a note to read."

Devon pulled it from her pocket and carefully unfolded it.

"You'll have to excuse me," she said. "Those of you who have met my mom know that her language can sometimes be . . . salty." She took a deep breath and read the note with her exhale. "Don't mess with us you sonsuvbitches. I will fuck you up and I won't care how much it costs, how long it takes, or how many lawyers I need to hire."

Devon refolded the note, returned it to her pocket, and smiled.

"Thank you for your time," she said.

Devon returned to her seat amid the loudest cheers of the evening.

"I like her," Special Agent Colgin said.

"So do I."

"Her brother was dating Emily Denys, wasn't he?"

"So I have been led to believe."

"Her mother, Eleanor Barrington, stands accused of Emily's murder. Must be hard on her. Devon, I mean."

"What's your point, Rachel?"

"You used my given name. I'm going to use yours, too, because we're friends now."

"What do you want me to do, Rachel?"

"I want you to do your job, Holland. I'm going to help."

"Help me what?"

"Find someone else to blame for killing Emily Denys."

"Anyone I know?"

She patted my knee some more.

CHAPTER TWENTY-FIVE

The Everheart Resort, Restaurant, and Bar was as busy after the town hall meeting as it had been before. If there was a difference it was the mood. It was celebratory, almost euphoric, as if the kids *had* won the Friday night football game. Although nothing had been resolved at the meeting, everyone getting a chance to have their say had apparently expelled much of the tension that I had felt in the town since I arrived. At least for now. The cliques had temporarily dissolved. Now sand supporters were bellying up to the bar with the enviros as if they had been pals all along. Personal insults became jokes instead of additional volleys in never-ending political conflicts.

I was able to secure the same chair at the same table where I had sat before the meeting and observed it all over a double bourbon on the rocks. The place became increasingly crowded and noisy. They had cranked up the karaoke machine, and patrons with iffy voices were singing songs that only vaguely sounded like something I'd heard before. Most of the other customers ignored them. I thought about going to my room for a bit of peace and quiet. Lord knows it had been a long day. Except I didn't want to miss Cynthia.

I watched the door. It opened and Esther Tibbits entered, a not entirely unwelcome sight in her blue-on-blue ensemble. She had arrived sans Kaufman and Palo, and for the first time I saw her smile. Friends young and old, male and female shook her hand and hugged her shoulders as if they hadn't seen her for a while and had missed her. She proved to be more popular than I would have guessed, seeing how many townspeople probably thought she had gone over to the dark side.

She swiveled her head as if she were looking for someone and paused when she saw me. She spent the next ten minutes glancing my way while pretending not to. After a while, she separated herself from the group and started to maneuver around the tables to where I sat. She halted when someone beat her to me.

"Taylor, what are you doing here?" Devon Barrington said.

She and Ophira had somehow managed to enter the place without my noticing.

"I came to hear you speak to the crowd," I said.

I stood, and Devon gave me a hug. I didn't expect it and did a poor job of hugging back. The expression on Ophira's face suggested that she was alarmed by the public display, and I quickly unhanded the girl. I offered them both a seat.

"Did you see me?" Devon asked.

"I was up in the balcony. You were great."

"Omigod, I was so scared."

"You didn't look it."

"I was shaking like a leaf. I could barely unfold my mother's note. Can you believe what she made me read? Omigod."

A waitress appeared.

"Can I get you anything?" I asked.

"I'll have what you're having," Devon said.

"No, you will not," her companion said.

Devon shook her shoulder.

"Ophiraaaaaaaa," she said. "It's Wisconsin. Everyone drinks in Wisconsin."

"Everyone but you."

"Taylor, say something."

"The young lady will have an iced tea, unsweetened, with a wedge of lemon," I said, ordering the same drink that Cynthia Grey always requested. "Ophira?"

Ophira ordered a Coke. The waitress wrote it down and went away.

"What are you doing here, Taylor?" Devon asked.

"I told you."

"No, seriously."

"The representatives for U.S. Sand who were on the stage tonight . . ."

"Yeah."

"They were the ones who were meeting with your brother in the conference room the day you and Emily went to visit him, the day she became so upset."

"The day before she was killed? I didn't know that. The reception-ist told us that Joel was in a meeting. She didn't tell us who with. Do you think . . ."

"I don't know what to think, yet. I'm here because they're here. Maybe there's a connection, maybe there's not."

"I hope you can prove they did it. Otherwise . . ."

The waitress returned with the drinks and set them on the table. Devon didn't touch her tea. Instead, she merely stared at it. I had no idea what thoughts were spinning in her head, although I didn't think they were pleasant.

"You don't speak much, do you, Ophira," I said just to be saying something.

"I speak when I have something to say," she told me.

Devon shook the woman's shoulder again.

"She's upset because Mother made her come with me," she said.

"Don't be saying that," Ophira said.

"You know it's true. You have your own life. You don't want to ba-bysit me."

"Your mother asked if I would look out for you, and I said yes. I always say yes."

"Because you were afraid she'd fire you. She might have, too."

"Because I like you."

"You do?"

"Because you *do* need someone to look out for you."

"Oh, Ophira."

Devon wrapped an arm around Ophira and rested her head on the woman's shoulder. Ophira shook it off.

"Stop it now," she said. "People are watchin'."

I wondered if she did it because, like me, she didn't approve of public displays of affection or because she was the only nonwhite person in the room, probably the entire county. Devon's response was to kiss Ophira's cheek like she meant it.

"So there," she said.

Ophira shook her head and drank her Coke.

"Where are you staying?" Devon asked. "Taylor, are you staying here? You should come with us back to Mereshack. Really. We have tons of room. Don't we, Ophira?"

"I'm sure he's made other plans," Ophira said.

"That's just your way of saying no. What are you afraid of? Do you think he'll ravish us in our sleep? Taylor, would you ravish us in our sleep?"

"Not tonight," I said. "Maybe tomorrow."

"Are you leaving tomorrow?"

"I haven't decided yet."

"I haven't decided yet, either. Ophira probably wants to leave."

"Child," Ophira said.

"I think I'd like to hang out for a while," Devon said. "It's so nice up here. The river . . ."

"I have a question."

"What?"

I pointed at Esther Tibbits.

"Do you see that woman dressed in blue standing over there talking to the two men?" I asked.

"The one with the big tits?" Devon's hand flew to her mouth. Her eyes glistened with both terror and glee. "I'm so sorry," she said. "I'm beginning to sound more and more like my mother."

"It's okay."

"What about the woman with, er, the woman dressed in blue?"

"Do you know her?"

"I don't think so. Should I?"

"Not necessarily. She works for the two men from U.S. Sand."

"Was she in the conference room, too?"

"Yes, she was."

"Huh."

"She also lives here. Or at least she did."

"In Arona? Kinda makes you wonder, doesn't it?"

"Yes, it does."

Devon looked me in the eye and grinned as if we were sharing a secret that no one else knew.

"I get it now," she said.

"Don't go jumping to conclusions," I said.

The man singing karaoke—badly—reached for a high note—also badly—causing Devon to turn in her seat toward the stage.

"Omigod," she said. "I'm next. Come on, Ophira." She grabbed the older woman's hand and gave it a yank. "I love to sing. I sing all the time around the house. It drives my mother crazy. See you later, Taylor."

I watched as the two women made their way across the room. A few moments later, the presence of a third woman at the table turned my head.

"Good evening, Esther," I said.

She seemed surprised by the greeting.

"Um, yeah, good evening," she said.

"Have a seat."

"Can I talk to you?"

"Sure. Have a seat."

"It's important."

"If you care to sit down . . ."

Esther sat reluctantly, occupying the edge of the chair as if she were preparing to jump up at a moment's notice. I fumbled with my smartphone. She knew what I was going to ask and turned her head away.

"I don't know who she is," Esther said.

"All things considered, I'm having a hard time believing you."

"What happened tonight, and before in St. Paul, that has nothing to do with her."

"What does it have to do with?"

"Can I speak to you in private?"

"We are speaking in private."

"I mean outside where there's no one around to see."

"So your brother and his friend can jump me in the parking lot? Absolutely not."

"No, nothing like that."

"You're saying you didn't come here to lure me into their clutches?"

"We just want to talk."

"We?"

"I meant me."

"So talk."

"Not here."

"How about the city jail? Chief McMahan wanted to arrest your brother tonight, but I wouldn't let her. I could change my mind."

"Taylor . . ."

I pulled up Emily's pic and showed it to her.

"Tell me who—"

I didn't even get a chance to finish the sentence before Esther finally launched herself off the chair and started walking away. She spoke over her shoulder.

"Never mind," she said. "Just never mind."

Esther moved past her friends without acknowledging them and went out the front entrance.

From the stage, Devon Barrington crooned in a sweet and surprisingly strong voice "Let It Go" from the Disney movie *Frozen*—an apt choice, I decided, given her attitude toward life.

Finally Cynthia Grey arrived at my table.

"Good evening," she said.

From the speakers, Devon sang "*. . . the cold never bothered me anyway.*"

I stood, said, "Good evening," and pulled out a chair for her. I'm not sure why. Force of habit, I guess.

I caught Devon watching us as I returned to my own seat. She smiled broadly, jabbed a finger in Cynthia's direction, and mouthed the word "Wow." I waved her away. She smiled some more and blew me a kiss. A few moments later, Ophira ushered her out of the resort.

Cynthia gestured at the untouched glass of iced tea on the table.

"Is that for me?" she asked.

"Who else?"

"Esther Tibbits. I saw the two of you talking. She seemed upset when she left. What was that about?"

"She wanted to have a private conversation with me. I declined the invitation."

"I wonder why."

"Why she wanted to get me alone or why I blew her off?"

"Your hand is swollen. You scraped the skin on your knuckles."

"Huh. I must have hit something."

"So, basically, you haven't changed a bit."

"Neither have you. You're still as beautiful as ever."

"Thank you, Taylor, for saying so even though I know it isn't true. I also want to thank you for what you said earlier. About being proud of me. I've been thinking about it all night. You're the only one who's ever said that to me, I think. In fact, of all the men I've known, and I've known so very many, you've been the kindest, the most considerate, and the most trustworthy."

"Unfortunately, you also want me to be the most forgetful."

Cynthia began stirring her iced tea with her fingernail, a habit that had never bothered me until now.

"Your mother never liked me," she said.

"My mother didn't like Laura, either. At least not until Jennifer was born. My father, on the other hand . . ."

Cynthia stirred her drink some more.

"Where are the boys?" I asked.

"The riffraff I hang out with now? I sent them home. For the most part, the town hall went very well. Why take the risk of losing what they gained by getting into a confrontation with a disgruntled resident? Besides, it's only a two-hour drive back to the Cities."

"What about Esther?"

"Apparently they wanted her to run a few errands at their field office tomorrow. Something about files. Taylor? Are you pumping me for information?"

"Who, me? How could you ask such a thing?"

"It reminds me of when we first met. As I recall, you were investigating a murder back then, too."

"Good times."

"Anyway"—Cynthia tapped the tabletop as if she were demanding my undivided attention—"now I get to use their room."

"What will you use their room for?"

"The possibilities are endless."

"That sounds like an invitation."

"The physical aspect of our relationship was never a problem."

"What happens in Arona stays in Arona, is that it?"

"Why not?"

"I'm just getting used to life without you."

"I wish I could say the same. All the time we were together, when I wasn't with you, I was alone. Now I'm alone all the time."

"Do you expect me to feel sorry for you?"

"Fuck, Taylor."

I didn't smile, yet it amused me just the same to see Cynthia's carefully constructed façade of upper-class gentility slip and the street kid peek over the top. She worked so hard and paid so much money to make sure the façade never slipped.

"I loved you, Cynthia," I said. "More to the point, I *liked* you. I liked you for the very things that you're trying so hard to hide from the rest of the world. Imagine breaking up with a guy over that. Twice."

"I hate that woman."

"What you've accomplished, what you continue to accomplish—"

"It's not enough."

Cynthia took a long pull on the iced tea. I knew she was wishing it were something stronger.

"How long has it been now?" I said.

She knew exactly what I was asking.

"Twelve years, eleven months, nine days," Cynthia said.

"You've kept track."

"If you're an addict, you had fucking better keep track."

"Why would you be ashamed of that, knowing precisely when you had your last drink?"

"Not ashamed, but . . . I don't want to talk about it."

"Why not?"

Cynthia glanced around the room, suddenly fearful that someone else might be listening. She leaned in.

"I don't want anyone to know. I would think you'd understand that by now."

"I do understand. You never knew your father, and your mother abandoned you at age six, leaving you in the care of elderly grandparents who both died when you were twelve."

"Taylor . . ."

"I understand you're the product of a brutal, loveless childhood and an adolescence squandered on the street. I know that you attempted to take your life on your seventeenth birthday. I also know that the experience shocked you into a peculiar kind of sanity and ignited a passion for survival that still burns red hot. I know that you embraced the straight life with both hands, earned your GED, and put yourself through college and law school on strength of will alone."

"How did I pay for my tuition?" she said. "Do you know that I danced on tables in a fucking strip club in front of assholes who threw dollar bills at me?"

"That was then. Now you're what my father calls 'a woman of substance.'"

"He doesn't know about me."

"He knows what he sees."

"He'd change his mind if he saw what was underneath."

"No, he wouldn't."

"Yes, he would. They all would."

"That's the problem, isn't it? That's always been the problem. You want to hide the woman you once were. Bury her so deep that no one will ever find her. I know she's there, though. It kills you that I know. Cynthia, I admire you so much."

"How can you if I don't?"

"Which brings us back to where we started. You've invested so much in yourself, hiring people to select your clothes and shop for furniture and teach you manners. Why not a therapist?"

"I've had doctors. They locked me away in a fucking asylum for six months, remember?"

"Now here you are, a senior partner in one of the biggest and richest law firms in Minnesota."

"One thing has nothing to do with the other. Look, you're trying to make me feel better about myself. I appreciate that, Taylor. You've always been good to me that way. If you really wanted to help a girl out, though, you'd come to my room."

"An out-of-town fling? Then what happens?"

"Like I said, I could meet you on the sidewalk with a bottle of water when you run past my house."

"I can't live like that. Not with you."

Cynthia reached across the table and took my hand. She squeezed it so hard it hurt.

"I wish I were a different person," she said.

"If you were, I don't think I'd love you as much."

She released my hand and left without another word.

I finished my bourbon, thought about another, and decided against it. Instead, I went to my room, took a shower, and went to bed. I half expected Cynthia to call, but she didn't. I was glad of that. I didn't think I could say no to her again. As it was, it took me a long time to fall asleep. When I finally did, I slept better than I had in a long, long time.

Do you want to hear something funny, though? Just before I dropped off, I remembered that I hadn't called Alexandra Campbell like I promised. I took that as a good sign, thinking of a woman besides Cynthia.

CHAPTER TWENTY-SIX

The sign was large with white lettering on a red background, its message succinct: PRIVATE PROPERTY NO TRESPASSING. A gate, similar to the one that I had encountered at Mereshack, blocked the dirt road. Beyond the gate, the road curved down and to the right behind the trees and the tall grass and the brush. There was a small hut next to the gate with a chair where someone could sit, only it was empty.

I spoke in a voice that wouldn't have startled a dragonfly if it had been perched on my shoulder.

"Hello, anyone there?"

There was no response.

"Guess I'll have to keep going."

A white van slowed on the county blacktop where I had parked my car, and sped up again. I waited until it was out of sight before I walked around the gate and the hut and forged ahead. I followed the road as it curved until I could no longer see the county blacktop behind me. It dipped down, angled to the left, and climbed a steep hill that made my thighs ache. Yes, I run three to five miles a couple times a week, except never uphill. There was a nice view at the summit if you like trees, but no buildings as far as the eye could see, and I looked hard while I rested my legs. I wondered briefly if Curtis Blevins and the Red Stone Patriots had camouflaged them, if they were deliberately hiding their compound from prying eyes, as well as government drones, black helicopters, and spy satellites.

I kept following the road as it dove into a valley and circled again to the right. The trees weren't as thick as they had been at Mrs. Barrington's place, and I could see deeper into the forest as I walked. I found a clearing. There had been a stand of trees in the clearing, the biggest about four inches in diameter. Only the trees had been cut down three feet above the ground; the trunks were splintered and dry and standing like shattered fence posts. I left the road and plowed through the brush to the trees. I bent to examine the trunks and found that slugs had mutilated the bark. A short distance away, sunlight reflected off metal shell casings. I bounced a few in the palm of my hand, listening to the metallic tinkle they made, and tossed them back to the ground.

I returned to the road.

"Apparently the Patriots wiped out a stand of trees with sustained fire from automatic weapons just for practice," I said. "I think we had better start taking them seriously."

The road zigged and zagged a few more times and suddenly there was a cluster of cabins no bigger than the ones I had found at Mereshack, all with small windows, all painted forest green, including the roofs. In the center of the cluster was a prefab pole barn made of corrugated steel and aluminum, also green. The huge door was flung open. Inside I could see two pickup trucks and an SUV; the owners are keeping them out of sight, I thought. At the edge of the compound, I spied a mobile home mounted on a cinder-block foundation. Beyond that there was a firing range setup with fresh bales of hay resting on top of old bales of hay. The hill behind the bales looked as if it had been torn up with a garden hoe.

I couldn't see or hear anyone. I called out.

"Hello." This time my voice was loud and clear. "Anyone home?"

I walked toward the buildings and shouted some more.

"Hello."

I heard them before I saw them. Four men. They seemed to burst out of the forest all around me. Young. Dressed in camo. Each was armed with an AK-47 assault rifle. The muzzles were all pointed at me.

I threw my hands into the air, holding them high as I slowly spun around so all could see that they were empty.

"Whoa, whoa, whoa," I chanted. "What's going on?"

"Down," a voice yelled. "On your knees."

I dropped to my knees, my hands still up.

"Why are the four of you pointing automatic weapons at me?" I asked.

I was careful to enunciate the number, although only two of the men were actually holding guns on me. The others had fanned out in the direction I had come, searching for friends.

"Listen," I said.

"Shut up," I was told.

The man who did the telling had a mustache. His partner looked like he was attempting to grow one and not having much success.

"Why are you snooping around?" the partner asked.

"I wasn't snooping," I said.

"Shut up," said the mustache.

"How the hell did you get here?" the partner said.

"I walked."

"Shut up," the mustache said again.

"You came up the road, past the gate?" asked the partner.

I kept quiet.

"Answer me. Didn't you see the signs? Can't you read?"

I gestured with my chin at the mustache. He stepped behind me and put a boot in the center of my back just below the neck. I fell face-first into the dirt.

"Someone asked you a question," he said.

"What are you doing, Tom?" his partner asked.

"What do you think I'm doing"—he spoke the name like an insult—"*Jerry?*"

"Let him answer the question," Jerry said.

"Search him first."

Hands patted my sides, the small of my back, the inside and outside of my legs. They were looking for weapons, not a wire. No one bothered to roll me over and pat my chest. What they did find was my wallet and smartphone. I turned my head enough to see both men examining them. At the same time, their two allies finished their sweep and returned to where I was lying.

"He's alone," one of them said.

"Now, what the hell are you doing here—Holland Taylor," Jerry said. "His first name is Holland. What kind of name is that?"

Tom nudged my ribs with the toe of his boot.

"Answer him," he said.

"It's the name my parents gave me."

"No, I meant—dammit." Tom kicked me again. "Why are you here?"

"I came to see Curtis Blevins."

"Hear that?" Tom said. "He's a fucking spy."

"Actually, I'm a private investigator."

"What did I tell you?"

"He *is* a private eye," Jerry said. "Says so on this card."

I heard the sound of a rifle bolt being pulled back and a round jacked into the chamber.

"I say we waste him right now," Tom said.

"Oh, for God's sake," Jerry said.

"Yeah? What do you suggest?"

"Put 'im in the barn and wait for Curtis to get back."

One of the other Patriots spoke up.

"I knew we should have left someone at the gate," he said.

"Fuck you, Charles," Tom said. "Sitting around there eight hours at a time. Besides, nobody ever comes 'round."

Charles casually pointed his weapon at my head. "'Cept him."

"I say we smoke this fuck right now and bury 'im in the woods," Tom said.

"What is wrong with you?" Jerry said.

Tom's answer was to again put his boot into my ribs, harder this time.

"Get 'im up," Jerry said.

Charles and the fourth Patriot slung their rifles over their shoulders and pulled me to my feet. Tom kept pointing his at my head.

"Really, fellas?" I said. "Russian-made AKs? You couldn't buy American?"

They urged me along to the pole barn and locked me in a small room in the corner. The outside walls of the room were iron, and the inside walls were made of wood and Sheetrock. The floor was concrete. There was an old mattress on the floor and a wooden chair next to it. A 60-watt bulb that I couldn't reach dangled from a black cord above my head. There were no windows. Just for fun, I tried the door. It was locked.

"That went well," I said aloud.

I sat in the chair. When I tired of that, I sat on the mattress, my back against the corrugated walls. I spent a lot of time staring at my watch. For a while I thought my battery was dying out, the second hand seemed to move so slowly. I closed my eyes, tried to nap, and failed.

"You're all probably wondering how I ended up here," I said to no one in particular. "I blame my mother. She was the original helicopter mom, hovering over me all the damn time, so naturally, when I became old enough, I ran away to join the cops so I would be in charge for a change. I took a wife and had a daughter. Then I lost my wife and daughter and started engaging in some, let's call it reckless behavior. Booze had a lot to do with it. Then George Meade ate his gun. He was my supervising officer back in the day, the guy I broke in with, and I was left wondering, is that my future, too? So I quit the cops and became a private investigator because, seriously, can you imagine me working a real job? Now I'm a prisoner of an anti-government militia. Like I said, it's my mom's fault. Plus, I fell in with bad company. You know who I'm talking about."

I closed my eyes. Voices outside my door caused me to open them again. I strained to hear. The voices went away. Changing of the guard, I told myself. I looked at my watch again.

"How time flies when you're having fun."

I tried to sleep again and succeeded. More voices jolted me awake. My watch told me eighty minutes had passed. Someone was unlocking the door. I made sure I was sitting in the chair, my legs outstretched and crossed at the ankles and my arms folded over my chest, a portrait of contentment, when the door was opened.

Tom and Jerry crowded into the room, followed by Curtis Blevins. They were armed. Blevins was not.

"Good morning, gentlemen," I said. I glanced at my watch. "Make that good afternoon."

"Stand up and put your hands behind your head," Tom said.

"No."

Tom whacked me on the forehead with the business end of his AK. I sat up straight in the chair and brought one hand up to rub the skin where he hit me.

"Get up," Tom said.

"Mr. Blevins, is that you? Will you please tell this moron to back off before someone gets hurt?"

"Do I know you?" he asked.

"He's a fucking spy," Tom said.

"Let's not go through that again," I said.

Tom pressed the muzzle of his AK against my forehead, which, believe it or not, was exactly what I wanted him to do.

I grabbed the barrel of the rifle just above Tom's hand and pushed it to the left even as I angled my head to the right, out of the line of fire. I yanked the gun forward. At the same time, I punched Tom in the groin just as hard as I could. The blow brought his head closer to me. I pivoted as I jumped to my feet and drove my elbow into his jaw. I grabbed the rifle with my other hand above the trigger guard and kept turning, pulling the rifle with me. Tom tried to hold on. My momentum dragged him over my leg. He released the rifle and fell with a loud thud on the concrete floor between the chair and the mattress. I brought the rifle up and centered it on the chest of the only other armed man in the room. Jerry froze in place.

"I promise I won't die alone," I said.

Blevins held out his hands as if he were attempting to ward off a collision.

"Wait, wait," he said.

Everyone waited.

I saw Eric Tibbits for the first time. He was standing behind Blevins's shoulder.

"Hey, Eric," I said. "The bruises on your face, did I do that? Sorry, man."

Blevins glanced over his shoulder. Eric lightly fingered his face where I had rammed it into the metal locker.

Tom reached out and grabbed my leg with both hands and tried to topple me over. I drove the rifle butt into his jaw, and he stopped moving. I brought it back up again and aimed it at Jerry's head.

"If it comes to it, I'll kill you all and take my chances with whoever's outside," I said.

"Stand down," Blevins said.

"Mr. B?"

"Jerry, stand down."

Jerry slowly stooped and rested his weapon on the concrete floor.

"Step back," I told him.

He moved backward until his shoulders and head were against the wall. I lowered the muzzle of the AK until it was pointed at the floor.

"Maybe now you'll tell me what this is all about," I said.

Blevins looked down at Tom.

"Maybe you'll tell me," he said.

"Happy to. My name is Taylor. I'm a private investigator. I came here to ask if you could identify a girl who was killed recently in St. Paul, but your guys went all militia on me. I think they've been in the woods too long."

"Why would I know a girl who was killed in St. Paul? I've never even been there."

I took my left hand off the rifle and used it to point at Eric.

"He knows her, yet he won't tell me her name," I said. "What's that all about, Eric?"

Blevins turned to look at the young man, whose expression changed quickly from surprise to terror.

"What *is* this all about, Eric?" Blevins said.

The young man shook his head.

"Eric?"

He shook his head some more and said, "I can't . . ."

"Can't what?"

Eric looked at me as if he were hoping I'd help him out.

"May I have my phone and wallet?" I said.

Blevins nodded, and Jerry took them out of his pocket. He gave me my wallet, which I promptly stuffed into my own pocket, and the smartphone, which I hung on to. In exchange, I handed him the AK-47. The gesture seemed to surprise him.

"We're all friends now, right?" I said.

"You're playing a dangerous game, Taylor," Blevins told me.

"Mr. Blevins, I'm not from the government. I'm not a cop. I don't care what you guys are doing here in the woods. You want to shoot down trees with automatic weapons, be my guest. I just want to ask a few simple questions, and then I'll be on my way."

"Ask your questions."

I activated my smartphone and called up the pic of Emily Denys. I held it up for Blevins to see.

"Do you know this girl?" I asked.

Blevins stared at the pic. His eyes blinked once, twice, three times, as if he were having a difficult time focusing. He reached out his hand slowly. I let him take the phone.

"What are you telling me?" he asked. His voice was low. I could barely hear it.

"Sir?"

"What are you telling me?"

"I just want to know—"

"What the fuck are you telling me!"

"What's wrong? Do you know her?"

"It's my daughter."

CHAPTER TWENTY-SEVEN

W ho killed her?" Blevins asked.

"I don't know."

"According to this, it was that Barrington bitch." Blevins spun the laptop on his kitchen table so that the screen was facing me. It displayed an article from the website of the St. Paul *Pioneer Press.* "It says you helped."

"It's what the county attorney told the paper. It's not what happened."

"You tell me, then, you sonuvabitch. You tell me what happened."

Blevins was angry, to say the least. That was okay. Anger was good. I could work with anger. There were times when I was forced to tell parents the unthinkable when I was with the cops. I watched them melt before my eyes, their brains becoming emotional mush that I couldn't access. It's a sight that stays with you, too. A sight that haunts your dreams. I thought Blevins would do the same. Back in the pole barn he kept chanting the same question—"What are you telling me?"—until I spelled it out.

"The girl in the pic is dead. She was murdered last week in St. Paul."

He collapsed to his knees and started hammering the concrete floor with his fists. His wail was painful to hear. Instead of attempting to comfort him, his people dragged Tom out of the tiny cell and disappeared. That left it to me.

"I'm so sorry," I told him. "I didn't know. I would have found a better way to tell you if I had known."

Blevins wasn't listening. He rocked on his knees and pressed his head to the floor and hammered the concrete and wailed.

"It's my fault, it's my fault," he told me.

I said nothing. Hell, maybe it was his fault.

Yet the grieving didn't last long. Less than fifteen minutes by my watch. Blevins gathered himself together. He stood slowly, took a deep breath, and brushed the tears off his face.

"Come with me," he said. "I have questions for you, and you had better answer them."

We exited the pole barn, and Blevins led me across the compound to the trailer mounted on the cinder blocks. A half dozen of the Red Stone Patriots watched us pass, including Eric, yet no one spoke a word.

Blevins fired up his personal computer and started searching news archives from his tiny kitchen table as if he needed independent confirmation of what had I told him. Maybe he was hoping I was a liar.

"I don't know who killed Emily," I said.

"Her name was Julie. Julie Elizabeth Blevins."

"I didn't know that."

"What do you know? Why are you even here?"

"We traced Emily's . . . we traced Julie's movements. She was seeing Joel Barrington—"

"That's what the media said."

"What they didn't say is that she visited him at his office. He was meeting with representatives from U.S. Sand."

"The Barringtons are dealing with those bastards?"

"Let me finish. Joel Barrington was meeting with representatives from U.S. Sand—"

"Kaufman and Palo."

"Yes. This seemed to upset her. No one knows why. The next day she was killed."

Blevins grimaced at my words.

"Later, I asked Kaufman and Palo about it. They claimed they had no idea who Julie was, claimed they didn't even remember seeing her in the office. Their administrative assistant said the same thing."

"Esther."

"Yes."

"Esther who works for them."

"Yes."

"My niece. Julie's cousin."

"She told me she didn't know who the girl, who Julie was. The next day I was at Julie's duplex. That's when Eric and his pal tried to shoot me. I didn't know who he was at the time. Or Esther, either, for that matter. I found out yesterday. When I went to the town hall meeting, Eric and his pal attacked me again. The bruises on Eric's face, that was from me. Yet he still insisted he didn't know who Julie was. That's why I'm here."

Blevins went to the thin trailer door and flung it open.

"Eric, get your ass in here," he said.

He stood back, leaving the door ajar. A moment later, Eric entered. He moved cautiously. Blevins grabbed his arm, pulled him all the way into the trailer, and pushed him down to the floor.

"Tell me about this," he said.

Eric pointed at me. "It was him," he said.

"Tell me about him."

There were a lot of hems and haws and ums in his answer, a lot of backtracking and repetitions, but eventually the story came out. Esther simply had not recognized her cousin in the brief moments she saw Julie in the conference room. Julie had kept her blond hair long and wore glasses; Emily had short black hair and didn't. She realized it was Julie only after I gave her a look at Emily's pic on my smartphone. I asked why Esther didn't identify Julie then.

"She was afraid," Eric said.

"Afraid of what?" I asked.

Instead of answering, Eric said that Esther called him the first chance she got after I left the offices of U.S. Sand. Eric came to St. Paul to see if he could find out what was going on and encountered me. He insisted that he had only wanted to ask a few questions. When I started running, his partner lost his head.

"Why did you ambush me at the high school last night?" I asked.

"We wanted to scare you into leaving town."

"Why?"

"They thought they were protecting me," Blevins said.

"Protecting you from what?"

"They thought I killed her." Blevins bent to Eric and cocked his hand as if he wanted to slap him, yet stopped himself. "Didn't you? You thought I killed her."

Eric didn't answer. He didn't move an inch.

Blevins turned on me. His nostrils flared and his fists clenched and his breath started coming in short gasps. I was convinced that he was about to attack. Instead, he turned on his nephew. Eric used his feet to propel himself backward across the floor.

"Get out," Blevins said. "Get out, get out, get out."

Eric scrambled to his feet and literally jumped out the door, leaving his uncle to slam it shut behind him. Blevins glared at me for a moment, went to a chair in what amounted to the trailer's living room, and sat down. He rubbed his face with both hands and spoke into the palms.

"I didn't kill my daughter," he said.

"I didn't think for a moment that you did."

"Julie never lived in Arona. Not for a day."

"I know."

"How did you trace her here, then?"

I couldn't answer his question, so I asked one of my own.

"Why was your daughter living under the name Emily Denys? Mr. Blevins? Why was she hiding?"

He hesitated before answering.

"She was hiding from me," he said.

"Why?"

"I did something."

"What did you do?"

"What do you know about me?"

"Almost nothing."

"Before I came here, before I moved to Arona, I lived in a small town in Michigan called Menominee, me and Julie. Ever hear of it?"

"No."

"People confuse it with Menominee, Wisconsin."

Blevins explained it to me. I admit the story of how he lost his home seemed much more compelling the way he told it as compared to Special Agent Rachel Colgin's version. He ended it by saying, "The morning we left, someone blew up the city's so-called Welcome Center."

"Did Emily—excuse me," I said. "Did Julie know that you bombed the building?"

"Who said I did?"

"Call it a lucky guess."

"Julie had nothing to do with it."

"Okay."

"It's all on me."

"Okay."

"She's the one who bought the hydrazine, the ammonium nitrate, the aluminum powder, that's true. She didn't know at the time what I planned to do with it, though. Do you believe me?"

"Why not?"

"Later she thought it made her an accomplice, and it shook her. I explained about the corrupt government and people's rights and how we must fight tyranny wherever we find it. She wouldn't listen. We had people in Arona. A sister, brother-in-law, nieces and nephews. I told her it would be a new start for us, that we would put the past behind us. Jules knew about the Patriots, though. She knew that my family was involved and that I intended to join them and continue the fight against injustice. She wanted no part of it. My daughter—she wanted no part of me, either. She said she was afraid of me. She said . . . When we reached a gas station in Eau Claire, Julie took her bag out of the trunk of the SUV and left. Just walked away without a word. Didn't even say good-bye. She was over twenty-one; I had no hold on her. If that's what she wanted to do . . ."

"Did you look for her?"

"No."

"I guess she thought you might. That's why she changed her name."

"Funny. I actually thought she would turn me in to the FBI. For the longest time I waited for a knock on the door."

"She didn't turn you in."

"No. Taylor, you didn't answer my question. Why did you come here?"

I answered without thinking.

"I believe whoever killed the mayor might have also killed your daughter."

"Todd Franson? That makes no sense. Julie never lived here. She never met the man. There's no connection between him and her."

"Tell me about Esther."

"What about her?"

"She worked for Mayor Franson right up until he was killed. Now she works for U.S. Sand."

"So?"

"You said there's no connection between the mayor and Julie. Esther connects them."

"That's ridiculous."

"Is it?"

Blevins went to his feet and crossed the trailer to a window. He gazed out as if he wanted to make sure there was no one near enough to eavesdrop.

"I'm going to tell you something in absolute secret. Only me and Eric know."

"Know what?"

"Esther is a spy."

Oh, for God's sake, I thought yet didn't say.

"She was keeping tabs on the mayor for me, and now she's doing the same with U.S. Sand."

"Then you knew that Franson was attempting to seize private property through eminent domain and give it to the sand miners long before it was announced in the *Kamin County Record*."

"I knew, but . . ."

Blevins stopped speaking, his eyes grew wide, and he became very still. I understood why, too. He had all but confessed that he blew up the Welcome Center in Menominee, and now he'd just admitted he had a motive for killing the mayor. Certainly he had the means. That left opportunity, and I bet he had that, too.

"Where were you the night Franson was killed?" I asked.

"I didn't kill the bastard. The Patriots didn't do it, either."

"Okay."

"Something else—I never actually said that I bombed a building in Menominee, did I?"

"No, you didn't." Although, I thought, you said enough.

"Even if I did do those things, I would never have hurt my daughter. Never."

"That's the only thing I care about, Mr. Blevins—finding out who killed your daughter."

"So you can get the Barrington bitch off."

"So I can get the Barrington bitch off. What about you? What do you care about?"

Blevins sat in the chair again and buried his face in his hands. I heard him say, "What am I going to do?" in a muffled voice.

"How should I know?"

I could have been more empathetic, I know. Then again, why would I? In any case, I figured it was as good a time as any to make an exit, so I moved to the door and opened it. I glanced back over my shoulder at the man. His face was stained with tears, and for a moment, I did feel empathy. I had lost a daughter, too.

"Mr. Blevins," I said. "For what it's worth, the medical examiner said Julie died instantly. She never knew what hit her. If that's true, she died happy. She was living a good life. She had many friends. They all loved her."

I stepped out of the trailer and closed the door. I could hear him weeping behind it.

Thirty minutes later, I found Special Agent Rachel Colgin of the Bureau of Alcohol, Tobacco, Firearms, and Explosives waiting for me in the front seat of a white van. The van was parked at the mouth of the road that led to the compound of the Red Stone Patriots, about fifty yards from where my own car was parked. The side door slid open, and Colgin hopped out, followed by a man who looked even younger than she did. I removed my jacket and shirt and winced as the tech peeled off the tape that held the wire to my chest.

"I'm sorry about your wife and daughter," Colgin said.

"I talk too much. Did you get what you needed?"

"Yes," she said. "Thank you. The number of Patriots, how they were armed—I appreciate that, too. Now all I need to do is travel to the office of the U.S. attorney of the Northern Division of the Western District of Michigan, which is all the way up in Marquette on the south shore of Lake Superior, prove that we have enough evidence to prosecute, get a warrant complaint because I don't think Blevins is going to respond well to a simple court summons, assemble a team, come back down here, and arrest the man without triggering a siege of a militia compound like they had in Waco or the Bundy ranch in Nevada. Easy peasy puddin' and pie."

"While you're at it, tell me what's the penalty for slapping the hell out of a federal agent, because right now I think it might be worth it."

"Hey, I'm the one who has to deal with the bureaucracy."

"You knew Emily Denys was Blevins's daughter before you sent me in there."

"Yeah."

"You heartless bitch. You made me tell the man his daughter was dead. That someone shot her in the fucking head."

"There's no need for obscenities."

Colgin's colleague smirked as he crawled back into the van and shut the door. Colgin hooked her arm around mine as if we were on a second date and walked me along the county blacktop toward my Camry.

"I'm sorry," she said. "I figured the fact you clearly didn't know who Emily was would only add confusion to the old man's grief, thereby increasing the likelihood that Blevins would do exactly what I needed

him to do—confess his crimes. It was a cruddy thing. My only consolation is that it worked."

"Did you know Julie Blevins?"

"Of course I did. We were onto her two days after she ditched the
old man. I tried to turn her, only she would have none of it. Blevins was
a jerk, but there was no way she was going to testify against him, not
even when I offered her a new life in WITSEC. I liked her for that,
believe it or not, standing by her father."

"Rachel, how could Julie get a birth certificate and an authentic
Social Security card with you watching? How did she become the
ghost of Emily Denys?"

"I suppose it's possible that someone felt sorry for her and helped
her out off the books. She needed help, too. It took a devious mind to
do what she planned to do, and she didn't have a devious mind."

"On the other hand, a special agent for the Bureau of Alcohol, Tobacco, Firearms, and Explosives . . ."

"I don't know what you're talking about, Taylor."

I gave her hand a squeeze.

"You have a kind heart," I said.

"Yeah, well, keep it to yourself. Something like that gets out it can
only hurt my career."

"Especially if Emily . . . Julie was playing you like she had so many
others."

"What's that supposed to mean?"

"Blevins taking the blame for the bomb, insisting Julie had nothing
to do with it—what if Julie had planted it and he was just trying to protect her name, the image people have of her?"

"Why would he do that?"

"Because he loves his daughter, why do you think?"

"You honestly believe he'd risk going to prison . . ."

"He didn't know he was providing evidence to the ATF, did he? He
didn't know anything he said could be used against him in a court of
law."

We reached my car.

"What are you going to do?" Colgin asked.

"Keep at it until I learn who killed Julie."

"What if you discover it really was Eleanor Barrington?"

"Then I'll stop."

"Take care, Taylor."

"Don't forget. We have a deal."

"I won't forget."

CHAPTER TWENTY-EIGHT

I was hungry, yet I wanted to check in before I ate, so I went to my room, sprawled out on the bed, and called Freddie.

"I have some good news and I have some bad news," he said. "The good news—according to her credit card statements, Eleanor Barrington bought cheesecake at a joint called Junior's Restaurant and Bakery in New York City exactly ninety-seven minutes before the mayor got dead in Wisconsin."

"That should make Helin happy," I said. "More to the point, it'll make the county attorney very unhappy."

"I hear that."

"What's the bad news?"

"The kid—Joel Barrington? He was with her. They shared a suite at the Park Savoy Hotel."

"That doesn't mean they shared—you know what? I don't want to know what those freaks shared in New York, only that they weren't here when the killing took place."

"Kinda makes you want to take a shower, though, doesn't it?"

"That sounds like a good idea."

"Have you called the professor yet?"

"I haven't had time."

"I'm telling Echo."

"C'mon . . . Freddie?" He hung up. "Dammit."

Next I called David Helin. I caught him between meetings. He once told me that seventy percent of his job was meetings of one sort or another. I told him everything that had transpired since I arrived in Arona, including my adventures with the ATF and Freddie placing Eleanor Barrington in New York at the time of Mayor Franson's murder. I knew he was taking notes because he kept saying, "Wait, wait," when I spoke too quickly.

"You know, I'll be sending you a written report like always," I said.

"This thing about Emily actually being the fugitive daughter of a crazed anti-government bombing suspect who's also a suspect in the murder of the mayor, that's pure gold, Taylor. This special agent—"

"Rachel Colgin."

"You say she's agreed to testify that Emily was afraid of her father, afraid that he would find her?"

"That was the deal we made."

"Pure gold. It might even be enough to get Marianne Haukass to drop the charges against Mrs. Barrington. Are you sure the county attorney knows nothing about this?"

"I don't know how she could, but David, I don't think he did it."

"Blevins?"

"I don't think he killed his daughter."

"You're missing the point."

"I get the point. I'm telling you, though, if we could actually find the real killer, it would be better all around."

"I'm not Perry Mason, I'm not—who was the guy that Andy Griffith played?"

"Matlock."

"I'm not Matlock, either. I'm not interested in finding the real killer. I only want to get my client off."

"Colgin said it would take at least twenty-four hours before she's ready to drop the hammer on Blevins and all hell breaks loose around here, assuming someone higher up on the food chain doesn't take the case away from her. I'd like to use the time."

"All right, sure."

"We're good, then?"

"You know how it works. The more suspects I can throw at a jury, the better."

"There're no lack of suspects for the mayor's murder, that's for sure."

"If you can connect any of them to Emily, I mean Julie, that's gold, too."

"Okay. By the way, did you know that Devon Barrington was in Arona?"

"I did not."

"She delivered a message for her mother at the town hall meeting I told you about. She did very well."

"Stay away from her, Taylor."

"The girl isn't even seventeen. Of course I'm going to stay away from her."

"That's not what I meant."

"What do you mean?"

"Just keep your distance, okay? Eleanor's orders."

"Sure."

I went downstairs searching for food and found Devon Barrington. She and Ophira were in the restaurant eating a late lunch. I might have avoided them, except Devon saw that I was standing in the doorway and waved me over to the table.

"Taylor, you're still here," she said.

"So are you."

"Do you believe it? There isn't any real food at Mereshack at all. Just cans. Is this a nuclear holocaust, I'm going to eat out of a can?"

"I eat canned food all the time," Ophira said.

"After lunch we're going grocery shopping. Sit, sit; please join us."

"I was just told to stay away from you," I said. "Your mother's orders."

"Then you should go," Ophira said.

Devon was visibly jolted by the remark. She turned her head and stared at her companion; an expression of anger seized her face.

"I asked him to join us," she said.

"Your mother—"

"Fuck my mother."

Ophira rested a hand on Devon's wrist as if she were a piece of machinery that required delicate handling.

"Now, now," she chanted. "We all be friends here."

Devon rested her hand on top of Ophira's and gave it a squeeze. Just like that, the flash of temper disappeared; Devon's expression became one of playful rebellion. She shook Ophira's shoulder the way she did the evening before and smiled.

"*Resist much, obey little*—that's what Walt Whitman wrote," Devon told us. "Geez you guys, worrying about my mother."

The transformation from light to dark and back again was so pronounced, and happened so quickly, that for a moment I lost my breath.

"Are you going to sit down, Taylor?" Devon asked.

I sat.

"Are you hungry?"

"I'm going to eat later," I said. "I need to interview a few people before it gets too late in the day."

"You'll have to come out to Mereshack, then. I'll show you around. It's really nice."

"I'll do that."

I glanced at Ophira as I spoke. Clearly she didn't think it was a good idea, yet refused to challenge the girl again.

"Give me your phone," Devon said.

I did. She inputted her number into it and pressed CALL. Her own cell started ringing. She ended the call and handed back my phone.

"See, it works," she said. "I expect you to call, too. Don't you dare blow me off."

"I won't."

"Not even for the woman you were sitting with last night."

"That was no woman. That was an attorney."

I smiled. To my surprise, so did Ophira, if only for a moment.

"I don't get it," Devon said.

"It plays off an old joke. Man says, Who was that lady I saw you with last night? The second man answers, That was no lady; that was my wife. Ba-da dum."

"I still don't get it."

"I didn't say it was a good joke."

"She was very beautiful, the attorney. I mean like freaky beautiful."

"Yes, she was."

"Did you—?"

"Dev," Ophira said.

"The woman works for U.S. Sand," I said.

"Oh, those guys," Devon said.

"Yes, those guys."

"What did she want?"

"She wanted me to leave them alone."

"Are you going to leave them alone?"

"We'll see."

Devon rested her hand on mine.

"Afterward, did you and the attorney, you know?" she said.

"What kind of question is that?"

The expression on her face—it was like I slapped her. She quickly pulled her hand back.

"I'm sorry," Devon said.

"Don't worry about it," I said.

"Taylor, do you think all teenagers are insane? This guy on National Public Radio thinks so. He thinks that for about a three-to-four-year period we just all go completely nuts."

"No, I don't believe it."

"I say and do things sometimes . . ."

I rested my own hand on her wrist the way Ophira had.

"Pretty girls who are almost seventeen always get a bye. Everyone knows that."

"You're nice, always nice to me. It's too bad you're so old. Don't you think, Ophira?"

"Just terrible," she said.

"I need to go back to work," I said. Yet before I could, a large man appeared at the table and called my name.

"Martin McGaney, as I live and breathe," I said.

"I'd like a word," he said.

"Ladies, this is Martin McGaney, an old friend from my crime-fighting days. Martin, this is Ophira."

He shook her hand, and she smiled brightly. I didn't know if it was because she liked what she saw or because now there were two African Americans in Kamin County.

"This young lady is Devon Barrington."

I thought the name might give him a start, yet he simply said, "Hi, how are you?"

"Join us," Devon said.

McGaney grabbed a chair and sat without hesitation. I didn't think I had ever seen him smile so much as when he returned Ophira's smile.

I stood up.

"Time to scoot," I said. "Before I leave, though, I should tell you. Martin, here? He works for the woman who's trying to put Devon's mother in prison for murder."

I turned and strolled away. Behind me, I heard a confusion of voices. McGaney's was the most prominent. I heard it say "Sorry" and "Not my fault" and "Excuse me," followed by the sound of a chair falling over, followed by another "Excuse me." I was in the lobby of the resort when I felt his hand on my arm pulling me to a halt.

"Sonuvabitch, Taylor," McGaney said. "What was that?"

I lifted his hand off my arm by his sleeve as if it were something contagious.

"Interviewing a minor without permission from her parents, what's wrong with you?" I said.

"I had no intention of questioning the girl."

"If it's about Ophira, then I did you both a favor. What would have happened when she found out who you were? Think of the heartache I saved you guys."

"What a bitter old man you turned out to be."

"Why is everyone calling me old today? I'm not old."

"Old, old, old—old before your time."

"What exactly are you doing here anyway, Martin?"

"Trying to find out what you're doing here."

"No license holder shall divulge to anyone other than the employer, or as the employer may direct, except as required by law, any information acquired during—"

"Ah, Jesus, stop it, wouldja."

"If you guys would give me a little cooperation, maybe I would give you a little cooperation. I've worked with the cops before, and you know it. All PIs do. It's always a strict quid pro quo relationship. So, if you want a little this, why don't you give me a little that?"

"You first."

"What do you want to know?"

"Have you identified the girl yet?"

"No one in town seems to know who she is. I know for a fact that Emily didn't go to school here, so . . ."

"Looks like a dead end."

"Looks like."

"Then tell me, Taylor—why are you still here?"

I gestured toward the restaurant.

"Just keeping an eye on the kid for Momma," I said.

"Why don't I believe you?"

"Because you have a suspicious nature."

"The skirt seems to think you're trying to connect Emily's murder to the Red Stone Patriots."

"The skirt? Everyone picks on Maureen. I think she's a fine chief of police."

"Oh, you do not."

"Unlike some big-city policemen I could name, she is without guile."

"If you say so."

"Although she did have as much reason to pop the mayor as anyone else. What's more, the chief carries a nine-mil. Kind of makes you pause, doesn't it?"

I knew what McGaney was thinking as he stared at me. He was thinking that I was thinking that he should investigate the chief.

"Cut it out, Taylor," he said. "Not even you would dump on a cop unless it was for certain. Not even to save your client."

He was probably right, although . . . "I'm surprised more and more, Martin, by what I'm willing to do," I said.

"Yeah? Me, too."

Martin left the lobby. I decided to give him a head start so I wouldn't bump into him in the parking lot. I hate multiple good-byes. While I lingered, Bill Everheart called me over to the front desk.

"Taylor," he said. "Sorry I missed you this morning. You snuck out before I could deliver this."

It was a neatly folded sheet of resort stationery; my name was written on top in a careful cursive.

"Lady left it when she checked out. She left before sunrise. She didn't look happy."

I unfolded the note and read what Cynthia had written there.

I love you, Taylor. I will always love you. You shall not see me again. C—

"Well, that's that," I said aloud.

"Excuse me?" Everheart said.

I didn't answer. Instead, I crumpled the note into a ball with the intention of throwing it away. I changed my mind, though, smoothed out the wrinkles, refolded it, and slipped it into my wallet.

CHAPTER TWENTY-NINE

I drove the county highway until it left the forest and revealed the long, flat field. The sight of the silica sand mine still jolted me. Something had changed, though; I felt it before I knew it. The pyramids of topsoil and shifting yellow sand were still there. My car kicked up the particles, trailing clouds behind it as I drove just as before. Yet there was no shrieking of heavy machinery. There was no noise at all except for the steady hum of the Camry.

I followed the road past the Franson farm. Bridgette and Mark were sitting on their stoop drinking from travel mugs as I passed. A couple more turns and I was heading toward a cluster of offices and porta-potties. Unlike the gash in the earth, the offices looked temporary.

I parked next to a Ford Crown Victoria Police Interceptor with the words ARONA POLICE DEPARTMENT painted on the door. Heads turned toward me as if they were waiting for something and hoping I was it. Most of them turned away when I emerged from the Camry.

Chief Maureen McMahan approached. Skip Zetzman and Doug Pinter trailed behind.

"What are you doing here, Taylor?" the chief asked.

"What's going on?"

"Answer me."

"I'm here to see Esther Tibbits. I heard she was out here."

Along with McMahan, Zetzman, and Pinter, there were at least twenty men milling around the cluster of buildings. They reminded me of baseball fans during a rain delay wondering if the game would resume. Leaning against the wall of one of the offices, I found Esther. She was wearing a black skirt and a white shirt, both tinged with yellow. The men were showing a great deal of interest in her, yet she didn't seem interested in them.

"Why do you want to speak to Esther?" Zetzman asked.

"It's a personal matter." I waved at the site. "What happened?"

Heads turned. I followed their gaze to what used to be a high-volume storage silo but was now a heap of twisted scrap metal that looked as if it had been dropped there from outer space. Next to it was a pile of charred steel resting on melted rubber that used to be a tractor and frack-sand trailer. Smoke lingered close to the ground. Blackened sand was everywhere.

"My, my, my, what a mess," I said.

"I got the call ninety minutes ago," the chief said.

"Then where is everybody?"

"The Kamin Independent Citizens Against Silica Sand cannot condone the destruction of private property," Pinter said. "However, given the urgency of the problem, the destructive nature of fracking and silica sand mining, we feel—"

"David, will you kindly shut up?" the chief said.

Zetzman held up his reporter's notebook.

"I got it, Pinter," he said. "I got it."

I took the chief's arm and led her away. Zetzman and Pinter attempted to follow, but I gave them a look that froze them in their tracks. As soon as we were safe from eavesdroppers, I leaned in.

"Dammit, Chief, this is no way to protect the integrity of a crime scene," I said.

"No one has gone near the silo and truck. I've seen to that."

"The crime scene isn't just the truck. It's everything. It's everywhere. You let the media hang around? Some environmental extremist who should actually be a suspect?"

"I've known David for years. He wouldn't hurt a fly."

"A silo isn't a fly. Where's the county sheriff? Where's the DCI?"

"I never called them. This is my jurisdiction."

"Maureen, this isn't a simple case of vandalism. Given the nature of this site—hell, even Doug Pinter knows eco-terrorism when he sees it. Which the federal government translates into domestic terrorism—"

"Don't you think I know that? I called the Feds."

"Who specifically? Homeland Security? The FBI?"

"Since I'm pretty sure it was a bomb that destroyed the equipment, I called the ATF."

I watched the white van approach, a yellow cloud trailing behind it. The vehicle followed the same path I had used and parked next to my Camry. Special Agent Rachel Colgin alighted from the passenger side, and the tech I had met earlier slipped past the driver's door. A third agent I had not seen before joined them. The two men halted and gazed at the scene as if they thought it was amusing. Colgin kept walking toward the chief. I stepped away from Maureen.

"You," Colgin said.

"Ma'am?" I said.

"Where are you going?"

"Umm . . ."

"Stick around."

"Yes, ma'am. Happy to assist the federal government in any way I can."

Colgin kept walking until she reached the chief. Without hesitation, she draped an arm around the older woman's shoulder and squired her toward the bomb site. Halfway there, they stopped. Colgin left her arm around the chief's shoulder and even gave it an encouraging hug as she spoke. I couldn't see the chief's face, but I knew something about body language, and hers was not confident. Finally Colgin removed her arm, turned, and walked away. The chief did not move, however, and Colgin halted. She walked backward until she was parallel to the chief. She said something. I don't know what, yet it was enough to cause the chief to turn and walk ever so briskly to her car and speak rapidly into the radio. Fifteen minutes later, an army of Kamin County sheriff's deputies descended on the place. It wasn't long before agents from the Wisconsin Division of Criminal Investigation joined them.

Meanwhile, Esther Tibbits continued to lean against the wall of the temporary office, looking as if she wished she were somewhere else.

"May I ask a few questions?" I said.

"I've got nothing to say to you."

"Don't be so sure. I just left your uncle."

"What did you do?"

"I told him what you and your brother wouldn't."

"About?"

"About Julie."

"Are you sure he didn't already know?"

"Whatever that means."

Esther went to the office door, opened it, and stepped inside. I followed. She closed the door behind us and locked it.

"I didn't recognize Julie when she came to the conference room in the Barrington building," Esther said. "That's the truth. I saw her only for a second, and I thought, Joel Barrington is doing a pretty girl, but that's all I thought. I didn't know it was Julie until you showed me the pic on your smartphone."

"Why didn't you tell me then?"

"Did you really speak to Uncle Curtis?"

"Yes. A couple hours ago in his trailer. You can call him."

I was relieved when she didn't. Instead, Esther said, "What did he say?"

"He was very upset about Julie's murder."

"But what did he say?"

"He told me about Menominee, if that's what you mean."

"Then you know that Julie betrayed the cause. That she ran out on the Patriots, on her father. She was just as guilty of the crime as he was. If it was a crime. More so because it was her idea."

"Blowing up the Welcome Center with a liquid explosive was her idea?"

"What did Uncle Curtis tell you?"

"He said that Julie bought the anhydrous hydrazine and ammonium nitrate."

"So you know, then."

"Know what?"

"That Jules was responsible."

"Your uncle said he did it."

"No, it was all her. She built the bomb and planted it. Don't you think she didn't. She ran away because she knew the Feds would come a-knockin'. Well, they came and they went and nothing happened. But we all knew if they ever caught up with Jules, she'd rat us out in a heartbeat. Turn government informant and get a cushy life in the Witness Security Program while the rest of us went to federal prison."

"So she had to die."

"That's how the Patriots looked at it."

Esther smirked then.

"Doesn't mean we killed her, though," she said. "After you left the office, I called my brother. Neither Eric nor the rest of the Patriots knew anything about Julie. No one knew she was in the Cities. No one knew she had changed her name to Emily."

"Are you sure of that?"

"Eric came down to make sure."

"Eric, but not your uncle."

"The Patriots operate on a need-to-know basis like any other paramilitary organization."

"Who's the one who didn't need to know? You or Curtis?"

"I know what you're asking, and—I'm speaking hypothetically now—it's possible he had it done without telling us because he didn't know how we'd take it, executing our own blood."

"How did you take it?"

Esther smirked some more.

"I don't know if Jules was killed by the Patriots. You never heard me say that any of us had anything to do with it. We're just talking here."

"That's right."

"I'm saying, if the Patriots did it or if someone else killed Jules for their own reasons, the bitch had it coming. There's no crime in saying that, is there?"

"Not to my knowledge."

"If someone else did kill Julie for his own reasons, let's just say me and Eric were protecting my uncle from some unnecessary grief by keeping it to ourselves and let it go at that."

"You're talking about your own cousin."

"I'm talking about a traitor."

"Are you really this cynical, Esther? Are you really this tough?"

"Tough enough to be my uncle's whore. Do you think Todd Franson would have hired me if I didn't put out? Do you think I'd be working for those shits at U.S. Sand if I didn't get down on my knees every now and again? I do what I have to for the cause. I do what's necessary to help protect this country from its enemies both foreign and domestic."

"That's the saddest thing I've heard in a long time."

"Fuck you."

"Just between you and me and the empty room, did you blow up that silo out there? Is that why you stayed in Arona instead of going back to the Cities with Frick and Frack?"

"I didn't blow up anything. You believe what you want, though. You can't prove shit."

I exited the office and hung around like any other innocent bystander. By now the investigation was humming along. Yellow crime scene tape was everywhere. Local TV cameras took video from behind the yellow tape. Pinter tried to attract their attention and actually succeeded. Guys crawled over the silo and truck with magnifying glasses and tweezers. Someone had even set up a table with coffee and donuts. A man wearing a flannel shirt kept asking Special Agent Colgin when his crew could get back to work, and she kept saying, "I'll let you know." After a while Colgin waved me over. Chief McMahan was standing near enough to hear our conversation.

"What's your name?" Colgin asked.

"Holland Taylor."

"What the hell kind of name is Holland for a guy?"

"My mother wanted a daughter."

"I can imagine her disappointment. What are you doing here?"

"I'm a private investigator working a case that has nothing to do with the bombing."

"I'll be the judge of that. Let me see some ID."

I showed it to her. At the same time, Colgin slowly nudged me away until the chief couldn't hear us.

"That woman," Colgin said. "Where the hell did she get her badge? A box of Cracker Jack?"

"I was told that she slept her way to the top."

"I'm not surprised."

"I like her, though."

"You like too many people."

"Actually, I've been accused of the exact opposite."

"My guys gave me a preliminary on the IED. Anhydrous hydrazine mixed with ammonium nitrate in a glass jar detonated by a cell phone. Sound familiar?"

"Vaguely."

"Makes you wonder where Curtis Blevins was when the bomb was planted, doesn't it?"

"We know he wasn't at the compound; otherwise I wouldn't have had to wait for so long. By the way, why aren't you in Marquette?"

"I was headed that way until this call turned me around. But you know what? I don't actually need to *go* to Marquette to get a warrant. They have all these wonderful newfangled inventions now. Email, Skype, the telephone."

"When you start building your case, I recommend that you interview Esther Tibbits."

"Blevins's niece?"

"She's a true believer. Give her an audience and she'll talk her head off."

"Good to know."

"She claims that it was Julie who planted the bomb in Menominee."

"Does she?"

"Yep."

"Does she also say that Blevins was innocent?"

"No, she doesn't say that."

"Okay, then."

"I'll be getting out of your way now. I'm sure my guy will be contacting you soon. In the meantime, good luck."

"Where are you going?"

"Home."

"No, no, no. I want you to hang around for a while, at least until tomorrow."

"Forget it. I've had enough of small-town American values."

"What about your case?"

"I have more than I need to help get Mrs. Barrington off."

"Seriously. Stay."

"Seriously, I'm outta here."

"C'mon, Taylor. Don't make me get all large and emphatic."

"I don't know what more I can do for you that I haven't already done."

"You never know what tomorrow might bring. The sun might even come out."

"Is that an allusion to the musical *Annie*?"

"*Bet your bottom dollar that tomorrow there'll be sun.*"

"I like a girl who likes her job."

"So, you'll stick around?"

"Since you asked so sweetly."

By then, Richard Kaufman and Allen Palo had arrived. I figured they must have broken every existing traffic law to get there from the Cities on such short notice. They approached Chief McMahan and demanded action in voices loud enough to be heard by the media standing behind the tape.

"This is an unforgivable act of domestic terrorism," they said.

Chief McMahan agreed.

Colgin drifted toward them, probably to let them know that she was in charge. I followed because I had nothing better to do.

"We demand a thorough investigation," Kaufman said.

"You'll get it," McMahan said. "In the meantime, I have some questions for you."

"What questions?" Palo asked.

"I have been conducting my own investigation into illegal activities involving U.S. Sand . . ."

Kaufman and Palo glanced at each other as if they couldn't believe what they were hearing.

"If you prefer that we speak in my office . . . ," McMahan continued.

"We have nothing to say," Palo said.

"I have Bob Barcott's emails. The ones where you and he discuss how you want him to retaliate against Arona citizens who oppose the sand mines. I especially like the one where you tell him to write a scathing letter to the nursing home that you helped finance, demanding that it fire a nurse who complained about a sand mine near her property. What was it you wanted Barcott to tell her boss? That the nurse used her work email to file the complaint, which brought the integrity of the nursing home's entire staff into question, especially management?"

"We have nothing to say," Palo repeated.

"I'll quote you when I send all my findings to the county attorney."

Kaufman and Palo glanced at each other some more.

"If you think some rinky-dink small town cop—" Kaufman said.

"Chief. I'm chief of police."

"What do you think that will get you?" Palo asked. "Hmm? This, this bombing"—he waved at the bomb site—"makes us look like the victims. We are the victims, too. That's what ninety percent of the media reports are going to say, and the rest—no one cares about the rest. As for this paltry investigation of yours, how many people did you interview. Two? Three?"

"Twenty-seven."

"I don't care if it's a hundred and twenty-seven. Do you know what's going to happen at the end of it all? Allen and I will be suspended for three days and given mandatory ethics training. At least that's what the company will announce to the media. Afterward, we'll be sent somewhere else to do the exact same job that we're doing here. You *opposers*"—he spoke the word as if it were an obscenity. "Frac sand is never going away. Never. Not as long as there's a nickel to be made from it. Get used to the idea. Best you can do, the best you'll ever do, is shut us down for an hour."

"Long enough to take a shower and get the shit out of my hair. This is a crime scene. Leave immediately."

"Who do you think—"

Chief McMahan stepped backward and tilted her head at Rachel.

"Special Agent Colgin," she said.

Rachel stepped between the chief and the boys. She held up her ID for them to see.

"Move along, gentlemen," she said.

Kaufman and Palo glanced at each other again. They seemed to do a lot of that. They smirked and shrugged and turned and left.

"I don't know," I said. "Telling them what you're going to do before you do it . . ."

"You too, Taylor," the chief said. "Beat it."

"Maureen . . ."

"You heard the woman," Colgin told me.

I bowed my head and spoke as respectfully as possible.

"Chief McMahan," I said.

It took me some time to maneuver my Camry out of the now-crowded parking lot. I followed the county road toward the Franson farmhouse. Bridgette and Mark were still sitting on their stoop drinking from travel mugs. I slowed to a stop and powered down my window.

"Good evening," I said.

"Beautiful, isn't it?" Bridgette said. "The way the setting sun reflects off all that golden sand."

"Peaceful, too," Mark added. "Quiet. You can hear the birds calling to each other."

"Wooo, wooo," Bridgette said.

The two of them giggled just the way they had when I caught them fooling around in their backyard.

I might have told them that if Kaufman and Palo had their way, the mine would be back to full operation before sunrise, except I guessed they already knew that. Instead, I wished them a good night and drove back toward the Everheart Resort, Restaurant, and Bar.

CHAPTER THIRTY

I was thinking of the food I hadn't eaten for nearly twelve hours. And bourbon. Lots and lots of bourbon. I passed through the lobby of the resort and walked a straight line toward the restaurant. I nearly made it, too. Except I was intercepted by Cheryl Turk.

"Detective Taylor? You said . . ." Cheryl held up a ledger for me to see. "You asked if I could tell you about Mereshack before the mayor was killed."

"Yes, yes I did. It's kind of you to get back to me."

I nearly added that I had forgotten all about it, but managed to check myself in time.

"Do you want to look at this?" Cheryl asked.

"Absolutely."

Cheryl led me back into the lobby to a table that we both could lean against. Her ledger was actually a blue three-ring binder like the kind school kids carry that she used to keep copies of her invoices, a running tally of her income, and instructions from her clients. She showed me a page from over a year ago and proceeded to tell me what was printed on it.

"It was a Sunday afternoon, and Mrs. Barrington was getting ready to leave, and she called me down to Mereshack to tell me what she wanted done while she was gone, and when I arrived she was standing on her deck, the back deck facing the woods, and she was talking to the mayor. Yelling at him, really. See here." Cheryl pointed at a notation on the sheet that read *Mayor Franson on deck during conversation.*

"Conversation?" I said.

"What happened, I arrived and I parked my car and I was walking toward them, and Mrs. Barrington was shouting until she saw me, then she starting doing this with her hand."

Cheryl waved her own hand like Catherine the Great dismissing her subjects.

"Mrs. Barrington was always doing that," Cheryl said.

She waved her hand some more.

"I'm like, I came all the way down here on a Sunday. She's like, it's all a terrible mistake, you're doing a wonderful job, I'll call you next week. I'm like, fine. I wrote it all down, though. See?"

Cheryl pointed at the ledger again.

"She was always telling me to do stuff or not telling me to do stuff and then forgetting about it, so I write it down to, you know, cover my ass, like I told you yesterday."

"When did this meeting take place?" I asked.

"Right here. I got the date right here at the top."

Cheryl tapped it with a fingernail in case I missed it.

"Two days later, someone shot the mayor," I said.

"Except two days later, Mrs. Barrington wasn't here. I know because . . ." Cheryl turned a page in her ledger. "Two days later—it was a Tuesday—I was out there cleaning the place and she was like gone. Only Devon was there, and what's-her-face, the black woman. You know, Mr. Taylor, I know you're a real detective and all that, but really, no one believes that Mrs. Barrington shot the mayor. I'm telling you, it was the wife. Maybe the brother helped."

I managed to get into the restaurant. The hostess apparently preferred that I didn't take up an entire table by myself during the peak dinner hour and suggested I sit at the bar. I told her I wanted a table, and she gave me the worst one they had, near the kitchen door. A few moments later, a waitress appeared with a menu and asked if I wanted a beverage before ordering.

"Maker's Mark on the rocks," I told her.

She shuffled away, and I began to study the menu. That's when my smartphone chirped. Someone sent me a text. I rarely get texts and seldom send them myself. I checked. It was from Devon.

How come you haven't called?

I replied, *I was at a crime scene.*

Devon's reply—*Who was shot?*—came with a smiling emoji.

Not shot—a bomb.

Who got blown up?—with two giggling emoticons and one with its fingers crossed.

Oh, for Christ's sake, I told myself. I called Devon's number.

"Hey," I said.

"Who got blown up?"

"No one. Just some equipment at the silica sand mine at the edge of town."

"Was it bad?"

"The damage was confined to a storage silo and a truck. They'll probably be back in business by tomorrow morning if not sooner."

"What does this have to do with my mother's case?"

"Probably nothing at all."

"Oh. Well, then, Taylor, have you eaten yet?"

"No."

"Come over. Come to Mereshack. Ophira is making Cajun stew. It's really good. Sausage and shrimp. Okra. The only time I ever eat okra is when I'm having Ophira's Cajun stew. Taylor . . ."

"Probably not a good idea. Your mother wouldn't like it."

"What Mommy doesn't know won't hurt her."

"What does Ophira say?"

Devon's voice sounded like she was a long way off, and I pictured her holding up the cell phone as she spoke. "Ophira, is it all right if Taylor comes for dinner?"

Silence. A moment later, Devon was back on the phone.

"She said it was all right."

"I didn't hear a thing."

"That's because she was nodding her head. Taylor, please?"

Neither Mrs. Barrington nor David Helin would like it if they heard, but I needed to ask the girl a question for my own peace of mind.

"I'll be there in a few minutes," I said.

The waitress arrived as I stood up and slipped the smartphone back into my pocket. She was carrying the glass of bourbon on a tray. I took the glass and drained its contents without pause. She looked at me as if I were the first raging alcoholic she had ever met.

I paid for the drink and headed to my Camry. My smartphone rang just as I reached it. I thought it was Devon calling back, but the caller ID read ALEXANDRA CAMPBELL.

"Hello," I said.

"Taylor? Is this a bad time?"

"It is, but Alex, how are you?"

"We're still on the first-name basis, then."

"I'm sorry. I really am. I know you called. I've been trying to get back to you, but it's been one thing after another. Are you all right?"

"I am. I had a couple of bad moments after the shooting. Now, though, looking back at what happened, I feel exhilarated. What does that say about me?"

"It says you're tough as nails. Alex, how did you get this number?"

"I called your office the other day. Your partner—Freddie?"

"Sidney Poitier Fredericks."

"No kidding? Sidney Poitier? Anyway, he said he'd tell you that I called. When I didn't hear from you I decided, well, he's not interested—"

"No, no, honestly. I've been meaning to call."

"What I'm trying to say is, Freddie called me back, just a few minutes ago, and gave me your cell number and said it would be better if I called you instead of waiting for you to call me."

That sonuvabitch, I'm going to kill him, I told myself. Out loud I said, "Absolutely. I'm going to have to thank him for doing that."

"You said this was a bad time."

"I need to interview a suspect."

"That sounds like fun, interview a suspect."

"The suspect is an almost-seventeen-year-old girl who's being guarded by a very fierce nanny, governess, I'm not sure what to call her. I doubt it'll be much fun."

"More fun than what I do every day."

"I'd like very much to learn what you do every day, but—"

"You need to go."

"I promise I'll call you back."

"Don't make any promises you can't keep."

"I promise I'll *try* to call you back."

"I'm a night owl, so if it's late, don't worry about it."

I told her I wouldn't.

CHAPTER THIRTY-ONE

I turned off the county blacktop and discovered that the gate to Mereshack was open. I followed the road. My odometer told me that it went on for just over a mile, yet it seemed longer in the darkness. Finally I reached the clearing at the top of the hill. I maneuvered the car down the hill toward the collection of buildings that lay between it and the river. My headlights swept the forest as I turned. There was also a lamp on top of a pole near the center of the buildings.

The only other bright light came through the sliding glass door in the back of the main house that opened onto the deck where the hot tub was located. I could see through the doors. Devon was studying a fistful of shirts on hangers and tossing them one at a time on top of the bed. She was dressed only in pink panties and a matching bra. Her hair was in a ponytail.

I swung the car in a half circle so that it was facing away from the house and parked. I went to the front door and knocked. Ophira answered.

"Dev, your date is here," she said.

"Don't, don't, don't say that," I told her.

"Mrs. Barrington said to keep away from her children. What are you doing, man?"

Before I could answer, Devon came bounding into the room. She was wearing shorts that displayed every inch of her long, slender legs and a top that was fitted to show off the rest of her. Her hair was undone and fell around her face to her shoulders. She grabbed my hand with both of hers and pulled me into the house. She didn't let it go until Ophira shut the door behind me.

"You've never been here before, have you?" Devon said.

"I looked around the outside, but not the inside."

"I'll give you a tour. Ophira?"

"Devon?" the older woman asked.

"When will dinner be ready?"

"My biscuits come out of the oven in ten minutes." Ophira looked me in the eye. "Maybe less," she said.

"Then we don't have much time," Devon said.

She pulled my hand again, this time leading me up the stairs to the second floor, where she proceeded to show the place like a real estate agent, one bedroom at a time, emphasizing the highlights. Mereshack reminded me of a well-appointed bed-and-breakfast built to cater to an army of well-to-do visitors or businessmen on an executive retreat. I had to keep reminding myself that only one family used the place, and mostly on weekends and holidays.

Eventually we descended to the ground floor. Ophira watched us carefully.

"We'll be ready in a minute," she said.

Devon showed off the library, dining room, and living room, finally ending at the bedroom in the back of the house.

"There's a hot tub just outside the sliding door," she told me. "I never use it, but my mom likes it, and so does Joel."

"Is this your room?"

"God no. I'm upstairs. I showed you my room."

"Yes, you did."

"This is my mother's room. She has a master bedroom upstairs. I showed you that one, too, only she also uses this one sometimes. I think because it's close to the hot tub. She keeps some of her clothes in the closet."

The young woman tugged at the collar of her shirt.

"This is hers," she said.

I came *this*close to explaining that I had witnessed her getting dressed and that she was foolish for not closing the drapes even if the house was in the middle of nowhere, literally miles from her nearest neighbor. I was afraid I'd embarrass her, though. And myself.

"The shirt looks good on you," I said.

Devon smiled as if it were the best compliment she had ever received.

"Thank you," she said.

Her breathless little-girl voice reminded me—almost seventeen, almost seventeen, almost seventeen.

"Dev." Ophira called to us from the kitchen. "Devon. Child, we're ready to eat."

Devon took my hand again and led me to the kitchen. Three places were set at the table.

"We have a perfectly good dining room," Devon said. "That's what my mom calls it. Perfectly good. I've always liked eating here instead. Is that okay?"

"Perfect," I said.

Ophira's Cajun stew was a collection of andouille sausage, shrimp, red onion, garlic, celery, carrots, potatoes, bell pepper, tomatoes, okra, and cayenne pepper simmering in a pot, with the homemade biscuits on the side. Devon reached for a biscuit. Ophira gave her a look, and the girl pulled her hand back. She bowed her head and folded her hands in her lap.

Ophira prayed aloud. "Bless this food to our use, and us to thy service. Fill our hearts with grateful praise. Amen."

"Amen," Devon said.

"Amen," I added so I wouldn't feel left out.

Devon retrieved her biscuit.

"Are you religious, Taylor?" she asked.

Ophira filled both Devon's bowl and my bowl with her stew. It smelled delicious.

"Not as much as my mother wants me to be," I said.

"My family isn't religious at all," Devon said. "The only time I've ever been in a church was with Ophira. Ophira is really religious, aren't you,

Ophira? God and family, she says, are the only important things. It's because of her that I pray sometimes."

I glanced at the woman. She was busy eating her stew without even a suggestion that she wanted to join in the conversation.

"I'm glad she takes me to church when my mother isn't looking," Devon said. "It gives me an idea of how things work."

"I haven't heard church described quite that way before," I said.

"You won't tell Mother?"

"Of course not."

"Then I won't tell her that we had dinner together even though she told me to stay away from you."

"I appreciate it. Ophira?"

She lifted her head, and I pointed at her stew with my spoon.

"Eating this is as close to a religious experience as I've come in a long time. Your biscuits—manna from heaven."

She smiled, if only for a moment. I might have missed it if I hadn't been watching closely.

"Be better if I had more time to let it simmer." Ophira gestured toward Devon. "This one, she wants what she wants."

Devon threw her head back and laughed.

"Oh, right," she said. "Like I give the orders around here."

Devon waved her spoon at Ophira as if she were slashing at her with a cutlass. Ophira frowned and shook her head. Devon set the spoon down and picked up a biscuit. She took a bite and spoke as she chewed.

"Is my mother going to prison?" Devon asked.

"Manners," Ophira said.

Devon finished chewing.

"Excuse me," she said. "Taylor, is my mother going to prison?"

"I don't think so."

"Then she didn't kill Emily like they said."

"There isn't very much evidence to prove that she did it, yet there's plenty to prove that someone else might have."

Devon's blueberry eyes narrowed, and she leaned in close.

"Who?" she said. "Who did it?"

"I'm afraid I can't really tell you much more than what I already have.

I work for your mother and her attorney. What I learn in the course of an investigation belongs to them. I'm ethically and legally bound to keep it private unless they tell me otherwise."

An expression of utter rage clouded Devon's pretty face. She gripped her spoon as if she actually intended to use it like a sword.

"But I'm your friend," she said.

I leaned away from her.

Ophira reached over and tapped Devon's shoulder.

"Child," she said. "Eat your dinner before it gets cold."

"Right, right."

The anger disappeared just like that. Devon bowed her head over her bowl and took a bite of shrimp and okra. She was smiling when her head came back up.

"This is really fabulous, isn't it," she said. "Ophira is a great cook. I keep telling Mom to hire her as a chef, but she has this guy who thinks if you smother something in enough sauce it becomes gourmet."

I asked Devon about school and what plans she had for college just to get her thinking about something else. She named a number of universities that interested her, none of them close to home. She said she was looking forward to touring the campuses that summer. This led to a spirited discussion about the value of higher education versus its cost. Ophira actually joined in for a change, arguing that onerous student loans were crushing the middle class. Devon agreed, which didn't surprise me, her agreeing with Ophira, even though it was unlikely the girl would ever know a moment of financial anxiety in her life. What surprised me was her clear-eyed theory that high student debt could cripple the economy. "You can't buy a house, you can't buy a car, if you need half of your income to pay Northwestern University," she said. It suggested to me that the young lady actually paid attention to the problems of the world around her despite the fact that she lived so far above them.

After dinner, we settled in the living room. Devon attempted again to pump me for information.

"This someone else who might have killed Emily, does he live in Arona?"

"Could be," I said.

"Was it U.S. Sand like you suspected? Was it part of a giant conspiracy like they have on *Hawaii Five-0?*"

"Sorry."

"Oh, c'mon, Taylor. I've never been involved in a murder investigation before."

"I didn't know you were involved."

"My mother was charged with the crime, so yeah, I'm involved."

Devon glanced at Ophira as if seeking confirmation, but the woman gave her nothing.

"What about Mayor Franson?" I asked. "Were you involved in that investigation?"

"No," Devon said. "No one even asked me a question."

"Why would they?" Ophira asked.

I asked the question I had come there to ask.

"You were here when the mayor was shot, weren't you?" I asked.

"You mean in Arona?" Devon said. "Sure I was. Well, I was here at Mereshack, anyway. It was spring break or something."

"Were you alone?"

Devon chuckled at the suggestion.

"Mother never lets me go anywhere alone. Besides, that was over a year ago. I was almost sixteen. I didn't even have a driver's license back then."

Mayor Franson's house was over ten miles away, I reminded myself.

"I was with her," Ophira said. "Why does it matter?"

"The mayor was trying to rip off my family," Devon said. "That makes us suspects. Isn't that right, Taylor?"

"Yes, it does," I said. "But . . . Okay, I'll tell you something about the investigation."

Both women leaned forward, which made me grin.

"The county attorney has evidence that proves whoever killed Mayor Franson also killed Emily," I said.

"What evidence?" Ophira asked.

"Now, I can prove that your mother and Joel were in New York at the time the mayor was killed, so they're in the clear. You and Ophira have each other for alibis, so—"

"Oh," Devon said. She sounded disappointed. She leaned back in her chair. "So Mom really isn't going to prison. I thought you were just being nice before. Did you hear that, Ophira?"

"What evidence?" Ophira asked again.

It was easy to lie to her; I did it automatically.

"To be honest, I'm not entirely sure," I said. "Martin McGaney—you met him this morning. I've known him for a long time. He gave me the heads-up, although he wouldn't be specific."

"Is it an ethical thing again?" Devon asked.

"He works for the county attorney, and I work for your mother's attorney so, yeah, something like that."

"Do the police have any idea who done it?" Ophira said.

"I don't think so."

"You don't, neither?"

"What you need to understand, it's not our job to find out who killed Emily or the mayor. Our job, your mother's attorney and mine, is to prove that your mother didn't do it, and it looks like we're going to be able to do that."

"That's good news," Ophira said. "Ain't it, child?"

"Don't you care, Taylor?" Devon said. "Don't you want to know who killed Emily?"

"Of course I care. From what I've been able to learn, Emily was a wonderful woman and well loved by everyone who knew her."

"I loved her," Devon said.

"I'm sorry about what happened to her, and yes, I'd like see the person responsible get what's coming to him. Only that's not what I was hired to do."

"The police, though. If they can't find who killed the mayor after all this time, how are they going to find who killed Emily?"

"As sad as it sounds, they might never find out. It's not like TV where everything gets wrapped up in forty-four minutes plus commercials."

"What you're saying, someone got away with murder."

"We'll see. You know the cops; they're never going to stop looking. After a while, Emily's murder will cease being a priority with them. There're always new crimes to solve. At the same time, they'll never completely forget about it."

"What about you?"

"What about me?"

"Someone could hire you."

"Dev," Ophira said.

"Hire me to do what?" I asked.

"Find Emily's killer. I mean, if it's not your job now, someone could make it your job, though, couldn't they?"

"One thing TV gets right, the police don't like it when private investigators meddle in open homicide investigations. In fact, they can get downright cranky."

"Do you care?"

"Not particularly."

"Well, then?"

"You're a minor."

"Yes, she is," Ophira said.

"What does that have to do with anything?" Devon asked.

"If you're thinking of hiring me, legally, I'm not sure we can make that happen unless your mother agrees."

Devon tucked her long legs beneath her and smiled brightly like a girl with a plan.

"Me?" she said. "I wasn't thinking of me." She glanced in Ophira's direction before turning her eyes back. "I wouldn't worry about it, though. One way or the other, I always find a way to get what I want."

Soon after, I announced it was time for me to leave.

Devon said, "So soon?"

Ophira stood up and opened the door.

"I need to get some sleep," I said. "I'm going home tomorrow morning."

"Then I might not see you again," Devon said. "Taylor, I miss you already."

I believed Devon wanted to hug me as she had the evening before. Yet as she moved toward me, I offered her my hand instead. She shook it, but she wasn't happy about it.

"You don't have to worry, Taylor," she said. "It's not a crush or anything. I just like you."

"I like you, too. Have a wonderful life."

Ophira waved me out the door.

Twenty minutes later, I was in my room at the Everheart Resort. My phone chirped with another text. It was from Alex Campbell.

Hello?

I answered, *Good evening.*

Wanted to call since you didn't—afraid to interrupt interview.

Finished. Just got back.

Where are you?

In my room.

In your bed in your room?

On my bed.

Are you still dressed?

Yes. Why?

Just curious.

Where are you?

In my bedroom—in my bed—alone.

What are you doing?

Texting, silly.

I'm not used to this.

Used to what?

Texting.

It's called sexting.

Then I'm really not used to it.

Kids do it all the time.

I haven't been a kid for many, many years.

Spoilsport.

If you say so.

Should I tell you what I'm wearing?

Please.

Start at the top and work down or at the bottom and work up?

Why don't I just call you?

We can do it that way, too.

CHAPTER THIRTY-TWO

Four forty-five A.M. and my cell phone rang. My first thought was of Alex and what I told her when last we spoke.

"I'm not into cyber, sexting, telephone sex, whatever you call it. I'm strictly a hands-on kind of guy."

"That's my preferred method as well," she said.

Which segued into a long and pleasant conversation about her and me and everything in between that lasted until—geez, was it only four hours ago?

I snatched the smartphone off the bedside table and spoke into it without checking the caller ID.

"What?"

"Good morning, sunshine."

The drapes on my windows were tightly drawn, yet there was enough of a crack to tell me that it was a very dark gray outside.

"Who's this?"

"Rachel Colgin."

"What do you want?"

"I need a favor."

"I already did you a favor."

"No. You did something for me, and in exchange, I'm going to do something for you. This is completely different."

"What?"

"Get dressed. Meet me in the parking lot."

"What parking lot?"

"The parking lot of the Everheart Resort. Taylor, please hurry."

I put on yesterday's jeans and yesterday's shirt and my all-purpose sports jacket and made my way downstairs. The lights were on, yet there was no one in the lobby. Just a bell on the front desk with a sign that read RING ME.

I stepped outside.

"Hey."

Special Agent Rachel Colgin's voice startled me. I moved to cover it with some macho posing.

"What the hell is going on?" I asked.

Colgin answered by seizing my arm and leading me away from the lights of the front entrance and deep into the parking lot. She was wearing body armor beneath a dark blue windbreaker with the letters ATF plastered in white over the front and back. The sun was threatening to rise, but that did little to keep me from shivering in the morning chill. Colgin, on the other hand, appeared as comfortable as could be. She brushed my hair with the fingers of her free hand.

"I like the bed hair," she said. "Gives you that outdoorsy windswept look."

"So I have that going for me."

"I like the day-old beard, too."

I exhaled hard in her direction.

"How 'bout that?" I asked. "I haven't had time to brush my teeth, either."

Colgin fanned the invisible air.

"Try to stay downwind," she said.

"Seriously, Rachel. What do you want from me?"

By then we had reached her white van and a knot of agents. They were all wearing bulletproof vests and ATF windbreakers, too.

"A slight glitch," Colgin said. "Because of your unannounced visit yesterday, the Patriots decided it would be prudent to put a guard back on the gate. It makes our predawn assault on their compound that much more difficult."

"Why?"

"There's only one road leading in and out. I have agents manning a perimeter in the woods, but they're there to cut off escape routes. It's on us to hit 'em. With a guard in constant contact with the compound, though, it'll be tough. The road is nearly a mile long. They'll have too much warning. The chance of my people getting hurt has increased exponentially."

"What does this have to do with me?"

"The Patriots know you."

"So?"

"So, you're going to drive to the gate."

"I am?"

"Yes, you are. You're going to drive to the gate and tell the guard that you're there to see Blevins about something important."

"He's going to ask what."

"I don't care what you say. Tell him that the ATF is onto him. Whatever. Just get the guard to open the gate. If you can get him to ride with you to the compound, that would be very, very good, too. We'll be following right behind you. Once you're in the compound, just park somewhere out of the way and we'll do the rest."

"It seems to me that a guy could get killed doing something like that."

Colgin gestured at her fellow agents.

"Yes," she said. "A guy could get killed."

"Since you put it that way . . ."

"Look at the bright side, Taylor. The ATF will owe you one."

"Rachel, please. I stopped believing in Santa Claus a long time ago."

I started walking toward my Camry. Colgin followed behind with some last-minute instructions. When I got near, I pointed my remote and pressed a button. The car's lights flickered, and my locks clicked open. I hit another button and popped my trunk lid.

"What are you doing?" Colgin asked.

I answered by digging into the compartment where the spare tire was stored and coming up with my Beretta.

"No, no," Colgin said. "I'm sorry, Taylor. You're a civilian. I can't have you shooting up the place."

"What am I going to do about the armed guard who will be sitting next to me on the front seat of my car while you assault the compound?"

"I didn't think of that."

I racked the slide and released it, jacking a round into the chamber. I thumbed the safety on.

"Fortunately, I did," I said.

"Taylor, I'm begging you. Please don't shoot anyone unless you absolutely have to. You can't believe the paperwork."

I pulled off the county highway onto the dirt road and stopped in front of the gate. My headlights illuminated the sign attached to the iron bar that blocked the road—PRIVATE PROPERTY NO TRESPASSING. It was still dark enough that they also caused the guard to shield his eyes momentarily, and I wondered if I had caught him napping. He stepped out of the tiny guardhouse and crossed over to me. He was holding his assault rifle by one hand. I recognized him as I powered down my window.

"Jerry," I said. "It's Jerry, right? Open the gate. I need to see Blevins right away."

"No one gets in without permission."

"Get permission."

I heard the voice squawking from the radio attached to his shoulder.

"What's going on?" it said.

Jerry squeezed a button and replied.

"It's that private eye," he said. "Taylor."

"What's he want?"

"I want to see Blevins," I said.

Jerry spoke into the transmitter. "He wants to see Blevins."

"It's five-fucking-thirty in the morning. I ain't waking up nobody at five-fucking-thirty in the morning."

"Come back later," Jerry said.

"Later might be too late."

"Why? Why might it be too late?"

"Listen to me. I've been interrogated by the ATF most of the night. They're trying to get me to roll over on Blevins for that thing that happened in Menominee. Now open the damn gate."

"No. You wait here."

Jerry turned his back and moved away. I heard him say, "Tom? You had better wake up Curtis. Here's why . . ." After that it was all just dull murmurs. They lasted for a couple of minutes. Finally Jerry returned to the car. He was holding the radio up. I heard Blevins's voice.

"Talk to me, Taylor," it said.

"I went to see Esther yesterday after I spoke to you. She was at the bomb site. Did you know someone planted a bomb at the silica sand mine?"

"I heard. Go on."

"The place was crawling with ATF agents. One of them must have overheard my conversation with Esther. Your blabbermouth niece told me basically the same thing that you told me about Menominee and Julie and everything else. Later, the agents grabbed me up. They wanted me to repeat what Esther said on the record, turn hearsay into evidence, I guess. I told them I didn't know what they were talking about. Look, man, they could yank my license for this."

"You better come in. Jerry?"

"Yes, sir," Jerry said.

"You come with him."

"Yes, sir."

"Search him first."

"Oh, for God's sake," I said.

I opened the car door and slid out. I put my hands on my head and spun around while Jerry frisked me. He did a much better job than he had the first time around. If I had been wearing a wire, he would have known.

"He's cool," Jerry spoke into the radio.

"Come ahead," Blevins told him.

I returned to the Camry. It took a few moments before Jerry was able to disengage the large lock and unwind the chain that kept the gate closed. He swung it open and hopped into the passenger side of the Camry, carrying his rifle straight up between his knees. I passed through the gate and kept going. Jerry glanced through the rear window.

"I wanted to lock it again," he said.

"I'll only be here for ten minutes," I said.

The sun had been rising steadily and now gave the forest a golden hue. Birds I could not identify began singing their morning songs.

"It's going to be a beautiful day," Jerry said.

"How did you get involved in all this nonsense, anyway?" I asked.

"What nonsense?"

"The Red Stone Patriots."

"Things are getting out of hand."

"I agree, but is an armed militia part of the solution or part of the problem?"

"We're a constitutional militia. We believe in the rule of law, not the arbitrary rule of fat-cat politicians who are bought and paid for by special interest groups. I mean, there's got to be a limit to their power, a limit to government, or you get shitheads like U.S. Sand paying 'em off with campaign checks so they can do whatever they fucking want and t' hell with the people, you know?"

"It's not the philosophy that makes me nervous. It's the guns. The bombs."

"What bombs?"

I followed one last long curve to the entrance of the compound. I turned off the road and drove past the small green cabins and the pole barn. The only people I could see were Tom and Curtis Blevins. They were both standing at the foot of the wooden staircase that led to the front door of Blevins's trailer. Tom was hugging his AK-47 to his body like a teddy bear. Blevins merely stood there watching, his hands on his hips and an expression of curiosity on his face, while I swung the Camry away from the trailer and slowed to a stop. I powered down the passenger side window and turned off the ignition.

"It's okay to park closer," Jerry said.

He reached for the door handle.

"Jerry," I said.

He turned his head to look at me and saw the nine-millimeter Beretta semiautomatic handgun I was pointing at his chest. I had stowed it in the storage compartment attached to the driver's side door when he had searched me earlier.

"Do what I say," I told him. "We'll both get out of this in one piece."

"You sonuvabitch," he said.

"Slide your rifle out of the window, muzzle first. Do it slowly. Do it now."

He did. The sight of the rifle being tossed out of the car window caused both Tom and Blevins to flinch. Tom uncradled his rifle and began to hold it like he knew what it was used for. Blevins folded his arms across his chest and took a couple of tentative steps forward as if he were expecting an explanation.

"I'm going to kill you," Jerry said.

"Hands on the dash."

Jerry complied.

"Believe it or not, I'm doing you a favor," I said. "As far as I know, you haven't actually committed a crime, so you should be able to walk away from this."

"Walk away from what?"

That's when the cavalry arrived. Four vehicles carrying agents of the Bureau of Alcohol, Tobacco, Firearms, and Explosives, as well as deputies of the Kamin County Sheriff's Department, scattered to all sides of the compound. The vans unloaded, and the occupants quickly spread out among the cabins and pole barn as if their movements had all been carefully choreographed ahead of time.

Tom screamed an obscenity, brought the AK to his shoulder, and squeezed off a dozen rounds at the agents.

He missed.

A single ATF agent fired back and did not miss.

At least one bullet caught Tom high in the shoulder. He spun around. The rifle went flying from his grasp. He fell in a heap. The agent ran to his side. He secured Tom's weapon. He secured Tom. He waved a deputy over, and together they began administering first aid.

Other agents led dazed Patriots from the cabins, their hands high in the air; all of them were dressed for bed. One by one they were handcuffed and made to kneel in a group. A circle of agents guarded them.

The huge doors of the pole barn were opened, and agents began searching the vehicles parked inside, as well as any unopened room and cabinet they came across. A couple of agents carried cameras and took video of the weapons and other contraband their colleagues discovered.

Jerry and I watched it all through the windshield of my car.

"You're a traitor," Jerry said.

"No, I'm not."

"What do you call it?"

"I'm just a guy doing a favor for a girl."

Special Agent Rachel Colgin moved from one group of agents to another. She paused where they were treating Tom. Apparently he wasn't badly hurt, because he answered Colgin's questions by spitting in her face. She wiped off the spittle with the back of her hand and walked toward my Camry. She saw me holding the Beretta on Jerry through the windshield and waved a couple of deputies over. They pulled Jerry from the car, cuffed him, and made him kneel, too.

"Have you seen Blevins?" Colgin asked.

"Fuck you," Jerry said.

Colgin actually smiled and pointed in my direction.

"I was talking to him," she said.

"Last I saw, Blevins was standing by his trailer," I said. "When you arrived, he must have hightailed it around the trailer and through the firing range they have back there into the woods."

"Why didn't you stop him?"

"What would you have had me do? Shoot him? I'm a civilian, remember? I'm not even supposed to be here."

Colgin turned to stare at the route I had described.

"My people will pick him up," she said.

"Your agents don't know the ground. He does. If he's smart, he had already planned his escape route."

Colgin started shouting.

"All right. Curtis Blevins is in the wind." She moved closer to her agents. "I want a hard-target search starting right now."

Jerry smirked. "You got nothing," he said.

"That's okay. I wasn't expecting all that much. Anyway, unlike you, I'm going home."

CHAPTER THIRTY-THREE

It was just after eight when I returned to the parking lot of the Everheart Resort, Restaurant, and Bar. The adrenaline rush I had received during the raid on the Red Stone Patriots had already worn off, and I felt bone tired.

I slipped the Beretta under my belt at the small of my back and covered it with the sports jacket because I was just too exhausted to go through the trouble of stashing it in my trunk again. I walked toward the main entrance. Many of the resort's other guests were already up and about, their faces fresh from a good night's sleep. I, on the other hand, looked like death warmed over. At least that's the impression I got from Bill Everheart, who called to me from behind the registration desk.

"Man, you look like you cut the candle in half and burned it on all four ends," he said. "What the hell happened?"

I was too tired to explain it to him.

"When's checkout?" I asked.

"Eleven. You're leaving us, huh?"

"Time to go home. Can you put my bill together?"

"Happy to. Did you hear? The county attorney is asking for a thirty-day injunction against U.S. Sand. There's going to be a court hearing tomorrow. This after the mine got bombed yesterday. I thought things were going to quiet down after the town hall."

"It's going to get worse."

"What?"

I told him about the raid.

"This is sure to hurt business," Everheart said.

"Is that all you care about? I have no love for either the militias or the environmentalists, but at least they're making a stand for what they believe. But you—pick a side, man."

"Easy for you to say. You're leaving. I live here. I'm not going anywhere."

I glanced at my watch. Breakfast or shower? I asked myself.

"Breakfast first," I decided.

"Feel free to charge it to your room. Your bill will be waiting."

"Just so you know, if they were pulling this shit in my backyard, I'd be tempted to blow up something, too."

I drifted into the dining room and found my table, the one with a view of the restaurant, bar, and lobby entrance. The waitress didn't even bother to ask if I wanted coffee. Instead, she brought a pot over and began filling a mug.

"Bless you," I said.

"You look like you need it."

"That bad, huh?"

"Sugar, cream?"

"I wouldn't dream of diluting it."

She dropped a menu in front of me and said she'd return in a moment. When she did, I ordered the Riverman's Special, which was your basic steak, eggs, and hash browns, except that it also came with a choice of cocktails—Bloody Mary, screwdriver, Irish coffee, mimosa, and something called the Corpse Reviver. I went with the screwdriver because of the vitamin C. I've always believed in a healthy diet.

I was just starting to enjoy the meal when Skip Zetzman arrived, carrying a tan reporter's notebook. I hoped he wasn't looking for me, but he was. He sat at my table without asking permission and started talking.

"The ATF raided the compound of the Red Stone Patriots this morning," he told me.

I chewed my steak and swallowed carefully before replying.

"Is that right?"

"Don't give me that, Taylor. You were there."

I scooped a forkful of hash browns onto a piece of toast. "Who says?" I took a bite.

"I have my sources."

Not the ATF, I told myself. It was probably one of the Kamin County deputies speaking out of turn.

"No, that's just an ugly rumor spread by loose-talking people," I said. "I'm a civilian. Why would I be there?"

"That's what I want to know."

Zetzman opened his notebook and prepared a pen as if he actually expected me to talk to him. Instead, I kept eating.

"I was told that the ATF has a warrant for Curtis Blevins, but he escaped," Zetzman said.

I swallowed a mouthful of food and took a long sip of the screwdriver.

"Dammit, Taylor," Zetzman said. "I answered your questions. The least you can do is answer mine."

He had a point. At the same time, I told myself, I might be able to strengthen my own cause.

I pointed at his notebook and said, "Close that."

Zetzman did.

"I promised the powers that be that I wouldn't answer any questions," I said. You have to admit there are damn few people who are capable of lying with greater dexterity than I can. "I would be happy, though, to *ask* a few questions if you don't attach my name to them."

Zetzman set his pen on top of the closed notebook.

"All right," he said. "Off the record."

"Who set the bomb that blew up the silica sand silo?"

"Was it Blevins?"

"I'm not saying anything, I'm just asking."

"All right."

"Who shot Mayor Franson?"

"You mean . . ."

"Who shot his own daughter in St. Paul seven days ago?"

"Sorry, what? This girl you were asking about, Emily Denys. She was Blevins's daughter?"

"Julie Elizabeth Blevins was her real name, only you didn't hear it from me. I suggest you contact the Ramsey County Attorney's Office for confirmation."

"Damn, Taylor. Damn."

"Now, leave me to my breakfast. Oh, and Skip? We never had this conversation."

He smiled and scurried away, happy about the scoop that I knew he would print in the *Record* before the week was out; a story that I was sure David Helin would happily quote to Marianne Haukass and a jury, should it come to that.

I finished my breakfast, drained both the screwdriver and my mug of black coffee, and stood up.

"My work here is done," I announced.

Unfortunately, no one was listening.

I paid for my meal and left the restaurant. I gave Everheart a quick wave as I passed through the lobby to the carpeted staircase that led to a long second-floor corridor with rooms parceled out equally on both sides. There was another flight of stairs at the far end of the corridor that led to the parking lot, as well as a small room filled with vending and ice machines. A large double-pane window looked down on all of it. The sun was shining brightly through the window.

It was because the sun was at his back that the man who stepped out of the vending room appeared as a shadow to me. The shadow didn't move, just stood there looking more or less in my direction. I was ten feet from my room when he started shooting.

He shot high. A steady rat-a-tat-tat of bullets tore into the walls and ceiling above me.

I went low, diving to the floor.

My right hand found the Beretta behind my back and pulled it from my jeans.

The man ceased firing his automatic rifle for a moment.

Then promptly resumed shooting.

This time he aimed low. Bullets tore into the floor only a foot or so in front of my head, sending shards of wood and carpet fibers flying through the air.

I gripped the Beretta in both hands and returned fire.

I was off target, too, the bullets slamming into the wall just off his right shoulder.

He fired again. This time his aim was even wilder. Bullets seemed to fly everywhere, yet somehow managed to avoid hitting me.

I fired again.

And missed.

The shadow turned and started running. He became a man when he stepped into the sunlight at the end of the corridor—Curtis Blevins. I could see him fumbling with a magazine, trying to reload his assault rifle as he reached the staircase and started down.

I jumped to my feet and began pursuit.

Room doors opened. Frightened faces peered out at me. I yelled at them as I passed.

"Stay in your rooms, stay in your rooms."

I stopped running when I hit the staircase.

I couldn't see the shooter, but that didn't mean he couldn't see me. It didn't mean Blevins wasn't waiting.

I descended the staircase cautiously, the Beretta leading the way.

I was halfway down the staircase when I heard gunshots coming from outside.

I dashed down the remaining steps and hit the glass door with my shoulder.

The door flew open, and I found myself standing between two rows of parked cars. The sound of automatic rifle fire drew me toward the front of the resort.

I started running through the parking lot.

I could see a Ford Crown Victoria Police Interceptor with the words ARONA POLICE DEPARTMENT painted on the door blocking the exit.

A woman dressed in sneakers, black Dockers, and a blue short-sleeve knit shirt was sprawled on the asphalt near the Interceptor's open door. A nine-millimeter Glock was lying just inches from her hand.

Curtis Blevins stood over her. He was carrying an AK-47.

I screamed his name and started shooting as I ran at him.

He never got the rifle up. To this day, I'm not sure he even saw me before I took half his head off.

I sat on the asphalt, my knees drawn up to my chest, my back resting against the front quarter panel of the Interceptor, and looked at her. Just looked. Sheriff deputies came and went, yet no one touched her body. Or Blevins's body, either, for that matter. Finally the ME arrived, along with an army of techs. The sheriff stood next to me. Together, we watched them work.

"What did I tell you about not carrying a gun in my county?" the sheriff asked.

The sun was in my eyes when I looked up at him, and I had to shield them with the flat of my hand. I didn't say anything, though. I returned my gaze to the body of Chief of Police Maureen McMahan.

"You're coming with me to Tintori Falls," the sheriff said. "I have a lot of questions, and you're going to answer every fucking one. Then the county prosecutor is going to ask questions, and you're going to answer them, too."

"Okay."

"You can start by telling me why this Blevins character was trying to kill you."

"He thought I ratted out him and his militia to the ATF."

"Did you?"

"I suppose."

"You're saying you were involved in that raid they used my people for this morning."

"You need to talk to Special Agent Rachel Colgin."

"I'll talk to the fucking ATF when I'm good and ready to talk to the fucking ATF. You act like you're doing me a favor. You're not doing anyone any favors."

"I know. I've been through this before."

"I bet you have. Every day and twice on goddamn fucking Sunday."

I kept my mouth shut and watched the techs and the ME working around the chief's body.

"She was a good cop," the sheriff said.

"She was a lousy cop," I said. "She deserved better than this, though. She deserved better than what we gave her."

"What I gave her," the sheriff said.

"She was going after U.S. Sand. Tilting at windmills, I suppose."

"I heard."

"Now . . ."

He surprised me by reaching down and gently squeezing my shoulder.

"I have her files," the sheriff said. "I'll keep the investigation alive."

"In an election year? How's that going to play?"

"Don't know," he said. "Don't think I much care."

CHAPTER THIRTY-FOUR

Everything happened slowly after that. My endless interrogation in Tintori Falls. A telephone call and later a face-to-face meeting with David Helin that seemed to last longer. His subsequent conversations with Special Agent Colgin, the Kamin County sheriff, and finally Ramsey County Attorney Marianne Haukass. Three days passed before I was invited to yet another meeting with Helin at his office in the Wells Fargo Center in downtown Minneapolis.

The door was solid oak, yet the walls were made of glass, so I could see inside as I approached. Helin was standing behind his opulent desk and leaning down to converse with someone using his speakerphone. Eleanor Barrington was sitting in a chair on the other side of the desk. Her skirt was too short and revealed more leg and thigh than Cynthia Grey would ever have. She looked bored.

Helin saw me as I was about to knock on the door and waved me inside after first putting a finger against his lips, the universal sign for silence. I heard Marianne Haukass's voice as I entered.

"I will not be holding a press conference," she said.

"You gave yourself a lot of publicity when you accused my client of murder," Helin said. "The least you can do is go before the cameras to admit she's innocent."

"We don't know that she's innocent."

"Oh? Tell me, Marianne. What do you know?"

"The press release will state that there is insufficient evidence to pursue charges against Mrs. Barrington at this time."

"You can do better than that."

"But we won't."

"All we're asking for is a simple apology."

"This office has conducted itself in a professional manner. We have nothing to apologize for."

"I guess we'll hold our own press conference, then. Maybe we'll announce a lawsuit for malicious prosecution."

"Go ahead, David. See what that gets you. Good-bye."

Haukass hung up her phone, and Helin pressed a button on the speaker to hang up his.

"I didn't think that would work," he said.

"Should we have a press conference?" Mrs. Barrington asked. "Should we sue?"

"No to the first part. Once the media gets wind of this, they'll be calling us. We can deal with them one at a time. Or I should say, I'll deal with them. I don't want you answering question one from here on in. If someone gets to you, just refer them to me."

"All right."

"As for part two—there's nothing to be gained by a lawsuit. We'll never win, and you don't want to be put in a position where you're forced to answer any question Marianne Haukass can think to ask. Taylor, you're just in time to hear the news."

"I guess the CA dropped all charges," I said.

"Like a hot rock."

"I want to thank you, Taylor," Mrs. Barrington said. "Thank you for everything you've done. It's because of you that that odious Curtis Blevins stands accused of Emily's murder and I'm free to go. I should say Julie, but she'll always be Emily to me and Joel. To Devon, too, I'm sure."

"All in a day's work," I said.

"I'm paying David and his firm a hefty bonus for all of this, and I've left clear instructions that he's to share with you."

"That's good to hear. Thank you."

"Now, gentlemen, let me buy you lunch."

"Before you do, there's something we need to talk about."

"Not now, Taylor," Helin said.

"Yes. Now."

"What, Taylor?" Mrs. Barrington said. "What do you want to talk about?"

"The person who really killed Emily. And Mayor Franson, too."

"I don't know what you mean."

"She needs help, Eleanor. She needs a doctor's care. Who knows, they might even be able to fix her. It's been done before."

Mrs. Barrington stared at me for a few beats. I don't know what I expected, but it wasn't the subdued response she gave me.

"When did you figure it out?" she asked.

"When I saw her get out of your car at the coffeehouse, dressed like an adult, wearing her strawberry-blond hair down around her shoulders like you do. It wasn't you that Professor Campbell saw that night. It was Devon. If the county investigators had thought to include Devon's pic in the photo array instead of yours, it would have been her that the professor would have pointed at."

"Then you knew before I did. David, what's my position here?"

"You're protected by attorney-client privilege. Anything you say—"

"That's not what I mean."

Mrs. Barrington pointed at me.

"It extends to him, too," Helin said. "Taylor, you have a legal obligation to keep quiet."

"I understand."

"No license holder shall divulge to anyone other than the employer, or as the employer may direct, except as required by law, any information acquired during an investigation."

"I know the rules, David. I quote them all the damn time."

"Only when they suit you."

"I don't trust the law, and I stopped believing in real justice a long time ago. Eleanor, this is about your little girl. I'm not going to call the CA anonymously or otherwise. I'm not going to drop a dime on Devon.

I just want to make sure she gets the care she needs. Eleanor, she murdered two people."

"I know," Mrs. Barrington said. "I know that now. I didn't—I didn't know it at the time they arrested me, and later . . . the only thing I could think to do was wait and see what happened."

"You allowed yourself to be falsely accused of murder?"

"I couldn't give up my daughter."

For the first time, I found something to like about her.

"Devon is so perfect most of the time," Mrs. Barrington said. "Ninety-nine percent of the time she's smart and beautiful and caring and fun and utterly fearless. That one percent, though . . . She has these moments of pure rage. Sometimes they last for only a second. I mean that literally. A second. Sometimes they last much longer. Yet she would always come back. It was like flicking a light switch.

"I thought . . . I thought she would grow out of it, except . . . Ophira told me a year ago that Devon slid into one of her moods when she was down at Mereshack and took the car and disappeared for hours one night. Dev didn't have a license, but she did have a learner's permit. She was taking driver's ed. When she returned, she was her happy-go-lucky self; she even brought ice cream home. I discovered later that Todd Franson was killed at about the same time that Devon went on her joyride. I didn't put two and two together. Maybe I didn't want to add up the numbers, at least until you told me that the same gun that killed Emily also was used to kill that blackmailing prick.

"What happened, the asshole saw Joel and me together. Franson said he decided to drop by to discuss the land deal and saw us together through the windows of the downstairs bedroom when his car was at the top of the hill. He backed the car up and then the asshole snuck through the woods and took pictures. That was on Saturday night. On Sunday, he came back with his photographs and said he was going to go public with them, stick them on the internet, unless I consented to sell my property to the city. I told him to go fuck himself. I didn't give a goddamn about him and his fucking pictures. I told him I would crush him like a fucking grape if he messed with me.

"Only Dev . . . Devon must have overheard. She was still upset about what people had said after her father's plane crashed with him and his whore inside, the jokes, and she . . . I shouldn't have left. The next day Joel and I flew to New York for a business meeting while Devon remained at Mereshack with Ophira. I shouldn't have left."

"What did you think when Emily was killed?" I asked.

"I didn't think, not at first. When the police came for me, I figured it was just that fucking bitch of a county attorney trying to make a name for herself. Later, after Joel went off the rails, I decided it was my comeuppance. It was me paying for my many, many sins. Then we couldn't find my gun and I didn't know why, and then you told me about the gun and then I knew why."

"Why did Devon kill Emily?"

"I can only guess."

"Please do."

"That night Emily was with us in North Oaks, and she and Joel were talking about the future. Their future together. I kissed him. I kissed him in the most unmotherly-like way possible. I used my tongue and I used my hands just to show the bitch who was in charge. After I left the room, Emily and Joel had a discussion. It ended with her screaming at him and running out the door. Well, good riddance. Only Devon was upstairs at the time. She must have heard what was said. I know that she was devoted to her brother. My guess? She decided to protect her family one more time."

"Jesus."

"If it's any consolation, Joel moved out while I was in jail."

"What about Devon?"

"I was going to take the blame. I really was. I decided it was the least I could do for her considering everything I've done to her. Although . . ." Mrs. Barrington smiled the way she usually did, and my opinion of her slid back to where it started. "I knew you two would get me off. Now . . ."

"Now you're free to go," Helin said.

"What about Devon?" I asked again.

"I'll talk to her," Mrs. Barrington said.

"That's not even close to good enough."

"Whatever I do, it's none of your damn business."

"She's my friend."

"Taylor, you are not to go anywhere near my daughter ever again, is that understood? I believe I have the legal right to make such a demand, do I not?"

She directed that last part to Helin. He nodded.

"So, gentlemen, where would you like to have lunch? My treat."

"I'll pass," I said.

Mrs. Barrington directed her gaze on Helin.

"I have far too much work to do," he said.

"Boys, boys," Mrs. Barrington said. "I appreciate your concern, I really do. Devon is my daughter. I love her. I'll take care of her. Don't worry."

Yet I did.

I decided I had had enough of being a private investigator for a while. Instead of returning to the office, I called Freddie and told him that I needed some mental health time.

"Does that mean you're going to see the professor?" he asked.

"You just won't quit, will you?"

"I saw her photo, remember? I'm just sayin' the lady looks like she could change a brother's outlook on life."

"Listen to you. What would Echo say?"

"She agrees with me. She said if you don't do her, she will."

"She did not."

"Ask her."

"I'm not going to ask her. In fact, I don't want to talk to either of you for at least three days."

"Is that because your mouth is gonna be busy?"

"Good-bye, Freddie."

I parked the Camry in front of my apartment building. Amanda Wede-meyer was kneeling on the sidewalk and drawing pictures with pieces of colored chalk the size of her fist. I stopped to admire an orange dragon breathing green fire.

"Nice," I said.

An older woman was sitting in a folding lawn chair on the grass between the apartment building and the sidewalk. Her head came up and she leaned forward.

"A man walked by earlier," Amanda said. "He said that dragons weren't orange. He said they were purple."

"Clearly he's not from around here." I leaned closer. "Who's the woman in the chair?"

Amanda whispered back. "My father's aunt. She insists on keeping an eye on me while Mom is at work now that school is out for the summer. Yay."

"It's nice that she's willing to do that."

"She's the only one on my father's side of the family who still likes us."

"Introduce me."

Amanda stood up and brushed the chalk from her hands onto her jeans, which caused the woman in the chair to roll her eyes. The girl took me by the hand and led me across the lawn.

"Aunt Florence," she said. "This is my friend Taylor. He owns Ogilvy that he lets me play with."

Aunt Florence nodded her head as if she knew who I was all along. We shook hands.

"I know of people who keep rabbits for pets," Aunt Florence said. "Keep 'em in cages. I never knew of anyone who let them run around their house."

"Oh, they're just like cats," Amanda said. "Ogilvy has a litter box and everything. The only problem is he keeps chewing on computer cords and stuff, isn't that right, Taylor?"

"Not so much anymore," I said. "I think he chewed on the wrong cord and was shocked to the point where he now avoids them. May I borrow Mandy for a minute?"

"Of course," Aunt Florence said. She then made a production out of looking at her watch as if she were timing me.

I led Amanda to my apartment, unlocked the door, and held it open for her. I left it open and went to the kitchen counter, where I found a small package wrapped in red tissue paper and a blue ribbon. I gave it to the young girl.

"For me?" she said.

I half expected her to add "You shouldn't have," or words to that effect, before ripping open the package. Apparently only big girls say that.

"Omigod, it's a camera," Amanda announced. "A Nikon. Thank you."

"You're welcome."

"But why?"

"For taking care of Ogilvy while I was away. I would have paid you cash . . ."

"No way Mom would let me take your money."

"There you go."

"You know, you could have paid me money and we wouldn't have told Mom."

"No, honey. You and I—we keep no secrets from your mother, ever. Okay?"

"Okay."

"Speaking of secrets."

"Huh?"

Assistant Chief Anne Scalasi stood in my doorway. She was in full uniform, although the buttons of her dark blue jacket were undone.

"I called your office," she said. "Freddie told me you were taking the rest of the day off."

"You remember my friend," I said.

I was speaking to Amanda, yet it was Anne who replied first.

"Of course I do," she said. "How are you, Amanda?"

"I'm out of school for the summer."

"Good for you."

"Mandy," I said, "why don't you show your camera to your aunt Florence. I need to talk to Anne."

Amanda gave me a quick hug.

"Thank you, Taylor," she said.

Amanda went out the door and Anne came in, closing it behind her. When she was close, I hugged her. I hugged her hard. There was nothing sexual about it. I hugged her for comfort, the way you might hug your best friend if she happened to be a woman. I kissed her forehead. She wrinkled her nose at me.

I released her and moved to the sofa in my living room, resting my backside against the arm. Anne closed the distance between us. I grabbed the lapels of her jacket and pulled her closer. She rested her hands on my shoulders. I slowly buttoned her jacket. The gesture didn't seem to surprise her one bit.

"Are you trying to tell me something, Taylor?"

"We're not doing this anymore."

"You're saying we're done?"

"Not done. Just different. Annie, I love you. I always have. You're my best friend. Without you, I would feel outnumbered. I like your kids, too. Your husband's an ass, but he deserves better. We all do."

"What's this? Suddenly you're behaving like an adult?"

"It had to happen sooner or later."

"Is this because of the woman who lives across the hall? And her little girl?"

"No. No, Annie, it's just . . . I don't want to be that guy, anymore. I want to be—"

"Who do you want to be?"

"The person I was before."

"Before what?"

"Before this. Before Cynthia. Before . . . I don't know. It might take awhile until I figure it out."

"What happened in Arona, it messed with your head, didn't it?"

"Not just Arona. Annie, there are a lot of screwed-up people in the world."

"You're telling me? I'm a cop, remember?"

"I just want to get my name off the list."

She hugged me and kissed my cheek and hugged me again. Finally she released me and headed for the door.

"I meant to tell you," she said. "Barbecue, early Sunday afternoon, my place. There'll be a lot of cops there. You'll know most of them. My husband, too. Bring beer and plenty of ice."

"Okay."

She opened my door and paused, staring at Claire Wedemeyer's door across the way.

"If you bring a date," she said, "I will shoot her on sight."

I moved to where she stood and gave her another quick hug.

"From now on, I'll bring all my girls to you for approval before I get serious," I said. "How's that?"

"If you had done that with Cynthia, think of all the trouble you would have avoided."

"My point exactly."

The smartphone in my jacket pocket chirped. I checked the incoming text. It was from Devon Barrington.

"I need to deal with this," I said.

"Don't forget Sunday. Yeah, and you can bring a date. Bring Claire."

A moment later Anne was out the door. I closed it. With my back against the wood, I opened the text.

I need you to come to North Oaks right away, it read.

I replied, *Your mother would not like it.*

My mother is not here.

Even better reason to stay away.

I need you.

I'm sorry.

I'm alone.

Where's Ophira?

She's gone.

The text forced me to pause. Mrs. Barrington never left Devon alone. The girl told me so herself.

I texted, *Where did Ophira go?*

Please help me.

The case was over. If she wanted to, Mrs. Barrington could have me arrested for trespassing, if nothing else. I would get no help from David Helin. My license could even be endangered. What other reasons could I think of for ignoring the girl?

I replied, *I'll be there in 15 minutes.*

CHAPTER THIRTY-FIVE

The Kamin County Sheriff's Department had confiscated my Beretta. Fortunately, I had another. It was tucked under my belt at the small of my back as I drove to North Oaks.

I jumped on West Pleasant Lake Road and followed it as it wound its way through the North Oaks Golf Club to the lane that led to Mrs. Barrington's estate. I kept looking for the community service officer, but I didn't see his Chrysler 300. Then I did. Someone had rolled the big car off the lane into a clearing among the trees between the main road and Mrs. Barrington's house. I nearly missed it. If not for the reflection of the late afternoon sun on the rear window I probably would have.

I slowed my car and stopped. The way the Chrysler was parked, nose in, it was unlikely the CSO was guarding the place from interlopers—I love that word, interlopers—who might have learned that the charges against Mrs. Barrington had been dropped. Certainly he wasn't running a speed trap.

I left my car and walked back to the Chrysler. I circled it so that I would come up on the driver's side. That's when I saw the bullet holes. There were so many that they could only have come from an automatic weapon. The driver's side window was shattered into a thousand pieces.

I looked inside. The CSO was slumped sideways on the front seat, his eyes staring at nothing. There wasn't much blood. He must have died quickly, I told myself.

"North Oaks isn't going to like this," I said aloud.

I ran back to the Camry as fast as I could. I fumbled with my smartphone, punched the numbers I wanted, and made a call even as I drove up the remaining portion of the long driveway and parked in front of the garage. The operator wanted to keep me on the line, but I silenced the cell and slipped it into my pocket just as I reached the Barringtons' front door. I both rang the bell and knocked. The knocking caused the door to inch open. I pressed my hand against the wood and swung it open the rest of the way.

"Devon," I called.

There was no reply.

I stepped inside and saw her.

Ophira was lying on the stone floor of the foyer. A bullet had caught her high in the chest and thrown her backward. She had fallen with her arms and legs spread-eagle as if she were making snow angels.

I slipped the Beretta out from under my jacket and thumbed off the safety.

I bent to the woman and rested two fingers along her carotid artery.

She was cold to the touch. There was no pulse.

"Devon," I said softly. "Did you do this?"

I stood and called to her the way that Ophira had.

"Dev. Devon, child. Where are you?"

I felt movement near the arched entranceway that led to the Barringtons' dining room and spun that way. I brought the Beretta up and went into a Weaver stance, the gun in my right hand, my left supporting it, my left arm close to my body, my head tilted slightly to align the sights on the target.

Esther Tibbits appeared. She was dressed for business in a white shirt, black jacket, and black skirt. She was using Devon as a shield, standing directly behind her. Her left arm was wrapped around Devon's shoulder, her hand resting just above the girl's breast. She also had a gun. It was pressed against Devon's temple.

I aimed the Beretta at Esther's right eye. Devon's head was too close to the target. I was afraid to take the shot.

There was movement behind me. Someone had been hiding in the living room as well.

I turned my head for a quick peek. Eric, wearing camo again, carrying an AK-47 assault rifle.

I looked back at Esther.

I tried to relax my hands.

"Drop your gun," Esther said.

"No."

Devon smiled, actually smiled. It surprised me as much as the rest of her demeanor. Nothing about her expression or body language suggested fear.

"Drop it," Esther said again.

"No," I repeated.

"I'll kill her."

"You're going to kill her anyway. If you do, I'll kill you. Your brother might get a few shots off. He might even get me before I shoot him. On the other hand, he might miss. Your uncle Curtis did."

"I won't miss," Eric said.

"In either case, Esther, you'll be dead before I am."

I said it, but I wasn't sure I meant it. You're taught to always take the target directly in front of you first. Except Eric had an automatic weapon. Plus, he was trained. Or at least he had practice shooting trees. That made him the greater threat.

"We didn't come here to kill the girl," Esther said.

"Did you come here to kill the maid?"

"It was an accident."

"That makes all the difference."

"We came here for you. Because of what you did to Uncle Curtis. Because of what you did to the Patriots."

"Then you should have come to my house."

"We didn't know where you lived," Eric said. "We knew where the Barringtons lived, though. We knew you were friends."

"We saw you with the girl at Everheart's," Esther said. "You like her. You don't want to see her hurt."

"No, I don't."

I spun and shot Eric.

I shot him three times.

I dove to my left as I squeezed off the rounds.

He hadn't even been aiming his rifle. Instead, he was holding it like a fire hose.

His body twisted and he fell backward. The rifle clattered across the hardwood floor.

I landed on my shoulder, my back toward Esther.

I tried to roll into some kind of firing position, but I knew it was too late.

The floor exploded under my hands.

I kept rolling.

Esther moved deeper into the foyer. She was circling for a better angle, holding her gun with both hands as if she had done this sort of thing before.

I tried to bring my own gun up.

I heard the shots—one, two, three, four, five.

I saw the bullets tear into Esther's body. Two in the chest, her arm, her shoulder, her face.

Blood saturated her white shirt.

She bounced off the front door and fell forward.

Esther landed facedown next to Ophira.

I kept rolling until I could see Devon. She was standing next to the small table, the one with the silver tray on top, near the staircase. The drawer of the table that I had wanted to peek into so long ago was now open.

Devon was staring at the nine-millimeter Ruger LC9 she held in her hand. The slide had locked open when she fired her final round. It seemed to surprise her. She shook the gun and looked down at me.

"Did I break it?" she asked.

"You're out of bullets."

"Oh."

She carefully set down the gun and helped me stand up. We drifted to the staircase and sat next to each other. She took my hand in both of hers and squeezed tight.

"I'm in trouble, aren't I?" she said.

I was gazing at the Ruger on the floor. Marianne Haukass wasn't an idiot. Well, maybe she was, but Martin McGaney wasn't. He would match the Ruger to the slugs in Esther's body. That was SOP. He would also match it against the bullets that killed Emily and Mayor Franson. Mrs. Barrington would finally be forced to confront the darkness in her daughter.

"Why did you keep it?" I asked.

"The gun? I stole it from my mother. It's the only one I had."

"Bad things are going to happen to you, but they won't be as bad as they seem. Your mother has a very good lawyer. He'll do his best to make sure you're charged as a juvenile. He might even be able to make a mental-illness defense, get you sent to a hospital. You should be free by the time you're nineteen. Twenty-one at the latest."

"But Taylor, I didn't do anything wrong."

"Yes, you did, honey."

"The woman with the big tits—she had it coming, breaking into my house, shooting my friend. I was only defending myself. I was defending you."

"Emily. And the mayor."

"Oh. I forgot."

"Why did you shoot Emily?"

"She was going to blackmail Joel just like the mayor was going to blackmail Mom. She yelled at him as she was driving away that night. She said, 'This is going to cost you. This is going to cost you a lot.' Taylor, do you think I'm insane? I mean, I didn't even cry when they killed Ophira. I wasn't afraid at all when they were threatening to shoot you. Or me even. I must be crazy."

"No. Just sick."

"What's the difference?"

"You're going to get better."

"I hope it doesn't take too long. I have so much to do."

She leaned against my shoulder and started humming a tune that I had never heard before.

Outside, the sirens wailed.